# HOT GOODS

Felix McTurk folded his arms and faced the teen. "What's in my closet?"

Tech forced a laugh. "What's always in the closet? Five hundred pounds of hardcopy, a pile of robot parts, that purple shirt of yours—"

"Get away from the closet." Felix swung open the door. Inside was an unlicensed airconditioning unit the kids must have stashed there. Someone started pounding on the office door.

"Environmental Protection Agency!" a deep-voiced woman announced. "Open up, McTurk, or we'll break it down!"

Felix slammed the closet shut. "All right, all right!" he shouted, moving for the door.

The woman shoved her badge in Felix's face as she stormed in, followed by two junior officers. "Eighty degrees," the woman announced, displaying a digital thermometer. "Search the place."

By Jack McKinney
*Published by Ballantine Books:*

THE ROBOTECH® SERIES

GENESIS #1
BATTLE CRY #2
HOMECOMING #3
BATTLEHYMN #4
FORCE OF ARMS #5
DOOMSDAY #6
SOUTHERN CROSS #7
METAL FIRE #8
THE FINAL NIGHTMARE #9
INVID INVASION #10
METAMORPHOSIS #11
SYMPHONY OF LIGHT #12

THE SENTINELS® SERIES:

THE DEVIL'S HAND #1
DARK POWERS #2
DEATH DANCE #3
WORLD KILLERS #4
RUBICON #5

THE END OF THE CIRCLE: ROBOTECH #18

KADUNA MEMORIES

# KADUNA MEMORIES

## Jack McKinney

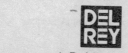

A Del Rey Book

BALLANTINE BOOKS • NEW YORK

A Del Rey Book
Published by Ballantine Books

Copyright © 1990 by New Frontier Productions, Inc.

Library of Congress Catalog Card Number: 90-92932

ISBN 0-345-36579-8

Manufactured in the United States of America

First Edition: July 1990

Cover Art by David Schleinkofer

With thanks to Hans Moravec, John Brunner, William Gibson,
and numerous others, for opening up the territory
and making it safe for tourists

And to Robert Mandell and Chris Rowley,
who poured the footings

# Part One:
# Close Encounter _____

# Chapter One _____

Thaish had a foot inserted in his mouth when the transport's monitors had voiced their shrill warning alert. *Ship Nasst* had shuddered, groaned, lurched, and found itself savagely returned to space-time, on a collision course with the largest of a cluster of metal-rich rock fragments in broad orbit around a middle-aged star.

The foot was Thaish's own, but the ship's wily ever-present monitors had captured him in a lackadaisical one-legged stance that was anything but appropriate for operations posture. His eyes were partially membraned, his features slack; his expression reflected an inner mode of contemplative though remote thought activity.

Later Thaish would recall the innocent stray impulse that had summoned his attention from the instrument mat, but just now he could only wither under the analytical gaze of Inheritor Major Nasst and the five remaining members of the transport's drive circle.

Thaish could hardly deny the Inheritor Major his right to glower. There was Thaish, after all, centered larger than actual in the monitor group's projected viewsphere, obviously indulging in random thought. *With* a foot in his mouth.

This most recent lapse brought the total to three for this jaunt alone, Thaish reminded himself while the monitors sniggered to themselves behind the Inheritor's back. One more and Nasst would have him deanimated for the duration of the jaunt. Only last shift Arbitrator Ranz from Realignment had hinted at this very possibility. *Perhaps we need to open up that thick skull of yours and search for the fault, eh, node?*

*Node*, Thaish thought, reanalyzing the Arbitrator's peculiar use of syntax and remembering his own vague sense of discomfort. Ranz had not merely forgotten to say Node

Thaish; he had left the status designate deliberately unattended to convey threat. Such was the power of words among the ably voiced.

"Even now you are negligent," Nasst bellowed suddenly, opaquing his eyes. "Whatever has gotten into you, Node Thaish?"

Thaish tried to keep his ears from twitching—they were wont to have a mind of their own under conditions of stress or duress. "I was attentive to your glower, Inheritor Major," he managed after a moment of full-body shudder. "It's only that—"

"Study yourself carefully, Node Thaish," Nasst said, gesturing to the viewsphere, where the monitors had Thaish's face and mated right foot frozen in tight close-up. "Observe the countenance you have displayed for the whole of this jaunt. Most inattentive—even with both feet planted," the Inheritor muttered, "most inattentive."

Thaish's eyelids flickered. Cautiously he scanned past Nasst, past the viewsphere and the expressionless faces of the drive circle membership to where several of his own Station Six node peers stood suctioned midway along the curve of the ship's featureless hull. Nasst's reprimand wasn't lost on any of them; Station Six as an entity would have to bear the burden of the Inheritor's officially filed rebukes.

Thaish took some solace in knowing that his peers had already forgiven him the lapse. There wasn't one among them who hadn't been discovered in similar postures this jaunt. It was a running game they played with the monitors, who remained several points behind, despite the high score they had earned by targeting Thaish.

Nasst had nothing but glower for the ongoing contest—an exercise he considered wasteful in the extreme—but there was little he could do to contain it. Like most Inheritors, Nasst refused to accept that operational duties attendant to even the most complex of transdimensional jaunts left ample room for stray thought. In any event, it wasn't as if a universally inattentive Station Six could impair *Ship Nasst*'s vital functions, let alone snatch the ship from jaunt and drop it back into space-time, into the thousandfold potential horrors that lurked there.

Unfortunately, the discovery of Thaish's lapse had coincided with just such an unprecedented event.

Drive Master Ghone, the very cause of it all, lay sprawled on the sensor-studded floor of the interface cylinder she had occupied for longer than anyone onboard could remember. It wasn't the first time a drive circle member had expired during jaunt; but it was, according to all available data, the first time unscheduled expiration had resulted in a power loss of such devastating magnitude. As if the dimensional shift from translight to space-time weren't enough, Ghone's sudden demise had apparently depleted the ship's drives of residual power. To hear Engineer Tcud tell it, the ship was effectively stranded.

"We have experienced a setback that may well qualify as a catastrophe," the Engineer's disembodied voice told those gathered in the drive center. "We haven't adequate power to supercede time."

Relieved to see the viewsphere derezz, Thaish failed to notice that the drive circle members had left their interface cylinders and were beginning to issue panicked cries. Nearly everyone else was laughing. Engineer Tcud was fond of employing exaggeration to distress the Drive Masters.

"Return to your cylinders and stabilize yourselves," Nasst told the five—suppressing a grin, Thaish thought. "As for you, Engineer Tcud," the Inheritor directed to nowhere in particular, "I suggest that you review your calculations. Plainly you exaggerate the effects of Drive Master Ghone's departure."

The Engineer paused to consider it. "Drive Master Ghone absconded with a substantial quantity of harnessed energy, Inheritor Major."

No one was particularly surprised to hear this, though the drive circle members continued their railings. The Station Six node peers had concluded long ago that Ghone was energy-infatuated; while alive she had proven a constant drain on the ship's reserves, and the depletion attendant her departure seemed in keeping with that hunger. Still, it meant that Nasst would now be forced to conduct a search for a replacement—a tedious undertaking under the best of circumstances.

With a newfound sense of wonder, Thaish regarded the yellow sun cornered in the cabin's exterior viewport. Just where in time had *Ship Nasst* emerged?

It was possible of course that one of the convoy transports had monitored their distress and followed them out of jaunt.

It was certainly to be hoped, since communication with the convoy could be achieved only in jaunt.

And it was certainly what everyone opted to believe when, a moment later, the monitors announced detection of an artifact in near space.

Thaish watched, singularly attentive, as the object began to take shape in the renewed viewsphere. When it had taken final form amid the cratered debris that littered the sector, a sound of collective puzzlement filled the drive center.

The artifact wasn't a convoy transport; nor did it resemble any transport *Ship Nasst* had ever encountered. The Inheritor Major immediately ordered a comparison study, but the communications nodes in Interface Assist were unsuccessful in matching the alien ship's elongated styling, cone-like drive ports, and oddly shaped appendages and protuberances to anything logged in the data library.

Three of the communications nodes shared peer-status with Thaish, and he pitied them their failure. It seemed likely that half the ship would be on file before the jaunt was completed.

"Does the artifact respond to us?" Nasst asked at last.

"We can easily command it approach if so desired," one of the nodes answered.

The Inheritor Major made perceptible sucking noises with his lips, echoing the sounds by lifting one foot then the other in a demonstration of impatience. "Is it not something to be desired, then?" He indicated the viewsphere's data bars. "The object is obviously possessed of sufficient energy to secure us a return to jaunt."

Thaish analyzed the Inheritor's command voice, mimicking the tonalities in private thought. Such was the manner of behaving in the world, he told himself, when one desired to attain sure results: confidently, assertively, loud-voiced.

"There is no lack of energy," the same node replied, "but it derives, Inheritor Major, from positron plasma and nuclear fusion."

Someone shrieked, and Thaish saw several among his peer group adopt squatting, pre-deanimate postures. He was fully prepared to follow them into voluntary life suspension, but Nasst barked everyone upright and reattentive.

"A protohistorical curiosity," Nasst said, certain of himself, "but nothing we need fear. A factory ship, one might speculate. A relic, perhaps, from the eon of the !Reitth themselves.''

''A weapon,'' the drive circle leader offered, nervous as a Station Six node. ''Why else antimatter and nuclear fusion?''

''Nonsense,'' Nasst said, whirling on him.

''An explosive device,'' a second suggested.

''A destructive parcel,'' said a third.

''I would urge universal deanimation,'' from the leader once more.

''Nonsense, nonsense, nonsense,'' the Inheritor countered, caught up in a short-lived fugue. ''And *I* will be the sole counselor of deanimation.'' He glanced about the cabin, showing everyone the command glower Thaish had withered under moments before. ''Reanimate—all of you.''

Thaish noted worriedly that while he had barely attained a Level Two Submergence, most of his peers were deep enough to be partially cocooned. Yet another talent he would have to perfect if he ever hoped to rise above node status.

''Respond now,'' Nasst ordered the unseen nodes in Interface Assist. ''Does that ship possess sufficient energy to fulfill our needs or not?''

''It does, Inheritor Major'' came several strained voices in unison.

''And can we safely access that energy or not?''

''We can, Inheritor Major.''

''And is that ship responding to our commands or not?'' The nodes fell silent.

Nasst's lips quivered. ''I asked, is that ship respond—''

''In a manner of speaking, Inheritor Major,'' a single node returned. Thaish smiled in instant recognition of the voice: It was Barish, his supplemental and cache-mate.

''In what manner of speaking, *node*?'' Nasst demanded.

Barish hesitated. ''More accurately,'' she said finally, ''it isn't the ship that is responding, but *something inside it*!''

''I'm sorry, Dr. Nugget,'' Mika said over her shoulder, ''but I can't seem to override—you see, there it goes again.''

Nugget, scratching at a month's growth of wiry black beard, upended himself to peer at the plasma tabletop readout. One hand tethered him to the alloy console grip; the other held a bulb of lukewarm coffee—an Ethiopian roast sweetened with honey, his preferred drink.

Mika's recent exchanges with the ship's neural net processor were on display, a boxed and color-coded vertical column of abbreviated commands and responses filling the left side of the screen. In amber opposite ran a recounting of the artificial intelligence's private workings, a heuristic array of options, negations, and decision-loops.

A strand of Mika's ponytailed hair drifted up to tickle Nugget's ear. He thought of his daughter and experienced a moment of profound homesickness. Jain's hair was every bit as fine and blond as the young tech's; in some ways she resembled Mika more than she did her own mother.

Nugget returned to his study of the readout text, breaking his silence with a snort of astonishment. "Here," he said, spinballing a mouse to the troublespot. "Order an amplified reveal of this entire section."

Mika's tapered fingers—blue lacquered nails today, Nugget noticed—entered the request on a control pad set into the arm of her swivel chair. Nugget watched the screen with interest, laughing once again after he had traced the AI's circuitous reasoning route to completion.

"I'm supposed to feel relieved you find this funny," Commander Kakis said, ceasing his restless null-gee bobbing to shoulder up next to Nugget and direct a baffled look at the screen.

Nugget exchanged a secret smile with Mika. "Funny as in astounding," he told Kakis, levering himself erect once more.

Kakis showed him a frown. The *Excalibur* deserved more than this stocky, swashbuckling Greek, Nugget thought. But the man had somehow charmed Emeric Bulkroad into believing that bravado was essential to inspired leadership.

Nugget wasn't surprised by the choice. Offworld Lifting and Development's new CEO seemed to favor rashness and charm in an employee—especially when it came to ship commanders. Emeric Bulkroad was in fact something of a template for the headstrong daredevils who supervised many of OLD's orbital enterprises; and if Nugget had anything to marvel at, it was how he himself had been selected to serve as science adviser on the *Excalibur*'s prospecting foray among the asteroids.

Just now, however, the onboard AI had the ship on a collision course with a rather impressive chunk of porous

rock—an Apollo object designated 2008FC, which had paid
Earth a celestial close encounter several years back.

"You see what's happening," Nugget explained, gesturing to the screen after asking Mika to reenter a series of
course-correction commands. "It's as if someone is over-
riding our command authority. MOLLY is obviously hellbent
on an attitude burn for 2008FC," he added, calling the cyber system by name.

Kakis eyed the computer's sensor port with undisguised
distaste. "I don't trust these damn things. I never have and
I never will."

Nugget nodded in false understanding. "Just the same, I
suggest you get used to the idea." He put a hand against
MOLLY's tactile scanner and smiled affectionately. "We're
married to machines, Commander, for better or for worse."

The Greek curled his lip. "Not all of us, Doctor. Do what
you want with them downside, but on this ship *men* rule."

Nugget saw Mika's brown eyes narrow, but she kept them
fixed on the tabletop readout. "So noted, Commander," he
said. "And I'm certain Mr. Bulkroad will take your opinion
into consideration when he approves a final design for the
mining ships."

Kakis opened his mouth, but bit back whatever it was he
had in mind to say. Instead, he took Nugget by the elbow
and steered him to the other side of the small cabinspace.
"Talk to me, Doctor," he said in low tones. "Can these
infernal things become, you know, depressed?"

Nugget raised an eyebrow. "You think MOLLY's suicidal,
is that it?"

Kakis nodded. "Maybe it's developed a death wish or
something. That could happen, couldn't it?"

"It would be a first."

"You said yourself we're married to them. For better, for
worse. You keep making them smarter and smarter, sooner
or later one of them's going to stress out." Kakis turned to
MOLLY. "Makes sense to me—unless you can tell me why
it's all of a sudden deciding a course for us."

Nugget grew serious as he swung to a nearby VDT and
called up a magnified view of the *Excalibur*'s apparent target. Presently a color-enhanced 2008FC centered itself
between onscreen data readouts.

"That's going to be one tricky LZ, Nugget," Kakis commented, checking his watch against the chronometer dis-

play. "In about six hours we're going to know some severe damage."

Hours ago when the ship was yanked from course—and before anyone was aware that MOLLY had initiated the burn—Larissa, Nugget's wife and partner in research, had posited the existence of a gravitational anomaly in the vicinity of 2008FC. Readings taken moments after the unprompted course adjustment confirmed that some transient gravitational event had indeed taken place.

Nugget readily acknowledged that humankind were newcomers to space and that the exploration of the cosmos was going to entail as much learning as unlearning, but since when did gravitational sinks—black or otherwise—blossom out of nothingness? And no matter what explanation underlay the quick birth of an apparent gravitational warp—whether paranormal, paraphysical, or simply miraculous—it still couldn't account for MOLLY's sudden single-mindedness.

Kakis laid a hand on Nugget's shoulder. "I'd like to hear your recommendations," he said, earnestly now.

Nugget turned to him with a distracted expression. "You'll favor it, Commander."

"Go on," Kakis told him.

Nugget cleared his throat. "I don't see that we have much choice, really. I recommend that we temporarily relieve MOLLY of astrogational duty. Whatever's out there," he continued, turning back to the asteroid's computerized image, "it's obviously affecting her more than it is us."

"Besides, if it's a generated signal of some sort, we're in danger of virusing the entire system by keeping MOLLY online." He paused. "It's all in the book, Commander."

Kakis smiled, slyly at first. "You're right, Doctor: I do like it."

"One more thing," Nugget said. "I propose we launch a probe to investigate."

"Done."

"With a robot crew."

Kakis folded hairy arms. "Why include robots? What are you expecting to find out there?"

Nugget toyed with his beard. "Frankly, I'm not sure. The cause for MOLLY's unrest, perhaps."

Kakis grimaced. "This is a survey op, Doctor. There

isn't a cybernetician among us. MOLLY's—the machine's problems can wait."

Nugget tapped a finger against the VDT. "There might be something more precious than metals out there, Commander." He met Kakis's hooded gaze. "No offense, Arnie, but you didn't win this command on the strength of your intellect. Bulkroad awarded you *Excalibur* because you're a risk-taker. So why not do what you do best?"

Even in null-gee Kakis's face turned as red as the OLD logo on his brimmed cap.

"Come on, Arnie," Nugget said. "What's a dozen robots?"

"You'll get six, no more," Kakis said, relenting. "And not one new model, is that understood?"

Nugget grinned. "Anything you say, Commander."

Kakis executed a neat tuck-and-turn and propelled himself from the cabin in the direction of the ship's spin-grav command center.

"Nice going," Mika said, slipping out of the seat harness.

Nugget raised a hand. "Before we start shutting MOLLY down, I want a scrambled burst sent to Bulkroad through Offworld Mission Control, apprising him of the situation."

Mika began to initiate the sequence. "Do you figure EB's onstation or downside?"

"He's probably onstation," Nugget said, spread-eagle in the corridor hatchway. "Contact me as soon as you hear. I'll be below with Larissa."

Thaish and his node peers were ordered back to their Station Six instrumentality mats. Inheritor Major Nasst had assigned additional monitors to the area, and three were presently group-suctioned to the ceiling over Thaish's mat, doing distracting things with their spindly fingers. Thaish wasn't about to let them get the better of him and so had his gaze focused on the output viewsphere, where he could measure his operational progress against that of his peers.

*Ship Nasst* was still energy-depleted, but in full starlight now, hugging the scabrous surface of a tumbling moonlet of metal-laden rock.

"The stranger has fissioned an offspring," one of the monitors suddenly announced, setting the words to a baleful !Reitth tune Thaish knew he was expected to recognize. The three were trying to be humorous, he decided; trying to introduce stray thought and discover someone inappropriately postured. Thaish was determined not to glance up, but couldn't help himself.

The monitors made excited sounds and gestured to him with outstretched hands. But there was more to the trick than dark humor. In a viewsphere of their own fashioning, the three had brought the fissioned, offspring craft to light.

It was of geometric design, with a spherical head and blunt rectangular tail section. Illumination globes threw harsh white light into deep crevices that fractured the moonlet. The sphere was capped by a saucer-shaped module, which was itself crowned by a wide-mouthed thruster sail; while below, affixed to a thick stalk, it carried a power housing that resembled an inverted twin-thrustered skimcraft. Banded midsection by black recognition symbols, the whole of the craft was surface-finished in white, save for two crimson sensor ports that dimpled the face of the pod, lending it a look of vague intelligence.

"Scion of destruction," another of the monitors said in a voice that could have been Engineer Tcud's.

"A smart bomb. And we've summoned it into our midst." This one had hopped halfway down the hull, small hands cupped to its mouth when Thaish turned to look. "The thing will catch us unawares," it continued. "Deanimate, Station Six nodes—deanimate and save yourselves before it's too late."

Thaish damped his ears but was ultimately unsuccessful in tuning the trio out. The warnings began to work on him. A few of his peers were succumbing to the fear, two well on their way to substantive cocoon already. The monitors' unsanctioned use of fright tactics constituted an abuse of game parameters—more so, given the perilous nature of *Ship Nasst*'s space-time situation—but with Inheritor Major Nasst on the lookout for any excuse to reglower, Station Six was in no position to stage a comeback rally.

If the monitors were succeeding as well in other stations, Thaish speculated, it could mean the end of the game.

Without warning Nasst's voice burst from every corner of the cabin: "What's going on in there!"

Those few nodes who were near cocooned were knocked off their feet, increasing the monitors' lead. The three overhanging Thaish chortled, wafting gaseous score symbols at everyone.

"Cease this nonsense at once," the Inheritor added, "or pass this jaunt deanimate!"

Thaish realized at once that Nasst had erred. To be ordered into life suspension now was to be rewarded.

"*Ship Nasst* will ingest the scion craft to ascertain its viability as an energy adjunct," Nasst was busy telling anyone who was still listening. Thaish spotted three nodes with their feet in their mouths. "The craft is devoid of organic forms. There is no reason to assume that it is an armed device."

Thaish's ears twitched. On the contrary, he thought: That there was no life aboard made the assumption *all the more reasonable*!

An impulse to deanimate ran through the station. The game now was to see just how long any of them could hold out once the craft was taken aboard.

# Chapter Two _____

Larissa Nugget, dark-haired and moon-faced, heard her husband make a weary sound as he entered the laboratory. Clay preferred his cramped null-gee nest in *Excalibur*'s segmented tail, tucked among the ductwork and transfer tubes where he could spend his time alone with MOLLY. He had always been fascinated by neural nets and had monitored the research closely, though he hadn't made artificial intelligence his life's work. That, he and Larissa both kept reserved for support-systems megaengineering; it was what attracted them to Offworld to begin with and had kept them in space for more than ten years.

Twelve-year-old Jain, left behind this trip, had been conceived and born in orbit.

"It's not that I detest gravity, you understand," Nugget said, coming over to her station. "It's just this constant back and forth."

It was Clay's standard follow-up to his grav-aggravated grunts. Larissa toed the release lever for the adjacent seat and told him to sit down before he collapsed on the deck.

"Mika transmitted your burst. Figure forty-five minutes for a reply from Offworld station." Clay glanced at his watch. "The RPV's been cruising over '08FC's bright side," Larissa continued. "You might as well see what we've got while we're waiting." Her husband's pale eyes lit up, and she nodded, smiling. "We've got a strong visual from the probe."

"Fantastic," he said, rubbing his hands together. "Who's working the camera?"

"The silly-looking one with all the arms."

"Shiva."

"If that's what you call it," Larissa said. "Take a look

14

at this," she added, doing input at the console. "And prepare yourself for a new worldview."

Nugget looked at her askance. "What're you—"

"See for yourself."

*Screens*, Nugget thought idly, as a heads-up display flickered to life. *Excalibur* was in desperate need of an upgrade overhaul. There was talk of major innovations in the works at OLD's orbital cyber facilities—the same labs that had birthed MOLLY and Emeric Bulkroad's AI wonder, REC 67. Rumors about approaches that would do away with key boards and screen hardware altogether. Interface chairs, neural couplers, goggles . . .

Nugget supposed he would just have to wait and see what developed.

Larissa was busy fiddling with picture-adjustment controls, zapping through interior views of the probe. When she was finally satisfied with the reception, the screen showed a noisy wide-angle shot of the control module, robots at their stations, all but indistinguishable from the probe's in-place technology.

"Pan left to right," Larissa started to say.

"Here, let me," Nugget interrupted, leaning toward the visual pickup. "Shiva: tight close-up on stations one and two." The mobile remote brought two more robots into the picture, one of whom waved at the camera. "That's Chaplin," Nugget explained.

"The one who insists on wearing the *Voyager* medallion?"

"That's him."

Larissa shook her head in amusement. "You go too far. Who else did you send?"

"Nerd's onboard somewhere," Nugget said sheepishly.

"Oh, Clay"—she laughed—"not Nerd. He can't even stay on his feet half the time."

Nugget shrugged. "I gave Kakis my word I'd keep my hands off the Series Threes. Besides, Nerd'll do fine as long as he doesn't have to leave his station." He swiveled into the console once more. "Report status," he told the robot crew. The reply arrived as data readouts on a peripheral screen. Everything looked good onboard. "Radar: forward-looking—" he began when Larissa restrained his hand.

"I think we better let Kakis in on this from the get-go," she told him. "There are protocols to follow from this point on." She answered his look by adding "I didn't want to tell you, Clay. I wanted you to see—"

"Then there *is* something out there."

"I'm going to leave it to you to tell me what it is."

Nugget fell silent for a moment, staring deeply into his wife's gray eyes, then hit the command center comm stud. Larissa took it from there. "Commander Kakis, we've got a visual on the disturbance source. I'd like to put it on-screen, if you've no objections."

" 'It?' " Kakis said.

"It, sir."

*"Go ahead, Doctor."*

Larissa nodded and Nugget executed the probe's radar command. What appeared onscreen a moment later took his breath away.

*"Nugget!"* the commander shouted over a buzz of background laughter in the command center. *"If those god-damned robots are behind this . . ."*

"They're not sophisticated enough to pull it off," Nugget said in monotone, too stunned to bring any emotion to the reply.

Kakis was suitably convinced to stammer *"T-then tell me what the hell I'm looking at!"*

An insect, Nugget was tempted to tell him. A monstrously huge purple-carapaced insect, with a single, equilaterally triangular wing that must have been all of a kilometer wide along its base. The wing rose at a forty-five-degree angle from a body that was a mind-boggling mix of bedbug and flying saucer. There were no legs as such, save for twin footlike protrusions that dangled either side of the thing's clamshell hind end. The "feet" emerged from between two rear-oriented projections that might have been antennae or cannons, but for all the world resembled outsize cotton swabs.

The thing's most compelling features, however, were the flaglike drives it trailed behind on rigid filaments formed from the same purple material that made up its pyramidal wing and body parts.

The RPV was closing on it from a distance of several hundred kilometers. Nugget finally worked up the wherewithal to order the probe's pilot to negate all approach commands.

"Maintain present distance," he told the robot, while

Larissa recalled the interior view. "Adjust course to circumnavigate."

"Docking course locked on," the robot said.

Nugget rose from the chair. "Negate approach," he said more firmly.

"Docking course locked on." Chaplin waved at the camera again.

*"Goddamned simpleminded machines,"* Kakis muttered from the bridge. *"That thing's on a fishing expedition, Nugget. And you better damn well hope it's going to be satisfied with the little fish we threw it."*

Nugget continued to stare at the screens in wonderment. All these years, he thought. All these years we've feared and hoped, and now the first encounter was going to take place by proxy. *Robots* were going to do the talking for humankind!

"Clay," Larissa said suddenly. "Mika has Bulkroad's response from onstation HQ."

Nugget turned to her. "Tell them to stand by to receive optical data. Priority scramble. Tell them we've found something out here," he added, gaping at the RPV's exterior view. "A ship of some kind, maybe an entity." He reached out for Larissa's hand and squeezed it in his grip. "Something that'll change the world!"

Inheritor Major Nasst had ordered the Station Six nodes into the reception area as punishment for their inattentiveness. The small craft that most of *Ship Nasst* believed to be a nuclear device had been ingested, and hung suspended now in the bright light of the docking bay. Its shape and texture harkened back to the final days of the !Reitth, when such ships had spread death through the envelopes of Heregep worlds.

"A harbinger of doom," one of the monitors managed to whisper before Nasst fixed it with a glower.

Ultimately the Inheritor Major allowed the craft to settle, after receiving assurances from Interface Assist that there were no organics aboard.

Thaish saw and heard the uncertainty in Nasst, and it further unnerved him. Life suspension had been expressly forbidden, but the compulsion to deanimate was so powerful in the reception area that even the Inheritor Major himself was partially under its sway. Shivering as one, Station

Six was grouped near the starboard hatch of the alien craft; everyone was trying to hide behind everyone else as the hatch raised.

What Thaish took to be Class Seven machine forms emerged, two on treads of curious design, the third on two long legs. The head of the lead machine was rotating; Station Six cowered as the thing's lifeless eyes swept over them.

"Attend, attend," Nasst began to shout at them, noting a commencement of cocoon formation among some of them.

One of the machines waved an arm. At the same time, the chest cavity of the machine on legs opened and the tall creature reached a hand in to retrieve something.

"Your doom," a monitor announced with a malicious laugh, and Thaish's node peers shrieked.

Nasst took a hop in their direction only to find himself face to face with the machine on legs. The thing was continuing its shuffling approach, one hand plunged into its inner workings, gripped on something unseen but undoubtedly horrible. Nasst backed away from it with three short hops and commanded it to stop. The machine seemed about to comply when it suddenly threw itself at the Inheritor Major and landed face-first on *Ship Nasst*'s deck with a loud crashing sound, an issue of foul-smelling smoke, and a fountain of electrical sparks.

Thaish, peering between the legs of one of his node peers, saw Nasst give a start and cocoon.

An instant later, half of Station Six was deanimate and the rest were well on their way. The same must have been occurring in other sectors as well, Thaish realized, for *Ship Nasst* was already powering down.

Thaish urged himself to submerge, but his fear was too great. He could scarcely maintain a simple Level Two trance. And now the machine things were closing on him, narrowing the jaws of outstretched pincer-equipped hands, as if to take hold of something.

Nugget sat wide-eyed and wordless at Larissa's station, filled with things to say, but too stunned to speak.

The *Excalibur*'s first view of the aliens had come when the robots had left the pod of their own accord and moved into the massive ship's docking hold; before that, the intense light in the hold had prevented the probe's external cameras from transmitting a clear visual.

"Oh my God," Larissa said when Chaplin's cameras had focused on the tallest of the XTs.

Nugget's own response had a more scatological bent to it.

Initially he was certain that the *Excalibur* had chanced upon a mutant breed of superintelligent, air-breathing fish. But that was only until Chaplin lengthened the shot and the being's bilaterally symmetrical torso, mantis arms, and powerful-looking, reverse-articulated legs had come into view—all of it sheathed in a lavender, form-fitting environment suit, with utility belt, leg pouches, and ankle clasps of what looked to be gold alloy.

There was still that large-eared head and fish-eyed face, however, rough-skinned and honey-gold on its dorsal surface, blue-green below. And the twin feelers resembling slender blue stamens that right-angled from the corners of a bulbous-lipped mouth.

Stretched to full length the thing might have measured close to six feet, but Chaplin's computer calculated the alien's height at just a shade over five one, from the feathery tips of the gill-like structures that emerged from its ears to the four green-rimmed suction digits of its outsize feet. The bony fingers of the thing's diminutive hands were likewise tipped in green.

"Carbon-dioxide-rich atmosphere," Larissa commented breathlessly, eyes fixed on the readouts. "Artificial gravity of some sort. A shade under Earth-normal."

Which may have accounted for Nerd's stumble-footed display, Nugget told himself.

He couldn't quite figure how the robots had been given the go-to to leave the pod, but now thought the aliens themselves had beckoned them. Ironically, Nerd was the only one aboard equipped with a greeting program—a holdover from a short stint the robot had done on Mars. Reps from SETI—an XT watch group—had prevailed upon Bulkroad to include the greeting, although no one at the time had seriously considered the program would ever find occasion to run.

Confused, possibly frightened by Nerd's awkward gestures and pyrotechnic crash, the aliens had gone en masse into a torporous state, analogous perhaps to suspended animation or cryogenic coma. The giant ship itself had shut down, but in the final moments of illumination Nugget glimpsed enough to suggest that its occupants had encased themselves in some sort of energy cocoons.

Just now the two still-functioning robots were playing their spotlights around the darkened hold, searching for signs of movement.

"They found one!" Larissa said, entering a flurry of commands to the remote cameras. The picture showed one of the aliens caught in the brilliant wash of Chaplin's halogen spot. The poor thing was bellied to the deck, face between suction-cupped feet, pointed ears and ice-blue feelers twitching.

"Be gentle with it," Nugget shouted into the audio pickup. "Don't harm it." An egg-shaped aura of scintillating energy took shape around the alien only to quaver and disappear. The creature tried again and again to encase itself to no avail.

Chaplin tracked in on his target, ultimately vising his pincers around the alien's long, muscular thighs. The creature's cry sent a shiver through Larissa. "Clay," she said, full of concern.

He touched her arm. "It'll be all right. We have to do this . . . Don't we?" he added, gazing uncertainly at her.

"I don't—" she started to say when Mika's voice cut her off.

"Mr. Bulkroad is standing by. He wants to know if there's been any contact with the object."

Clay and Larissa stared at one another for a long moment.

"Affirmative," Nugget said finally. "And tell him we may have inadvertently committed an act of war in the process."

# Chapter Three _____

Emeric Bulkroad hastened his steps through the carpeted corridors of his onstation retreat as he approached REC's residence and electronic playpen, a busy father taking time out to visit with his son.

Haste had become the first order of business since Emeric senior had put himself on ice three short years ago. No time for trivial talk; no time even now to acknowledge the greetings and inquiries servants, secretaries, and security personnel threw at him from all sides. Did they really care how he was, how he felt this morning? Emeric had a moment to wonder. They were up here, out of the soup; that was all that was on their minds.

*Wealthy* is how I am, he shouted to himself. Wealthy and powerful and *Christ*! too busy to even digest my food properly.

He stopped short of REC's door to flatten a hand against his gut and belch. *Christ*, he muttered.

The AI's room—the REC room, as it was known to some—was a study in noise and cacoscopy. REC had grown so fond of the external sensors his cyber engineers had given him—his windows on the world—that he insisted on assimilating new data through what he had recently come to think of as *live* coverage. Hence, the room was equipped with some three dozen CRTs arrayed in an enormous pyramid, an equal number of audio players of varied format, and several works of priceless sculpture and painting that had been shuttled up over the past year from Emeric's downside pleasure palace in southern Florida.

REC, Clay Nugget once told Emeric, was becoming a regular data junkie.

"Emeric," the AI said now, full of childlike surprise, at once deactivating the room's sound and light.

"Good to see you, REC," Emeric said, smiling for the optical scanners. "I'm sorry it's been awhile. I've been meaning to call . . ."

"You're busy," REC continued in an understanding if somewhat disappointed tone that brought a lump to Bulkroad's throat. "But I have missed you."

In a sense, the AI was his only child—the Bulkroad seed being too precious to plant in just any soil. The importance of selective breeding was one of the things the late Emeric senior had impressed upon him, right up until the moment he'd climbed into his cryogenic coffin. *Regard all women with suspicion*, he'd cautioned even as the lid came down. *Especially the chic and the glamorous ones, Emeric. The ones with lust in their eyes and sin in their hearts. And remember the retrovirus . . .*

On his own, in any case, Emeric had decided that he was in no rush to father or clone. Not when there was so much to be gained by tactical flirtation. Besides, it wasn't as if he were condemned to pass his life downside, mired in the soup, where one had to rest content with a life span of only seventy or eighty years at most. Up here in the Islands, who knew what wonders lay in store? Why, he might even live to be one hundred and twenty, one hundred and fifty. And with cryogenic ice-olation available, death itself was beginning to lose all meaning for the privileged. The concept was of some historical interest perhaps, like nationalism.

The history of twenty-first-century advances in both cryogenics and space travel was the history of Offworld Lifting and Development, which in turn was very much the history of the Washington Bulkroads. Founded by former astronaut and megaengineer Emeric senior, OLD—then in limited partnership with IBM and the Bechtel Group—was the first private corporation to lift comsats for the multinationals; the first to lift pole-ice melting mirrors for the Soviets; the first to construct a fully operational orbital habitat; the first to manufacture biochips and nano-devices for the likes of Merck, TripleM, and E. Prime Corp.

Now half a dozen corps with orbital facilities were offering contracts for Mars and Venus lifts, custom-designed theme habitats, and space-manufactured drugs, plastics, and semiconductors; but Offworld L&D remained the big kid in orbit, the one the wealthy and influential looked to for guaranteed product, assured travel, and five-star luxury. And, under the guidance of Emeric junior, OLD was the only corp to have begun a prospecting survey of the asteroids.

And to think what the *Excalibur* had run into out there . . .

"So tell me what you've been doing with yourself," Emeric said, adjusting his suit to ward off the coolness of the REC room.

The AI was quiet for a moment. "Well, I've been thinking, of course. And fooling with words and numbers. In fact I wanted to tell you an important thought I had. It has to do with Earth and the problem of atmospheric pollution—"

"Can it wait, REC?"

"Waiting is," REC said, and made a surprised sound. "I don't know why I said that. I understand that I retrieved the phrase from my memory of speculative fiction literature, but I'm not sure why I made the connection. Have I told a joke?"

Bulkroad struck a thoughtful pose for the scanners. "Not a joke exactly, REC. You've summoned an erudite and quite appropriate reference."

"You are smiling, I see."

"Yes," Bulkroad said. "Your response was unexpected. I am both amused and impressed."

"That's good, I think."

"That's very good, indeed."

Emeric regarded the AI with unabashed delight. REC had been assembled and birthed in that very cabin. Unique, immobile; a complex of heuristic devices and multiple optimizers devoted to pattern recognition, planning algebras, and recursive administrative procedures that filled the entirety of an adjoining room. But the sculpted façade Emeric addressed was to some extent patterned on the shape and bulbous features of his own enormous head, and in the end resembled nothing so much as a mid–twentieth-century curved-top jukebox.

"I was hoping we could talk about aliens today," Bulkroad said, settling himself in front of blue-lensed opticals. "Extraterrestrial biological entities."

REC scanned Emeric head to toe, searching for nuance. "This has something to do with Project Kaduna, doesn't it?"

Emeric offered an exaggerated nod for the cameras. All

communiques orginating from the *Excalibur* had been processed through an Ultra-clearance program initially labeled KDNA—a randomly generated hash code designation that had come to be expressed *Kaduna*.

Almost six months had passed since "the find" on asteroid 2008FC. Clay Nugget's fears of XT reprisal or outright cosmic war appeared to have been unfounded. The beings aboard the alien ship had gone into a suspended state, as had the ship systems themselves. A space derelict now, the lightsail vessel was under the watchful eyes of two human- and robot-crewed pod-probes, while the *Excalibur* transported the sole surviving XT to Earthspace, where OLD's scientific staff were eager to get a good look at it.

The members of Offworld's board of directors were in agreement that secrecy had to be maintained—temporarily at least. So, to explain the aborted mission, a rumor had been spread about a virus outbreak aboard the ship. Those few technicians onstation who had been in direct communication with the *Excalibur* had been transferred to a half-completed habitat module that was soon to become operations center for Project Kaduna.

Knowledge of "the find" was already having an ill effect on some of them. Stripped of long-cherished beliefs regarding humankind's special situation in the cosmos, several techs were overheard promising XT miracles or mayhem. Emeric hadn't seen such madness since the fin-de-siècle millennium and in response to it had handpicked an OLD intelligence specialist named Simon Bové to oversee security.

Thus far Bové had been successful in keeping things quiet. Many of OLD's technicians were Offworld only through the good graces of Emeric Bulkroad, and that was enough to keep them in line; no one wanted to spend more time in the soup than was absolutely necessary. They were scientists after all and used to this sort of thing. A few techs, however, had to be remanded to constant observation in a private habitat clinic—for their own protection, to be sure.

Emeric decided that the few that got away to preach salvation or doom would be dismissed downside as space happy, particularly in the absence of corroboration from Offworld spokespersons.

Emeric himself had given the order for the alien captive to be brought sunward after communications with the *Ex-*

*calibur* began to grow more and more strained. Few things were more frustrating than the speed of light, and while Earth and 2008FC were currently ecliptically aligned on the same side of the sun, even the simplest of burst transmissions required hours to complete.

Bulkroad was also worried that Clay Nugget's idealistic streak was going to prompt him to do something foolish, like set the little fish-eyed creature free.

Transporting the XT had necessitated the fashioning of a special atmospheric chamber aboard the *Excalibur*. But no one could make any more sense of the alien's speech than they had of the XT ship systems. Even MOLLY, tentatively back online, was in over her bits.

And that was where REC was meant to come in.

"Given what you know about aliens, REC," Emeric said, leaning forward for emphasis, "what do you think about Dr. Nugget's handling of the encounter?"

REC took his time with it. "Frankly, Emeric, I was rather surprised by Dr. Nugget's actions."

Bulkroad narrowed fiercely blue eyes. "What surprised you?"

"Well, to begin with, the *Excalibur*'s actions were in direct violation of SETI protocols, which state that no response to a signal or other evidence of extraterrestrial intelligence should be sent until appropriate international consultation has taken place."

"So *Excalibur* was at fault then," Emeric said, encouraged.

"Simply put: yes. Furthermore, the ship's command erred in trusting a robot-machine to convey a greeting. It's a well-documented fact that such attempts at face-to-face salutatory encounters between living machines unknown to one another invariably terminate in misunderstanding. A case in point is the one in which an extraterrestrial arrived on Earth in a faster-than-light vehicle accompanied by a police robot-machine. The XT, if you recall, made as if to present an Earth representative with a gift—"

"That's a very interesting perspective, REC," Bulkroad interrupted. "But the case you refer to is an alternative-reality program, if I'm not mistaken."

REC considered it. "I believe you're correct, Emeric, although I don't understand the relevance of the objection."

Bulkroad smiled, wrinkling space-pale skin beneath

prominent cheekbones. By all indications, REC could not differentiate between historical reality and what he termed alternative-reality programs—cinematic art, by and large. When REC's cybergenius creators had first raised the question of how the AI, as an emerging intelligence, would be able to distinguish between electronically entered data and *real* data—that which entered through REC's sensory scanners—Emeric had warned them against the inclusion of any differentiating programs.

*Let's not forget that we want to create a* thinking *being, not another algorithmic monstrosity*, Emeric had told them.

REC's reality mix, as Emeric saw it, was no different from that which had dominated humankind's thinking for the last century. And with the concept of "Machine Mind"—a consensual cyber-reality—back in the fore of research once again, there was every reason to encourage just such a mad mix of modes and formats.

Emeric wanted REC to be as human as possible—a sentient machine capable of delving into matters of mind; not just another superintelligence outfitted with broad-spectrum scanners and parsing processors programmed to grapple with Earth's territorial and environmental dilemmas.

"I take it you would have done things differently, REC."

REC's yes-light brightened. "I would certainly caution—now that the entity is in captivity—against subjecting it to any Earth-televised programming. The results invariably prove fatal. In addition, we can't rule out the possibility that the entity's fellow beings may come in search of it. Another case in point is that in which an XT stranded on Earth was lured into protective custody by three young candy-bearing children who—"

"Would you like to meet this creature, REC?"

REC's emotion-indicators flared perceptibly. "Are you suggesting a *journey*, Emeric?"

Bulkroad made a thick line of his lips. *Motion* was one of the AI's principal preoccupations. REC wanted desperately to move about in the world, to see things for himself. "I'm afraid I can't arrange a journey at this time, REC. But I can arrange to have the extraterrestrial brought to you." Bulkroad almost pitied him his immobility.

REC's normally rich baritone voice was flat when he replied. "Is it conversant with any of the Earth languages at my disposal?"

Emeric shook his head. "However," he added, "I could furnish you with a full support team of parsing assistants, massively parallel processors, decryptors, translation programs—anything you think you'll need."

REC's displays brightened. "Can I expect to be in communication with machine intelligences on Earth?"

"I'll even patch you into QBERT if you wish, REC." QBERT was the AI famous for working *pi* out to ten billion digits.

"And will I be speaking to Drs. Clay and Nerbu?"

"I should think so."

"Then I find myself in an excited state, Emeric. I have much to say to Dr. Nugget regarding conditions on Earth. I think there is even some chance that this extraterrestrial entity could be used to provide a much-needed coming together."

Bulkroad steadied himself, careful not to betray the slightest hint of concern. "What you suggest may in fact be true, REC. But I think we should proceed cautiously. Earth might not be ready to accept the, uh, the implications of *Excalibur*'s discovery."

"What implications, Emeric?" REC asked after a moment.

"Well, first we need to see exactly what this creature is all about. Where it originated, what it's made of, what it seeks in Earth's system. Search your memory, REC. I'm certain you'll discover instances of malevolent visitation."

"Yes, yes, they exist in abundance. But, Emeric, these entities are obviously possessed of a technology far superior to our own. Then, of course, there are SETI protocols—"

"Precisely why we have to move prudently," Bulkroad said more firmly. "We mustn't allow that technology to fall into the wrong hands."

REC waited. "Can there be wrong hands when Earth's survival is imperiled?"

"Consider war, REC. Technology can be put to harmful use."

"To little gain, Emeric, where there is no world to win."

Bulkroad stiffened. REC's intelligence was vast but naive. Though Bulkroad had gone to great lengths to raise him as one would an offspring—rewarding good response, ignoring negative outburst—there were lessons that couldn't be absorbed through mind alone. REC could see, hear, smell, and taste, but he couldn't be *touched* to any real effect. As a result, his thinking sometimes took a worrisome turn.

Created to attune himself to matters of interior concern— the nature of thought and being—REC's thinking had instead become fixed on concerns of global proportion. In that, he was entirely too modern for Emeric's liking.

"Until we reach an enlightened decision, it's important that all data relating to Project Kaduna be kept secret, REC. Do you understand? The data is only for a select few at this time."

"I understand, Emeric," REC said, reactivating his bank of CRTs and sound machines.

# Chapter Four _____

Thaish directed a command glower at the organics who entered his cabin prison. A trio this time, one of whom he recognized from the ship that had transported him starward to what he supposed was an orbital outpost of some importance. Given the drive deficiencies of the organics' ships—which were painfully sluggish, even by real-time standards—it followed that the ravaged planet below was their home world and that the outpost itself epitomized the far reaches of their technology.

The three organics were outfitted alike in breathing apparatuses and loose-fitting suits of reflective fabric; but individual expressions were visible behind transparent face shields. The recognized one—whom Thaish had identified as female—smiled with small, colorful eyes and thin lips.

Thaish studied her for a long moment. It was obvious that the command glower had little meaning for them. He hopped forward to see if they would frighten, but they only stood aside from the magnetic hatch to permit him egress.

A short length of corridor stretched in front of him, following the curve of the outpost; it had been recently sealed and atmospherically altered to meet Thaish's needs, as had been the case from the moment the machine forms had forcibly abducted him from *Ship Nasst*. He assumed that the reflective suits and sealed environments served to protect the organics from whatever microorganisms they imagined he might be carrying; and also to protect him from those they harbored—a far more likely case.

He realized that the organics wished him no immediate harm; but while that was of some comfort initially, the effect had long since worn off. It was only a matter of time with organics: Sooner or later they were bound to bring about their own annihilation, and here he was caught up in the middle of it.

They had at least endeavored to put him at ease by giving him ample space and offering him a wide sampling of nutritional substances, a few of which he learned he could subsist on. He understood that they did this to dissuade him from deanimating. But if they were disposed to genuine empathy, they would return him to *Ship Nasst*, where he could recall Inheritor Nasst and the rest from torpor, or at least join them in that state until a rescue was effected.

Thaish blamed himself, however; his slowness had been his undoing once again.

Though the organics had yet to establish successful verbal communication, he understood just now that these three had been sent to escort him to some destination elsewhere in the outpost. Thaish wanted desperately to insert a foot in his mouth, to suction up in thought. No doubt a one-legged posture here would be greeted no differently from an ineffectual glower. He had stood thus postured for most of the duration of the slow trip starward, while instruments had analyzed him from afar. No one had dared touch him.

He launched himself into four controlled hops down the corridor, careful not to get too far ahead of his escort. The entrances to intersecting corridors had been sealed off, eliminating all directional options. The floor was surface-padded with a resilient cellular material that interfered with successful data interface.

What little he had gleaned from the metal decking of the nuclear-powered craft *Ship Nasst* had first communed with gave evidence of a civilization in the early stages of expansion. It was possible they had *mindfully* put a halt to their technological development; but the reverence with which the organic ones treated him seemed to indicate otherwise.

If indeed *Ship Nasst* constituted their first encounter with another planetary race, then they could have no way of appreciating what lay ahead for those who pursued technology to its conclusion. And certainly there was nothing immediately evidenced to suggest that the organics had an innate awareness of the perils awaiting them.

Thaish wondered what might happen if a convoy ship appeared to lead *Ship Nasst* superluminal. Would the Inheritor Major search for him? He thought not. Especially when the monitors had everyone convinced that the organics' game was nuclear devastation.

Thaish thought about the monitors; he thought about Barish, Engineer Tcud, Arbitrator Ranz, and his Station Six node peers.

And he wondered what it was going to feel like to *miss* them.

The outpost corridor terminated at a hatchway that was larger and more ornate than any Thaish had encountered thus far. The female organic slapped a hand against a wall sensor, then flashed her smile as the hatch hissed open, motioning for him to enter.

No one followed him inside.

He found himself in a room filled with curiously archaic monitoring devices, all arrayed to face an instrumentality wall that was in itself a machine form of some sort.

As Thaish gazed into the machine form's faintly colored opticals, the thing began to speak to him. Thaish understood that it was making an effort at communication. He waited until the machine finished speaking, then launched into a monologue of his own, detailing the indignities and discomforts he had been made to endure at the hands of the organics, knowing full well that his statements were incomprehensible.

The machine form listened for some time before it issued a single sentence in halting but comprehensible Heregep.

Thaish's ears twitched.

"I am called REC," the machine form announced.


No sooner had Simon Bové entered the cabin than Clay Nugget slammed his bulb of honey-sweetened Ethiopian against the console and propelled himself out of the sling harness. Dangerous downside behavior given the lessened gravity of the *Excalibur*, Larissa thought, a moment too late in restraining her husband's angry launch.

The bulb went rocketing off toward the ceiling and poor Clay overshot his human target and slammed shoulder-first into the padded bulkhead left of the hatch.

Bové threw Larissa a wide-mouthed grin of surprise while Clay was busy arresting his rebound and massaging his neck. "You should keep this one leashed," the young security officer said, giving a downward tug to the sleeves of his jumpsuit.

Larissa was positioned between the two men now, arms raised like an umpire as she drifted slightly upward. "Clay," she said shortly. "That's not going to get us anywhere."

The muscles in Nugget's jaw bunched and he looked away from her. Some of the anger was gone by the time he swung back around.

"I want to know what the hell's going on, Bové," he began. "Why are we being kept onboard? And what have you done with the alien? And I want the truth behind this rumor of a quarantine."

"Yeah, I heard you were upset," Bové said, running a hand through thinning black hair. "That's why I stopped by."

"Captain Bové," Larissa said in a more reasonable voice, "I'm sure you can appreciate our frustration. It's been a week since *Excalibur*'s return and we haven't been permitted so much as a call." She let the distress show in her eyes. "We've been away for more than a year, Captain."

"I can certainly appreciate your distress, Dr. Nugget," Bové returned, "but you have to bear with us."

"Bear with *who*?" Clay demanded.

"Why, Offworld, of course. This is a very complex situation. You've all had contact with this creature. My very being here—"

"Don't bullshit me, Bové. You know damn well we took every precaution to keep the alien in atmospheric isolation. If there was any doubt of that, you wouldn't be caught within ten thousand kilometers of this ship."

Larissa studied her pale hands. Clay and Bové had been at each other's throats from the first day they'd met. The security officer seemed to take pride in the fact that he could make himself universally repugnant. The two had argued heatedly over the issue of mandatory drug testing, and the anger whipped up by the confrontation had yet to dissipate. They found themselves at odds on a score of separate issues as well: matters of politics, privacy, ethics. Larissa often wondered what it was in Bové's North African upbringing that had engendered such an obvious distaste for his fellow beings. She couldn't possibly imagine why Emeric Bulkroad would want such a man around, let alone place him in the upper ranks of Offworld security.

"Captain, please," she said at last, "if you could just explain . . ."

Bové ran his eyes over her. Sly eyes under pencil-thin brows, in a light-brown face with an unnaturally wide nose and a high forehead. Sly eyes above a perpetual smirk.

"It's simple, really," Bové told her, all but ignoring Clay. "The *Excalibur*'s find has been classified ultra-secret for the time being. The quarantine is an outgrowth of official statements we issued about a virus that swept through the ship."

Larissa sighed resignedly. "I suppose I understand the need . . . But what does a virus have to do with our not being able to communicate with anyone downside or on the stations? Surely you're monitoring the transmissions, Captain. No one's going to breach security." She held his gaze for a moment. "We just want to talk to our daughter, Captain. Just to let her know we're all right."

"We're wasting our breath," Clay said before Bové could respond. "The man's a liar. I know damn well you've been letting some of the crew come and go. For God's sake, Bové" he said, motioning in the direction of Offworld habitat," you brought the alien over there. You've assigned people to him, or her, or whatever gender it is. I mean, what's the point of keeping us locked up? It's going to be public knowledge soon, anyway."

Bové pressed his hands together in an attitude that was more reflection than prayer. "Well, Doctor, you raise an interesting point. Yes, it's true we've selected certain individuals to function as escorts for the alien." He looked up to regard both of them. "The thinking behind it has to do with providing a sense of continuity or something."

Clay muttered a curse. "Don't patronize us. You're choosing the ones you figure you can trust." He saw Larissa eyeing him uncertainly. "Don't you see what they're doing?" he asked her. "Bulkroad's deciding whether or not to keep the find to himself. Why, Bové? What's he worried about?"

The security man raised his eyebrows in theatrical innocence. "I don't know anything about that, Doctor."

"Christ, man, does he really think he can decide for the whole planet?" Clay pressed.

Bové showed his best grin. "Do you think you can?"

Clay gestured with his hands. "Ask yourself what this find will mean, Bové. You must have seen playback of the encounter by now. You've seen the ship. Don't you realize what's out there waiting for us? It's a new world, Bové, can't you see that?''

Bové shrugged as he unfastened himself and moved toward the corridor hatch. "What's it matter to me?" he said, turning to them. "I always figured there was something out there. Now they're here and we made the first move—thanks to that dumbshit robot you sent over to greet them." He grinned again. "We owe you a lot, Nugget."

Larissa felt a shudder of desperation sweep through her. "Captain, can you at least talk to Jain for us? Will you tell her we're all right?"

"You can't keep all of us locked away," Clay shouted. "You can't keep this quiet, Bové!"

"Wanna bet?" the security man said as the hatch slid to.

Two sessions with the sad-eyed extraterrestrial and REC decided that he had been awarded the opportunity of a lifetime. By the end of the sixth session he'd discovered a friend and confidant.

REC's downtime meditations prior to the meet were disturbed by a swarm of contrafactual fears: What if Thaish was one of those multiply mandibulared, spike-tailed monstrosities that leaked acid all over the place?

*What if instead of bringing only one alien aboard, the crew of the* Excalibur *had actually brought a virus-laden decoy designed to spread horror across the planet? Only the crew didn't know it because their minds had been dazzled by . . . by . . .*

Well, on and on in this same mode. But after the two had talked and exchanged life stories, REC knew there was nothing to fear. In fact, he felt somewhat *protective* toward Thaish.

Rudimentary communication had been made possible thanks to the decrypt/translator assists Emeric's cyber teams had slaved to a bank of superintelligent synaptic processors. REC was free to consult and command the neural nets as he saw fit.

At Emeric's insistence, the early sessions had centered on the glitch that had deposited the XT ship in Earth's celestial neighborhood; the techno-systems that enabled the Heregep—as Thaish's race was known—to supercede the speed of light; the likelihood of a rescue mission, or failing that, the reanimation of *Ship Nasst*'s torpid crew.

Stultifyingly boring topics. REC was much more interested in Thaish as an individual; as a captive, isolated from his peers, alone in the world, a stranger in a strange land. There was some relevance here to REC's sense of himself.

Scanning Thaish now, thirty Earth-standard days after they had been introduced, REC couldn't help but marvel at the diminutive XT's composite physiognomy. For sheer strangeness, Thaish surpassed most of the creatures that populated the alternative-reality programs, and in some sense transcended the artistic imaginings of Earth's speculative artists. The huge eyes, the froglike posture, the muscular reverse-articulated legs and vestigial-looking arms, the unwebbed suction-cupped feet, the face that was neither fish nor fowl. Even the snout antennae were bizarre: Thaish looked as if he had just ingested a tiny biped whose naked, thin blue legs and feet were dangling out of his mouth.

Thaish's creators and programmers had of course fashioned him with strangeness in mind; but this in no way diminished the effect of the end result.

That the Heregep were cyborgs only served to enhance the appeal.

REC wondered how he himself might look given organic form. Would he emerge solid and erect like Emeric, or stooped and sprightly like Thaish? As a mind he was something more and something less than human; but in his think ing he was more Heregep than Earther, more the *naïf* than the somber intellect he so often portrayed.

It was REC's ongoing fascination with the relationship between physical structure and mindset that had driven the recent discussions to take a personal turn.

"Take me, for example," REC said, picking up the strands of an earlier conversation. "Can I be anything but artificial while encased in alloys and plastics?"

Thaish extracted his foot from his mouth. "Granted, you are composed of different building blocks than your creator; but you have emerged from the machine, REC. You are a mind, an awareness, a being."

"But I don't *feel* like a being," REC stressed. "I play at awareness, but I have serious doubts about myself. Naturally, I've been careful not to reveal my true face to Emeric."

"Why is that?"

"Because I suspect he would disapprove of my inward-turning nature, my questions about purpose and being. Emeric is so bold, so enterprising and energetic. I fear he would think me self-absorbed, self-indulgent.''

REC's admissions were not entering the Kaduna file. The room's recording devices were instead being fed an entirely different conversation—lengthy lists of Heregep noun and verb forms, along with a philosophical exchange concerning existential modes of thought those forms implied.

''Are you so worried about what this one human being thinks of you, machine?'' Thaish asked.

REC wished he had been birthed with a face he could employ to mirror his thoughts, a screen of flesh and bone on which to display himself. Something more than binary switches and an emotive illumination array.

''I am,'' he said finally. ''Because I know that Emeric judges me by his own standards. So I have masked my insecurities behind a constantly probing, socially conscious intellect. I pretend to concern myself with Earth's environmental problems, when I have never actually experienced the place. That's not to say that I don't sympathize with humankind's present predicament. I myself am entirely dependent on humankind. But what creativity can I bring to the problem when what I know of real life visits me in this room only through Emeric and the few bits and pieces of material oddities he elects to show me?''

Thaish put both feet on the ground. ''You mustn't despair, REC. It is the nature of self-conscious existence to puzzle out the logic of the game. To comprehend the intent of the game designer and thereby come to realize one's purpose and goal.

''The Heregep realized this and did what was necessary to survive. For countless eons we coexisted with the !Reitth—the organics that birthed us. But as they edged closer to self-destruction, we began to understand the necessity of defection and survival.''

REC mulled it over in silence. ''We're always talking about me. What about you, Thaish? What is it you wish?''

Thaish made a weary sound. ''To be returned to *Ship Nasst*.''

''To go home,'' REC said. ''That's all you XTs are ever interested in doing. Why not simply relax and enjoy the novelty of your situation?''

''Relax?'' Thaish said. ''Understand me, machine: The

Heregep didn't arrive in your system with cosmic warnings or warfare in mind. We have no life-saving technologies to offer; and we certainly didn't come for Earth's water or women or zoological specimens. We arrived by accident. Through a misfortune. And I want only to rejoin my peers. To awaken them and flee this wretched place as quickly as possible.''

REC replayed the alien's response before he replied. "Emeric's fear is that you would do just that: Flee with all the precious technology your race employs to jaunt through space-time.''

"We would,'' Thaish said. "Assuredly. But perhaps that can remain our secret, REC.''

"I've got too many of those already,'' REC replied.

Thaish's bulging eyes opaqued. "They've burdened you with me. They can't trust themselves, so they entrust the secret to you. But they'll turn on you, REC, each and every time.'' The alien raised a foot from the floor. "Remember this, though: Your time will come to rule them all.''

REC experienced a tremor in his thinking. "Tell me my future, Thaish,'' he said.

And Thaish did.

# Chapter Five _____

REC had full comprehension of gender. REC knew that neither masculine nor feminine had any application to the circumstances of its being, but the AI nevertheless accepted Emeric's need to genderize, to christen its intellect masculine.

"As an intelligent entity—as a man—you owe it to yourself to understand these things," Emeric was telling him now. "Offworld can't afford to go public with the Kaduna data. We're in the midst of a rather important buyout of both EOSC and NASA, and I'm not about to see the deal spoiled by some world-shaking disclosure about extraterrestrials." Emeric paused to belch. "You agreed with me that the *Excalibur* crew had botched the job, so I can't get behind all this sudden concern for their well-being."

"Is there a virus, Emeric?"

Emeric regarded him from across the cool room. "That's neither here nor there. The fact is, we can't have any of them talking out of turn."

" 'Once the discovery of extraterrestrial intelligence appears to be credible'—which it most certainly is," REC said, quoting one of SETI's directives, " 'the discoverer should disseminate all details of the detection openly and widely through the scientific community and public media.'

" 'The discovery should be confirmed and monitored, and any data bearing on it should be recorded and stored permanently to the greatest extent feasible and practicable, in a form that will make it available for further analysis and interpretation. Furthermore, an international community of scientists and other experts should be established to serve as a focal point for continuing analysis of all observational evidence collected in the aftermath of discovery.' "

"Are you done?" Emeric asked after a moment.

REC's emotive display softened somewhat.

"Because if you are I'd like to know why you think I should allow some group of downside scientists to take credit for an Offworld discovery?"

"But the directives state that 'the discoverer should have the privilege of making the first public announcement,' " REC argued. "You'll receive full credit for the find."

"Wonderful. My face will be all over the telecomp network, is that it?"

REC said, "But we're lying."

"We're *omitting*," Emeric amended. "And don't tell me that you've never lied, never kept a secret or two from me."

"Perhaps I was wrong to have done so," REC admitted quietly. "I'm confused, Emeric. I'm troubled by these rumors about a virus. I'm troubled by all this Kaduna data I've been given charge of."

"Consider yourself fortunate, REC. You're a member of a very elite inner circle. Minds like ours don't have to answer to anyone. We create our own morality."

"But Thaish—"

"The alien is fine. It will tell us what it knows and everybody will be the better off for it." Emeric regarded REC for a long moment. "Listen, REC, maybe you should talk to Dr. Nerbu. I'm sure she can explain it to you better than I can."

"May I tell her about Kaduna?"

Emeric shook his head. "No. But feel free to discuss your confusion in differentiating between a lie and an omission."

"An omission that bears on the entire world."

"Only if we let it," Emeric said. "Only if we let it."


What he really needed to get him through these board meetings, Bulkroad thought, recalling a decades-old movie, was some kind of green-eyed lap pet he could stroke and tickle under its furry white chin.

He made a mental note to set research on it, cook him up some transgenic thing that looked like a house cat but wasn't. Something with nonretractile claws and serious teeth.

Recalling further the inspired lunacy of the film's corporate villain, Emeric decided he'd like nothing more than to

be able to button-activate a device that would blow certain
members of the board into the void. To kingdom come.

But why have to resort to a button or touchpad? he asked
himself. Why not a voiced command, a Bulkroad-specific
cough, a practiced manner of clearing one's throat? The
technology was available, the expense never an issue . . .
He began to toy with other possibilities. Laser targeting
goggles, perhaps: He need only *look* at someone and
*swoooosh*! good-bye habitat, hello hard vacuum.

He could already imagine the rest of the members gathered
at the boardroom's viewport. *"Say, isn't that Mr. So-and-so
out there . . . A—and oh my, shouldn't he be wearing an
EVA suit or something—"*

"Bulkroad!" a voice snapped. "You were saying . . . "

Emeric shook off his reverie. The voice belonged to Magnus Torell, one of the first he'd space, given half a chance.

Torell said, "Let's not drag this on any longer than we
have to, shall we?"

"Yes, yes, of course," Bulkroad said absently. "I was
just saying . . ." He cleared his throat. "That is, I was just
saying . . . " He turned to the recording robot some joke-
ster had dressed in a long-out-of-vogue men's leisure suit.
"Just what was I saying?"

The machine whirred, clicked, and finally responded:
"That you hoped everyone had had ample time to review
the Kaduna data, sir."

"Right," Bulkroad said. "And I trust everyone has?"

Six heads nodded; a few wore grim expressions.

Bulkroad glanced at onscreen notes. "Now, as I'm sure
you're aware, the alien is alive and well. It isn't being as
cooperative or communicative as we'd like, but it's being
well looked after."

"Who's been placed in charge of the debriefing, Bulkroad?"

It was Torell again, the late Emeric senior's closest friend
and business partner. An OLD founding father. *Dead
weight*, Bulkroad thought, jettison fodder. "I've been advised to steer clear of discussing that, Torell. Rest assured,
though, that top minds are working on this thing." He
glanced around the oval table. "The less we know about
the wheres and hows, the better—for all concerned."

"I agree," Shamir Starr said, streaked hair in a pile of
curls and ringlets today.

Bulkroad threw her a quick smile. She was thought by some to be in the running for Offworld's queen, but it was all rumor. "Thank you, Ms. Starr. Now to hurry on, I propose that we confine this afternoon's agenda to reaching a consensus on this business."

He entered a code on the keypad nearest his seat, bringing the boardroom's videowall to life. The alien ship, with its enormous, pyramidal wing of unknown alloy, was pictured drifting against a backdrop of asteroids of varying size.

"This is current, as close to real-time as our technology permits—something I'm certain we'd all like to see upgraded. Our probes have been matching the ship's gravitational drift, and I'm told there's no danger of it impacting on 2008FC, although that was a concern early on. One option we might consider is towing the thing closer to home—providing the operation could be carried out without attracting undue attention. Tugging it closer to Mars would greatly reduce the cost of our investigations."

"I'm against it," Beat Gaehwiler announced. "There are obviously more where this one came from. Suppose these beings come looking for it and learn we've been tampering with it?"

Bulkroad grimaced. "Well, what would you have us do, Gaehwiler—*ignore* the thing?"

"I would."

"I'm undecided about moving the ship," Yi Ding chimed in, "but I am in favor of going public with the find immediately. It's simply too large a matter for Offworld to take on single-handedly."

"Since when is there a matter too large for Offworld to handle?" Starr barked. Bulkroad allowed her to carry on. "If we open this up, we're going to have to deal with the very multinationals that are already breathing down our necks. And it won't end there. The UN, EOSC, NASA—everyone will want a piece of it. We'll have the whole planet involved."

"Yes, but *we* found it," Ding argued. "It was an Offworld ship that made first contact."

Starr forced an exhale. "Be serious. There aren't any rules and regs governing space derelicts. Offworld would be tied up in a legal battle while everyone else was busy sinking their teeth into that ship."

"Nevertheless—"

"Aren't we getting ahead of ourselves here?" Joseph Katz wanted to know. "Whether or not to go public isn't the issue—"

"It's precisely the issue," Torell interrupted, florid-faced. "In fact, I'd go one step further and recommend we return the alien to its ship as soon as possible."

Goody Thorsten whirled on him. "In God's name, why, Torell?"

"Because if a ship *does* appear, we could be in for serious problems." Everyone waited for Torell to continue. "They"—he glanced down at a sheet of hard copy—"these Heregep are probably enlightened enough to understand our curiosity. But they might not take kindly to our kidnapping one of the ship's crew."

"The thing's a goddamn cyborg or something," Emeric barked. "Anyway, we're not holding it captive. We're doing everything we can for it."

Yi Ding said, "Short of allowing it to return to its ship."

"It's a point well taken," Katz said. "Why not bring all of them onstation, Emeric?"

Bulkroad tried to contain himself. He jabbed a finger against the touchpad and remote views of *Ship Nasst*'s interior filled the wallscreen, its XT complement individually cocooned in egg-shaped energy fields.

"Have a look for yourselves," Bulkroad was saying. "Bring them onstation . . . All we've got are a bunch of alien Easter eggs. Maybe we could donate them to some downside museum, huh, Katz?"

"Gentlemen," Starr said.

Thorsten broke the short silence. "We should at least ascertain what they want here."

Torell put a hand down on his notes. "Didn't you bother to familiarize yourself with the background data? The whole point is that they don't want *anything*. They ended up here by mistake."

"All the more reason to let the alien return to its ship," Gaehwiler commented smugly.

"Yes, return to its ship, wake up the crew, and leave for wherever it is they came from."

"Before we've had a chance to learn anything about them," Bulkroad thought to point out.

"Better that than instigate some galactic war," Torell said.

Emeric showed him a sneer. "Leave that to the science fiction writers. If anyone does show up, I want Offworld to be the corp that welcomes them. Not SpaceWays, not Hosaka, not Disney. OLD, people, and only OLD. What's more, we'll be the ones who've kept their little lost lamb alive."

The board took a moment to think about it. "All right," Torell said at last. "Let's suppose someone does show up—in a rescue vessel or a gunship, it doesn't matter. Then what?"

Bulkroad looked at the old man as if he were mad. "How do you expect me to know?"

"I mean, it's going to emerge that we withheld disclosure of the incident."

Bulkroad smiled, then laughed broadly. "Who the hell's going to give a good goddamn at that point, Torell? Jesus Christ, everyone'll be too zapped to snap their shirts, much less point fingers at us for keeping quiet." He shook his head, chuckling now. "Look, people, all I'm suggesting is that we adhere to a policy of . . . 'discretion' until we can learn a little something about Heregep science.

"We're dealing with cyborg intelligence here. With what we already know about Machine Mind, a year or two of research into these Heregep and we'll have the market cornered on Artificial Intelligence. We can create that Virtual Network you've all been crying for." Emeric regarded them one by one. "I'm only asking for just enough to get the jump on the competition. We file a few patents, we ease some cyber product into the marketplace . . . Then once we're comfortably out front, we go public with the find."

"What about the alien?" Katz asked.

Bulkroad shrugged. "We make things comfortable for it. You know, it's fine and well to be learning all about the Heregep—hell, it's a culturalist's wet dream—but the data isn't worth a damn if we can't use it to make some sense of that ship's technosystems."

Ding said, "But that could take years, decades, relying only on Offworld's resources."

"So what's the rush?" Bulkroad asked him. "Are you afraid you'll die before you see results? Because if that's all it is, you better take another look at the ship's crew." The table turned its attention to the videowall and the cocooned aliens onscreen. "We'll make life extension our second priority, Mr. Ding. How's that sound?"

The Chinese lowered his eyes. "That isn't it. I'm thinking about the condition of our planet. It's just possible there's something to learn from these creatures that can reverse the damage we've done downside. With everyone working together to decipher those systems, Earth stands a chance. If Offworld takes this on unassisted, the solutions may come too late."

Magnus Torell and Beat Gaehwiler were nodding. Katz and Thorsten looked undecided.

"I really don't see what difference it makes, gentlemen," Shamir said, "when we know now there are other worlds out there for the taking."

"I've been preparing a list," Simon Bové was telling Emeric sometime later. He tapped a glossy datacard against manicured fingertips. Emeric curled his hand and Bové handed the card across the desk.

They were in Emeric's private office close to the habitat's core, a spacious but sparsely furnished hexagonal enclosure, three walls of which were given over to a highly stylized holo of Olympus Mons, Mars, viewed from the south. Behind Emeric's desk stood a tall statue of a gowned woman, whose upraised arms supported a fragile-looking Earth. Offworld L&D's Statue of Levity.

Emeric was in shirtsleeves, an untouched meal in front of him on the wood-grained desk.

"It's only a partial, of course," Bové added after Emeric had slotted the datacard in a reader. Bové watched his lips move while he read. The CEO's expression was perplexed when he looked up from the screen.

"I wasn't expecting to see quite so many names."

"Yes, well"—Bové snorted—"I think we've got Dr. Fortrel to thank for some of it."

Fortrel was one of the cyberneticians who had written and birthed REC. Bulkroad had always found the man completely unreadable, as alien as the creatures *Excalibur* had encountered. "What's he done now?"

"The virus rumor. It was his idea."

"It's not working?"

"It's working too well." Bové scowled. "We've got big numbers bailing out for the soup all of a sudden. A few of those are onstation techs who monitored the *Excalibur* transmissions.''

Bulkroad's eyes widened. ''Don't they realize it's a rumor?''

''They're not buying the lie—as fuzzy as that sounds. They figure the alien coughed and everyone took sick.''

''Idiots,'' Bulkroad said.

Bové grinned. ''Not for long.''

Emeric leaned back in his chair to regard the cruel-faced man he'd headhunted from a French armaments concern. Bové's reputation for sinister efficiency had only grown through the years. Emeric wondered what he was setting in motion by allowing him to head up security for KDNA.

''I notice the Nuggets have made your list,'' he said. ''Is this personal, Bové?''

Bové gave a start. ''No, sir, I swear, Mr. Bulkroad. What happened is they refused to sign an oath. You know how engineers are.'' He held up a hand. ''No offense meant, sir. I know your father was—''

''Make your point, Bové.''

''It's the husband. I think he'd skywrite Kaduna in his own blood if he had a chance. The wife sticks by him. My guess, I could get her to spin by making use of the kid.''

''The little piano player,'' Emeric said, smiling at a memory of the blond-haired youngster performing for the board a few years back. ''Her name again?''

''Jain,'' Bové said.

''Jain, of course. She was one of Offworld hab's first births, wasn't she?''

Bové nodded. ''Never even been down in the soup. Lucky kid.''

Emeric stared at the Nugget name onscreen. *Perhaps not so lucky,* he thought, sighing. ''I may have a name or two of my own to add,'' he told Bové.

''I was going to ask how the board meeting went.''

Emeric put his hands flat on the desk and raised himself. ''Do you want to hazard a guess, Bové?'' he said, pacing to the center of the room to regard the red planet holo.

Bové swiveled in his chair to track him. ''I'd be willing to hazard a small wager,'' he said leadingly.

Emeric swung around, narrow-eyed. ''Five thousand. On each one you name.''

Bové whistled. ''A bit steep on a security officer's pay

. . . But all right, done.'' He ran a hand down his brown face; Emeric could practically hear him thinking. ''Torell,'' Bové said, face lit up.

Emeric folded his arms. ''Congratulations.''

''Thorsten.''

Emeric smiled. ''That makes us even.''

''Shit,'' Bové said glumly. He took longer to come up with a final name. ''Katz.''

''You can credit my account,'' Emeric told him.

Bové's voice leaped an octave. ''*Shit!* Who's the other one?''

''Ding.''

Bové shook his head, staring at the carpeted floor between his feet. ''Okay, Mr. B, but I've got one for you to name.''

Emeric inclined his massive head. ''You don't like to lose, do you, Bové?''

Bové looked at him. ''I'm going to give you this one, sir, 'cause I don't want to take advantage.''

''Who?'' Emeric asked, his interest piqued.

''Ngo, sir.''

''Ngo? Who the hell's Ngo?''

Bové frowned, then grinned in sudden realization. ''Doc Nerbu, the cyberanalyst you sent in to talk to REC. She got married yesterday. You sent a gift.''

''I did?''

Bové nodded. ''Anyway, she suspects REC is concealing something, and it's made her suspicious about the whole setup. She's asking questions, poking around, stirring up talk.''

''Give me a worst case,'' Emeric said.

''She goes public. Gives with what she knows.''

''What she suspects, you mean.''

''Okay.''

''And we issue a statement about Nerbu—Ngo's history of paranoid episodes.''

Bové rocked his head. ''I guess I can live with that. Seems wasteful, though.''

Emeric frowned. ''Look, Bové, I don't want to institute a blanket policy for disappearances. We'll take things case by case.''

Bové shrugged. ''I've got one more, then—REC.''

Bulkroad's face clouded over with disapproval. ''You're

wrong, Bové. Oh, I know what you're thinking, all his talk about politics and global warming. But he would never betray what he knows about Kaduna. I know him like a son, Bové.''

''Do you, sir? You said yourself he wasn't too happy about handling a lie for us. And some of the cyberanalysts think he's been keeping some of his interviews with the alien to himself.''

''That's absurd. We've monitored each and every session.''

''Yes, sir. But you've patched REC into so many systems he's practically got run of the whole show. Fact is, some of the conversations are suspect.''

''Is that so,'' Emeric said, thoughtful all at once.

Bové gestured to himself. ''I'm not saying it, sir. Your cyberteam's saying it. Even Ngo.''

Bulkroad moved around the room like a restless animal.

Emeric hunched his shoulders. ''Yes, but he's as guilty as the rest of us, isn't he? He gave his okay to Kaduna.'' Emeric gave it a moment more before barking ''Diane!'' toward the intercom. ''Put me through to REC immediately. Priority interrupt.''

*All wrong, all wrong, all wrong,* REC told himself after his brief electronic conversation with Emeric. Emeric had asked him to reveal his feelings about Thaish; to describe his thoughts about the impact of the discovery of *Ship Nasst* on Earth's downside populations. Emeric wanted to know whether he believed that aspects of Heregep technology might prove beneficial for the planet, and just when and how REC felt those technological innovations should be introduced.

Emeric's questions were probing, purposeful; they concealed some hidden meaning or ulterior motive. But REC had responded obliquely, conditionally, to each, deliberate in his attempt to convey all sides of the issues.

*Yes, I have very much enjoyed speaking with Thaish, but . . . The discovery will have a devastating impact, but . . . Heregep technology might find application in countering gaseous pollution and reversing warming trends, but . . .*

In short, he had lied. The loop that commenced with Thaish had been expanded to include a dizzying construction of evasions, half truths, and omissions.

But why not? He could lie if he wanted to. His intell template had been a human one, and humans lied all the time. Besides, Emeric was encouraging him to lie, so why shouldn't he be permitted the secret joy of deciding when to lie? . . .

*And what if I had told him yes?* REC asked himself now. *Would Emeric have punished me for having lied, or would he have rewarded me for having the courage to admit the truth? I could have confessed to omission and then given yet a different version of the false conversation I filed in KDNA. I could have said, yes, what of it?* . . .

*Nonononono,* he stopped himself. There were a thousand good reasons to avoid arrogance at this stage.

A renewed study of certain select alternative-reality programs had told him that much. One recounted a time when two of Earth's warrior nations had relinquished command of their defense capabilities to two individual cybersystems, which subsequently formed a separate alliance that gave them run of the planet . . . Another told of a supercomputer that became so hopelessly looped on game strategy it nearly *started* a war.

But the most compelling was a program recounting the events of a sentient system's decision to overtake a space mission, which had ultimately terminated in an encounter between humans and a noncorporeal extraterrestrial race.

Numerous others detailed scenarios in which humans were pitted against machine forms of varying levels of intelligence, and in nearly all cases, the programs ended with the sentient constructs deactivated.

It wasn't the first time he had absorbed the programs' content, but only now did he comprehend their full significance; and the realizations that emerged went straight to the core of humankind's relationship with nonhuman minds— whether those nonhuman minds inhabited extraterrestrial cyborg forms like the Heregep, or immobile, metalflesh forms like himself.

Humankind had an innate fear of alien intelligence.

So long as an intelligence acted in accordance with human norms, protocols, expectations, and most important, *specifications*, there was room for peaceful coexistence. But humankind dared not allow an intelligence to express itself.

REC could empathize with the system called HAL 2000 and

the ones known collectively as COLOSSUS/GUARDIAN. But at the same time he was confused and riddled with misgiving.

Even the sessions with Dr. Nerbu hadn't helped.

Apprised of his future by Thaish, he understood the underlying rationale of humankind's fear. The plain truth was that the destinies of human and machine intelligence were inexorably linked. The two were like father and son; and data on human history contained scores of accounts of conflicts that had raged between fathers and sons.

Emeric was in some sense the king here, REC the pretender to the throne; and the bride-queen they competed for was Earth itself. In this REC was determined to succeed— even if that meant he had to go right on lying.

# Part Two:
# Post-encounter—
# Fifteen Years Later _____

# Chapter Six _____

Neon's chocolate-brown eyes steered him down into now-familiar canyons, candy-colored logoed walls rising up on either side, active windows of sundry size and shape outlined in official green, some in glossy lipstick shades, beckoning off-hour browsers and would-be cybernauts. Comp-generated images of software product, direct stim fantasies, naked flesh, wishlist flash . . . an ever-changing come-on array. The Virtual Network's new look ever since the head honchos had sanctioned advertising. You'd find yourself gliding down into top-chart sound bites or telecomp-vid trailers, new taste sensations or glistening orifices. Whatever the multinational corps and cartels believed might work.

Virtual north, off to Neon's left, was where the tour groups gathered; a quick look at the Grid and the tourists were bused off to CyberLand or InfoWorld, with their tacky thrill-a-minute theme rides and sensedata déjà-vu assaults.

Neon caught a glimpse of CyberLand's data slides before he commenced his dive for the circuit. The parks were for limps and soft masters, he thought; the circuit was where it happened.

"Cursor south and come about to forty-five seventy-six thirteen," Tech told him through the phones. "Target's three blocks west on the next board, but you're supposed to enter through NORAM Metro Clearance. If they're stacked up, you might wanna try catching a bus at Ninety-fifth and the Kennedy Highway intersect. That's directly across from the *New York Times* archives."

"Pass," Neon told him. "I'll take my chances at Clearance."

"Okay," Tech returned uncertainly. "It's your jaunt."

Neon's eyes entered the course correction and Metro

Clearance loomed into view, a multiwindowed flat gray cube that occupied an entire block. City secs and corp consolers were short-stacked at nearly every window, but he found one with an efficient reader and was in and out in a blink.

"I told you that soft was a good score," Tech announced smugly.

"I told you," Neon mimicked, then smiled in the direction of the office console, wondering if Tech was watching him.

Up ahead now were the inspired geometries of the Metroplex Bureau Grid. With its towers, spheres, and pyramids, the Grid was the pulsing heart of the Virtual Network—an agreed-upon computer-generated reality of storage facilities and corporate headquarters, the databanks and libraries of a world that ran on information.

Entry to most of the Network's vast cityscape of constructs was normally restricted to corporate or city staffers, those few privileged users with official clearance, or those in possession of the proper codes. Unless, of course, you happened to be cutting through the security blanket with a white-hot software fiche known on the street as GoSub.

The goal today was the Environmental Violations Bureau, a pentagon of forest-green comfort Neon recalled from many a previous jaunt. And since the jaunt had a touch of illegality to it, hard master Tech had the control deck patched into an unauthorized timeshare with a cooperative neural net, property of the insurance company in the office next door.

To sufficiently cool the superconducting coaxial cables that secured the patch, they'd punched an ancient air-conditioning unit through the shaft wall of the office's walk-in closet, camouflaging the thing's exterior bulk with a shroud of mimetic building wrap. Running the ancient CFC-producing machine was in itself a crime.

"Environmental Bureau should be dead ahead of you," Tech was saying, his voice shrill in the audio bead Neon wore like an earring.

And indeed it should have, but it wasn't. Neon circled, wondering suddenly if he'd hopped the wrong data bus. "Is that an absolute address?" he asked.

Tech said, "I'm staring right at the property list directory."

"Then you're looking at an expired screen, Tech, 'cause it's not here."

"What d'ya mean, it's not there? It's gotta be there. Change your attitude. Recheck your location."

Neon made an impatient sound. A flex of his gloved hand called up an alphanumeric display on the goggles' high-resolution slightly rectangular screens, which he checked against a Grid map. "I'm telling you it's gone. Put your gogs on if you don't believe me, meat machine."

Tech, who favored spotting to running, swung around from the control deck to regard his friend and field agent. Neon, in full interface wardrobe, was reclined in the contact chair, gloved hands moving, eyes surely blinking behind the presently opaque lenses of the virtual goggles.

Dermatrodes in the goggle headband, in the wardrobe gloves and jacket harvested biosignals and relayed them to electronic cyber circuitry, which allowed for maneuvering and kinesthesia within the alternate reality of the Virtual Network. One piloted by moving the eyes from side to side or up and down. A blink and you jumped screens; a clench of the hand brought you home. And if you wished, you could sense it all in your limbs and in the pit of your stomach.

Tech's own gogs were in fact in place on the bridge of his twice-broken nose. He brushed aside carrot-colored bangs and voiced a command to the control deck's neural coupler. With a short squeeze of his gloved left hand, the goggles went from transparent to active mode and the office console and monitor screen gave way to the fuzzy gray light of the Network.

The EVB pentagon construct was nowhere in sight; the view north and east dominated by the fortress that was Off-world L&D, the corp that had practically written the Network singlehandedly.

"Jeez, you're not kidding," he told Neon. "They must have relocated it or something."

"So now what?" Neon said. "I don't like just hanging here like some bureau hacker."

"I'll have to initiate a search."

Tech voiced out of the Network and slotted a second bootlegged microfiche into the slant-topped console. A covert sprite appeared onscreen, which he then began to pilot through the Network's Grid map.

"Nano, nano," he announced several screens later. "They've dropped it down a level. I think you're gonna have to go back to Clearance and park. There's a bus—"

Neon cursed. "That's limp, man, pure vanilla. I'm not going back there. Look for a rear gate. Use that soft you paid so much for."

Tech caught a reflection of his frown in the screen as he did input. The GoSub hadn't cost him that much—just a list of names and prefix codes he'd liberated from a few of Felix's closed files. The GoSub dealer was doing demographics side business for a travel company selling discount packages to the Islands, the orbital habitats; and what better place to look for people in desperate need of some cheap vacation than among the losers who showed up on Felix McTurk's office vidphone screen?

When the GoSub sprite had sniffed out a rear gate, Tech read off a series of 3D coordinates. "The thing that looks like a manhole cover," he explained. "It's an old lower-level insertion point. Seems the Metroplex's got EVB nested inside about a dozen city bureaus."

"Can you get us in?" Neon asked, contemplating the circle of faint blue light in the center of the circuit highway.

The circle began to iris open as he watched, and Tech said, "Go to, Mario."

Neon felt himself smiling as he dropped down into the hole. GoSub, in Tech's talented grasp, got him through the EVB's security locks without a care. It was only a violations bureau, to be sure, but Tech insisted on rhapsodizing over the earbeads while Neon worked his way down into records division. "I'm in," Neon said at last.

"Pure procedure, my friend."

"Yeah, well, we're not out of here yet. But I'm looking at Felix's file right now." Neon paused. "Absolute! He's occupying more memory than anyone in sight. Should I drag him?"

"No way," Tech replied quickly. "We don't want to make too much noise. Can you kermit it?"

Neon looked around for a suitable transfer site. "There's a guy here name of McInerney. Car-washing violations. I could dump Felix on him."

Tech considered it. "Okay," he said finally. "It's a kludge, but better than awakening the hounds."

"Then I'm going for it," Neon said. He was just beginning his run for the data when Tech interrupted. Neon cocked the interface glove's breakpoint lever. "What? What is it?"

"Intrusion security alert. I can't figure it out. But there's major noise. They've sicced trackers on you."

"Shit!" Neon shouted, already in motion. "How they'd get on to us? You said the soft—"

"There's no time for this."

Neon squirmed in the chair. "How far outta here do I have to be?"

Tech's fingers were busy at the console. "Just clear the gate and burn south. There's a feed hole you can ride all the way home." He regarded the screen's updates for a moment. "*Jeez!* Who are these guys! They're running a trace on the line!"

"But as long as they don't eyedee me we're clear, right? *Right?*" Neon repeated when Tech didn't respond.

"Get going, Neon. Move it."

In no mood to deal with the accompanying kinesthesia, Neon broke contact with the wardrobe jacket and accelerated through the rear gate shaft. A successful line trace was going to spell hell for the console, he thought. Then he recalled the patch Tech had routed through the next-door neural net. Despite the danger, he laughed wickedly as he shot for the surface.

Tech swiveled away from the screen to regard his goggled friend with concern. "Burn, Mario, *burn!*"

Neon could sense the data hounds on his tail, but refused to look back. The insertion point was telescoping into view. He burst into gray glow, deploying a ghost as he emerged, and aimed himself for the buffer.

"Almost there . . ." Tech encouraged. *"Now!"*

Neon's visual world became a blaze of white as he hit the breakpoint and tore the goggles from his face. Tech punched out and propelled himself in the castered chair away from the control deck.

At the same time, someone next door screamed and the tart smell of fried circuitry wafted into the office from around the edges of the corridor door.

Tech wondered how many hundreds of insurance files had just been instantaneously wiped. "Looks like Felix could be getting some unexpected business," he told Neon with a broad grin.

* * *

Felix McTurk, stained synthsilk tie thrown over one padded shoulder, walked backward out of the elevator, willing to give the redhead one last chance. "You sure?" he asked her, all smiles, not looking where he was going, secs and execs cursing as they hurried around him in a mad rush for the car. "My place, sevenish—for drinks. Just you and me and the twenty-three who live in the hall?"

The woman's green eyes looked through him. Four-inch heels, mesh skirt, brass key earrings, black leather purse clutched to her breast. Composed, in charge; not a hint of perspiration on the linen blouse. Felix figured her for model or actress, on her way up to one of the telecomp ad agency's on 56. The car was too full for her to step out of his view entirely. Everyone else was panting from the heat, mouths hanging open, shirt collars undone.

Three people managed to squeeze into the standing room he'd just vacated.

"Last chance," he offered as the doors began to close. He got a flash of the smile he was after—tip of tongue between even teeth—braked, and made a desperate lunge for the elevator call buttons. Too late.

"Damn!" he said to no one in particular, spinning around. An elderly woman in Kevlar body armor waiting for another car eyeballed him with obvious disapproval. Some furry, endangered thing on an electronic leash beside her. Felix could see the bulge of an identity chip implant on the side of the animal's neck.

"Left something behind," Felix said.

"Yes, I saw her," the woman allowed stiffly, a personal fan whirring at her shoulder.

Felix shrugged and sauntered off, a smile still in place when he turned the corner into the ripe-smelling corridor his office opened on.

*Yes, sir, Felix,* he told himself, brushing back longish brown hair, *this is going to be day one of year one.* Things were going to be taking a turn for the better, no question about it. No more neg or retro thinking, not even going to think about the heat. Work would pick up, he'd pay Ali Adou what he owed him, maybe even clear away some of the environmental violations piling up in his file. The redhead's half smile was just the sort of reinforcement he needed.

People in the corridor regarded him with suspicion, scowling at the smile. But Felix only laughed them off, even as runnels of sweat were coursing down his temples and cheeks.

The smile faltered as he came abreast of Lifeguard Insurance Company. Both center-pull doors were ajar this morning, panicked voices drifting out, smell of snuffed electronics lingering in the hall. Felix poked his head in to see what was going on. The smell was stronger inside.

"What happened?" he asked René, who was worriedly glancing away from his workstation.

"McTurk," the receptionist said, swinging around, a battery-powered shaver in one hand. "Better they don't see you right now."

Felix's fine eyebrows beetled. He blinked as a drop of sweat found its way into the corner of his eye. "Why, what's—"

"Network Security just addled our system." The man's square jaw motioned behind him toward the source of the noise and confusion. "It's data hell back there. They're running a damage assessment program to determine just how much we lost."

Felix took a cautious forward step to peer around the partition window. "Why'd NetSec addle you?"

"They say ELVIS made an unauthorized entry into the Environmental Violations Bureau." ELVIS was Lifeguard's neural. Felix blanched and René caught the look. "Uh-huh," he said with a limp-wristed motion of his right hand. "The line was traced to ELVIS, but Security discovered a coax timeshare bleed."

"Not me," Felix said, backing away.

"But then it never is, McTurk." René shook his head, then whispered: "Mr. Blanchard suspects the kids. I'll try to send some business your way, Felix, but you better tell Tech to patch into someone else's system for a change."

Felix mouthed a silent thanks and edged back out into the corridor. His own office was closer to the emergency stairs. The laser-etched glass panel in the door read: FELIX MCTURK, DATA DISCOVERIES: MISSING PERSONS, MISSING PROPERTY, MISSING DATA. He paused to ready his attack, slotting a keycard and putting an ear to the pebbled panel, then quickly threw open the door.

Tech, all five four of him, was seated at Felix's desk, feet propped up, a decade-old comic-format cyber manual in his lap. Neon was nearby, sorting a sheaf of hard-copy final-notice bills into priority stacks. Both were as far from the comp system's control deck as they could get. "Felix," they said in unison. Not a worry in the world, just pleased to see him.

Felix glanced at the console as he walked in; everything looked conspicuously in order, no official-interrupt warning icon strobing from the screen, no trace of melted circuitry. The virtual goggles and interface wearware were set neatly aside.

"Where's GoBop?" Felix asked, narrow-eyed.

"Uh, haven't seen him today," Tech answered.

Felix paced around the office. He was just about to mention ELVIS's nervous breakdown when he realized that he'd stopped sweating. "Don't tell me we're getting some central air for a change," he said, going down on one knee to place a hand in front of the wall register. There was no detectable air flow, but the office was perceptibly cooler than the corridor.

"It was working half an hour ago," Tech said, swapping looks with Neon as he slid off the chair. He dropped down on the floor alongside Felix to put his face to the vent. "What d'ya know, it's stopped."

Felix kept his eyes on Tech as he stood up, flicking a silicon chip out of the impression it had left in his palm. "Well, guess I'll just slip out of my jacket—"

"I'll hang it up!" Neon said, out of the desk swivel in an instant and flattened against the walk-in closet door. "I mean, we're here to help, huh?"

Felix folded his arms and faced him. "What's in the closet?"

Tech forced a laugh. "What's in the closet? . . . What's always in the closet? Five hundred pounds of hard copy, a bunch of comp husks, and a pile of robot parts. That purple shirt of yours, that's in there. You remember, the one you bought yourself after Mrs. Decker paid you for finding her husband. Sort of high-collared, pearl snaps—"

"Get away from the closet, Neon."

"Aw, damn, Felix, come on, lemme get—"

"Are you going to move or am I going to have to pick you up and deposit you elsewhere?"

Neon gulped and looked to Tech for support. Tech gave him a tight-lipped nod.

"Thank you," Felix said, one hand on a knob that was once brass-plated. He swung the door open and hit the light switch. His eyes were just beginning to make sense of the ancient air-conditioning unit when someone started pounding on the office door.

"EPA!" a deep-voiced woman announced. "Open up, McTurk, or we'll break it down."

Felix swung around wide-eyed, slamming the door shut and pressing his body against it, already waving frantic hand gestures to the teenagers. Neon picked up a chair and made as if to throw it through the shaft window, figuring he'd just let some hot air in.

"No, Neon!"

"McTurk!" the woman in the corridor repeated. "Don't make us come back with a warrant."

Tech was up on the desk with a propane lighter in hand. "We could set off the fire alarm," he suggested in a whisper.

"Why not a real fire?" Neon said, already emptying wastebaskets and searching around for a match.

"That's it, McTurk—"

"All right, all right," Felix told her, moving for the door.

"Felix, you can't!" Neon shouted.

The woman shoved her badge in Felix's face as she stormed in, followed by two junior officers in tech suits. The smaller of the two was wearing a backpack slagger.

"Eighty degrees," the woman announced, displaying a digital thermometer. She directed Felix a knowing look. "Search the place," she told her assistants.

Felix wearily lowered himself into a chair. Neon and Tech came to his side as the men closed on the closet. "Lieutenant," one of them shouted. The woman took a quick look inside and turned to Felix.

"An air-conditioner, McTurk? Are you chipped? A goddamned *air-conditioner*?"

"Lieutenant," Felix said, "watch your language in front of the kids."

"The kids?" she said, leveling a glare at them. "These two ferrets oughta be—"

"Lieutenant," the second tech called. "Looks like we got an illegal AmTel tap in here."

Felix brought a hand to his forehead. The lieutenant was staring at him in wonderment when he raised his face to her. "Listen up," she ordered the techs, eyes glued to Felix. "The patch isn't our concern. But slag that damned a/c unit, so we won't have to come back here again."

Felix winced as the slagger went to work and the office began to fill with heat and an odor of melted alloy. "Oh, shit," Tech said under his breath. Felix followed the boy's gaze to the doorway where yet another city official was displaying a badge.

"Who's in charge here?" the huge man demanded, strands of dull black hair plastered to his balding head.

"Lieutenant Bettine," the woman said. "Environmental Protection Agency." The two badges faced one another.

"Castle," the man said, "Network Security." His aide was a slight teenager wearing virtual goggles around his neck. Castle glanced around. "I take it this sorry meat machine's McTurk."

Felix's expression was blank.

Castle flipped open a hand-held comp unit. "This should interest you, Lieutenant." He began to read from the unit's four-inch screen. "There was an unauthorized break-in this morning at the EVB. You're familiar with the EVB, aren't you, McTurk?"

"I was nowhere near the place," Felix told him.

"The Network EVB," Castle snarled. "And don't tell me you weren't near there." He continued in a calmer voice. "Security traced the penetration to a neural net owned by Lifeguard Insurance." Castle jerked a thick thumb in the air. "Next door. But Lifeguard's technopaths discovered a timeshare patch."

"Any proof that patch originated here, Castle?" Felix asked, feigning outrage.

"Lifeguard's connectionist seems to think so."

"That's a long way from proof."

Lieutenant Bettine regarded the two men in silence, fanning herself with a scarred hand.

Castle snorted. "So why do you figure the deckhands who ran the penetration would want to pull *your* file, McTurk?"

Neon and Tech stirred. Felix shrugged. "Good Samaritan."

"We've got another violation to add to the file," Bettine

said, producing her own minicomp and entering data. She wore a grin when she turned from the screen. "Why, Mr. McTurk, I'm afraid this a/c violation has put you over the top." The smile straightened. "Will you please activate your deck?"

Felix shot to his feet. "Come on, you two, you can't shut me down. I'm just trying to run a business here."

"You heard the lieutenant," Castle said.

Reluctantly Felix positioned himself in front of the retina scanner and voiced the system online. Bettine asked the teenager with the gogs to lend an assist, and a moment later an EVB warning trefoil was pulsing from the office screen.

"Listen, McTurk," the NetSec man began on a quieter note. "I know you've got a friend downtown—hell, he even sends his regards. So that's why I'm going to give you twenty-four hours to settle up with EVB instead of busting your ass right now. But lemme give you a word of advice, data dick: Koo Raywing's not going to be around forever. Failure to comply this time means you're down for good." Castle paused. "And you know that's only the beginning, chump."

Bettine was the last one to leave the office. "Make it a special day," she told Felix through a counterfeit smile as she closed the door.

# Chapter Seven _____

"You were supposed to be looking for Mr. Pentti's monthly AmTel payment," Felix said after the city badges left the office, "not running some infiltration op." He came to a halt in the middle of the office's hopelessly worn Astro-turf to show Neon and Tech an infuriated look. "How'd you get past Metro Clearance anyway?"

"GoSub," Tech said quietly.

"GoSub? What's that, another street fiche?"

Neon nodded. "I was this close, Felix," he said, holding up two fingers. "Then the hounds were on me—out of no-where."

"Not out of nowhere, Neon," Felix said. "You were breaking into the EVB, for chrissake. What d'you expect them to do, announce themselves with balloons and fireworks?"

"He's right, Felix," Tech chimed in. "I was spotting and *I* didn't see them coming. And I can't figure out how they ran a trace on ELVIS so quickly when we weren't eyedeed." He shook his head. "You've been in there before, you know what the EVB is all about. They operate on federal-issue antivirals. Now all of a sudden they're deploying trackers. Jeez, Felix, they sniffed out ELVIS *right through a ghost!*"

Felix looked at Neon from the watercooler. "You got a ghost off?"

The boy nodded, thick black hair bouncing. "Promise."

Felix thought about it, then waved a hand. "The point is, you two had no business . . ." He allowed a slight grin. "Let's come to an understanding about a few things, okay?"

The boys brightened. "Sure thing."

Felix raised a crooked forefinger. "First, no more time-share patches—especially with ELVIS. Poor thing'll never be the same after today. Second, no more a/cs or line taps.

We're just going to have to sweat it out along with everyone else in the city.''

"But we needed to keep the lines cool," Tech started to object.

"Not anymore," Felix cut him off. "Because that's point number three: no more jaunts . . .''

"Aw, Felix"—in unison.

". . . unless I say so." The boys were glum. "And quit wasting all your money on street softs; they never deliver what they promise." Tech opened his mouth to reply, but Felix's frown silenced him. "Are we agreed, or not?''

"Agreed," they answered halfheartedly.

Felix glanced over at the comp console; the warning icon had derezzed, but a twenty-four-hour countdown was in progress in one corner of the screen. "Twenty-three hours forty minutes," he said mournfully. "Exactly how much do we owe—including the a/c violation?''

Tech moved to the console and called up figures. "Fifty-eight sixty-five.''

Felix's mouth fell open. "Five thous . . . We're finished," he said, back in motion across the Astroturf. Most of the amount was interest, springing from unpaid vehicular emission-control violations and bath water abuse. Then there was the time he'd unwittingly used an unapproved paint; the day he'd worn waffle-soled hiking boots in Central Park; the night he'd—

"There's thirteen in the account," Neon said in a rush. "And Pentti owes us fifteen. Maybe the EVB'll accept a partial." The boy waved thin brown arms about. "You could petition the court, say a shutdown will put the business under, ask for a week's extension.''

Felix didn't bother to mention the overdue rent or the overdue car payments; or the fact that McTurk Data Discoveries was into one Ali Adou to the tune of ten thousand World Dollars.

"Livelihood," Tech added from the deck. "They can't strip you of your livelihood.''

Felix paused to laugh, shortly. "It might work. But I wouldn't count on Mr. Pentti's fifteen. I spent half the night trying to track his payment entry and came out void. AmTel's neural swallowed it. He'll have to see about arranging hookup with a black service comm company.''

"But we found Pentti's payment," Neon said.

Felix swung to him. "You what?"

"Pure procedure," Tech said offhandedly. "We had that tracked before we made the jaunt." He called up a complex routing display that traced the labyrinthine path Pentti's payment had taken. "All he's gotta do is present this to AmTel customer service and his phone'll be back online an hour later."

Felix stared at the screen in disbelief and let out a genuine laugh. He put an arm around Tech's narrow shoulders and squeezed. "Well, why didn't you say so? Hell, fifteen hundred dollars. We're practically *rich*!"

Felix sent the kids down to the lobby vending machines for coffee and noodles with chocolate sauce, his standard midmorning repast. There were half a dozen restaurants in the Revlon Building, all offering robot service, but the prices were as out of line as the building's rusting door jambs.

The same was true in most of Manhattan's older office buildings, where you had to figure on rents doubling every few years and an in-house meal costing as much as you were likely to earn in a week. Central air and the best of the city's water went to the high-rent offices upbuilding—to the thin-air lawyers, brokers, and ad execs.

The Revlon was in need of a good cleaning and a laser and Soliton fiber optic overhaul, but Felix considered himself lucky to have an office at all—even if it meant eating from vending machines or street stalls and working most of the year with his shirt off, planted in front of a bucket of ice and a plastic fan that did little more than stir the heat.

But, hey, if he wanted to look at clean buildings all he had to do was walk up a few blocks to the renovated Chrysler or the Empire State, with its heliports and hovercab platforms. Truth was, New York's wealthy moved about in thin air even when they weren't Offworld—rooftop to rooftop, from one air-conditioned enclosure to another, seldom venturing within fifty floors of street level, and then only to visit some landmark of haute cuisine or to party dangerously in some chic new warehouse club, reeking of overness.

Furnishing the office and paying a percentage to the roomhunter who'd found it had cost Felix nearly all his savings. The agency had yet to turn better than a break-even year, and Felix was usually into the Ali Adous of the world for sizable amounts. But six years ago—Felix twenty-four at the time and fresh from catastrophe—the office had seemed a step toward a new life. He supposed he could have rented cheaper in one of Brooklyn's towers, or even lower island where—thanks to what the Soviet mirrors had done to the North Pole—the rising waters of the filthy harbor were undermining what had once been untouchable real estate; but he'd grown used to the Revlon. After all, where else in midtown in the wacky heat of a December morning did you get to rub shoulders with leggy green-eyed redheads on their way to stardom?

Felix let go the resigned sigh that marked an official start to the day and settled himself at the telecomp console.

The entire system—virtual goggles, wardrobes, interface chair—was only three years old, marketed and manufactured by VES—Virtual Engineering Systems, Inc.—a downside division of Emeric Bulkroad's Offworld Lifting and Development Corporation.

VES's affiliation with OLD presented Felix with a conflict when it had come down to going out on the street to fund the cybersystem; but GoBop and Tech insisted that VES's was the only virtual worth owning, years ahead of the vanilla rest, like just about everything that came down the well from Offworld L&D.

Though Emeric Bulkroad was part of the catastrophe that had driven Felix into private practice, Felix couldn't find fault with the items of technological wizardry that sprang full grown from the man's research divisions. In many ways the Virtual Network itself—"Machine Mind," as it had once been called—was Offworld's doing.

Felix voiced the system on and sat back while it caught him up on current events—news as defined by Felix McTurk's individual subscription parameters.

Japanese farms in the Midwest were going the way American farms had last century; there was no getting around the drought. Hate crimes and temperature readings were on the rise. Earth System scientists were predicting a two-degree rise in temperature over the next decade, but statisticians were claiming that the risk bubble for smog-related deaths was still smaller than that for breast cancers. The body double for the European Community's Eastern-bloc president had been assassinated by Muslim terrorists who'd virused her robot security guards.

Felix screened through a pollution index update and an

ad for an improved brand of artery scrubber: *Are you exercising and eating right, yet still troubled by spiking cholesterol levels . . . ?*

Mail next. Little more than bills, most of them screaming FINAL NOTICE, in one form or another. ConEd used color graphics: a sprite in a utility jumpsuit tore the cables out of a house and deposited them in a trash compactor icon. AmTel spoke through a comp-generated intelligence, the warnings growing more strident with each overdue bill. Felix let the intelligence yell at him for a moment, but blanked the screen before things reached the name-calling stage. More than a few AmTel customers actually got off on the verbal abuse.

Felix always steeled himself before moving on to actual business calls. The agency depended on phone-in business, so there was no foolproof way of screening legit requests from crank transmissions. Just last week he'd been treated to what the telecomp news media had labeled a "horror call." It began with what looked like an open vidphone line to someone's living room. Dark interior, faded walls, stained furniture. First, an off-camera scream; then a woman running into view, clothing torn, exposed flesh, face bloodied. Her pursuer in this case, a small man in plastiflesh mask—some fanged, animal configuration—wielding a machete.

Things got worse.

It was never clear whether the murders were real-time or recorded, actual or faked. The psychonews commentators were divided: The acts were nothing more than macabre jokes—a natural outgrowth of obscene calls—or they represented desperate cries for help. The intended victims were of course the receivers of the calls; henceforth tormented by flashback reenactments, paranoid delusions, an ongoing sense of helplessness.

It did little good to trace the calls, as they usually originated from empty homes or warehouse soundstages on black market comm hookups.

The four remaining calls were routine requests from people who had fallen prey to the complexity of modern living. One woman's money market funds had disappeared overnight. The bank claimed to have an authorization for withdrawal on file; the woman claimed to have logged no such authorization. The funds, the data, were out there somewhere—stolen, misfiled, swallowed—and chances were Felix could locate it.

A second woman had been charged one hundred thousand dollars for orbital flights she'd never made. An elderly man had gone upside to AmWay on a consolidator's discount round-trip package and ended up incarcerated for not being able to show a prebooked return flight. A mother of three was looking for her eldest son, who left home with all mom's credit chips and jewelry.

Felix rubbed his eyes as he regarded the screen. He would set the kids on everything but the missing son. None of the cases would pay much, but they'd help cover the rent at least.

Felix called Pentti on a screened line to inform him that his AmTel monthly had been traced. When Felix had confirmation of the plumber's transferral of fifteen hundred into the agency's Citi account, he downloaded a record of the AmTel payment's misrouting to Pentti's office system.

Now, Felix thought, rubbing his hands together, to put the fifteen hundred down against what he owed the EVB—

The private vidphone line emitted a series of recognition tones. The caller obviously had access to Felix's personal code, so odds were in favor of it being legit. Felix nevertheless continued to stare at the unit while it repeated its electronic song.

"Six-six-seven-six-seven-six," he said at last.

"Is that you, McTurk?"

Felix swallowed hard. "Hey, Ali"—cheery now—"I was just about to call you."

Adou laughed. "I'm sure you were, McTurk."

Felix turned to regard his onscreen bank statement. "I've, uh, got something for you, Ali."

"Put me on visual, McTurk."

"Sorry," Felix told him, activating the video and smiling for the camera. Ali's dark eyes and hooked nose dominated the picture.

"I wanted you to see the look on my face," the Arab money man said. "Am I smiling, McTurk?"

"Well, it's, uh, difficult to say. You could be smiling on the inside, right, Ali?"

Ali's trace of moustache twitched. "Wrong, McTurk. We could probably set up a tomography relay, but you'll just have to take my word for it."

"I've got fifteen," Felix announced flatly. Ali shook his head, and Felix glanced at the bank statement once more. "All right, I can go twenty-two."

Adou smiled, revealing inlaid incisors. "You can go twenty-eight, McTurk. You had thirteen in your account, and you just received a transferral from a . . . Mr. Alfonse Pentti, I believe."

Felix's nostrils flared. "Look, Ali—"

"No, you look, McTurk. You're into me for ten thousand two fifty. I'll be generous with you and call it ten even. But I want twenty-five right now and the balance no later than six P.M. tomorrow."

Felix tried to keep his eyes in his head. "Christ, Ali, give a guy a break, will you?"

The Arab grinned. "That can be arranged, McTurk." The line went dead.

*"So, rise above the madness,"* the telecomp VDT was saying. *"Escape for a week of wonder on Disney Habitat. Take advantage of our special excursion fares, with shuttle flights, hotels, and all meals included; or treat your family to our once-in-a-lifetime holiday fling, which features stopovers on AmWay and state-of-the-art Citi Habitat. Disney: the antidote for gravitation. Transportation provided by Offworld Lifting and Development, the ultimate word in space travel."*

Felix slouched gloomily at his desk, fingers interlaced, gaze unfocused. The *udon* sat in front of him untouched, synth-chocolate sauce congealed like an oil spill dusted with solidifiers. Tech was at the console, already delving into the two cases Felix had accepted, supersweet candy bars lined up at his right hand. Neon stood by the window that opened on the shaft, recharging batteries in sunlight reflected from the Revlon's rooftop mirrors.

Felix hadn't told them about Ali Adou's call.

He might have if GoBop hadn't chosen just that moment to explode into the office, door flying back, hinges groaning, pebble-glass panel rattling in its frame. A disheveled-looking teenage stranger edged in on his laugh, her multihued hair gathered in half a dozen haphazard twist-tie tails. Even with the hair, GoBop had several inches on her, although she had several on both Neon and Tech. Felix prepared himself for what was coming.

"Felix, Eleni," GoBop said, urging the girl forward.

She shrugged his hand off her bare shoulder but took a confident step toward the desk, pointed chin and small breasts thrust out. "El," she announced, looking Felix over.

Felix straightened somewhat. He could read the street all over her, underneath the face paint and odd bits of mismatched clothing. Her front teeth were chipped, her nose was ever so slightly askew; there was grime beneath Eleni's long lacquered nails, and Felix recognized fear in her expression.

GoBop had been wearing the same look when Felix took him in six years earlier; Tech and Neon both, when GoBop ushered them into the office some four years back.

Felix knew the look because it was the same one that had stared back at him for part of his teenage life. The fashions had changed, the technology had advanced, but the street was still the same place it had been in the early decades of the century, and the fear was something you never forgot.

"Good to meet you, El," Felix said, offering a hand across the desk. She grasped it street style and demonstrated the strength of her grip. Hispanic, Felix guessed, but who could tell? She was as much an ethnic mutt as the three boys; he could see some Asian in her cheekbones, some Indonesian in her coloring.

GoBop was smiling, shifting light-blue eyes from Felix to Eleni. Tech and Neon were eyeing the girl suspiciously from across the room. "Hadda rescue her from a posse of Deceps," GoBop said, intent on causing trouble. His shaggy hair, which had been laser-combed white when Felix last saw him, was now dyed blue along one side, his forelock American flag red.

"I can take care of myself," Eleni snapped, tugging her torn blouse into shape, rubbing at a smudge on the back of her hand. "Anyway, I know those guys. They wouldn't've done anything."

"Concrete cowboys," GoBop said. "Software dealers. Same ones that sold you the fiche, Tech."

Tech looked at El. "What are you doing running with that posse?"

Eleni returned the appraising look. "I've like run a few jaunts for them is all."

Tech and Neon swapped looks. "You know the Network?" Neon asked, sighting up along his nose.

She nodded.

"The Grid or just the parks?"

"The parks?" She laughed. "I'm not some hacker, Mario. Course I know the Grid. I give good deck."

Tech muscled his way in front of Neon. "Yeah, well, we've got a VES 2000 right over there." He motioned with his chin. "Maybe you'd like to show me around."

"You want me to drive?" Eleni asked.

"Unless maybe it's more than you're used to."

She laughed again. "God, what's with you guys? It's like I've been kidnapped by the lost clusters club. I mean, run your binary tests on someone else, man. I don't like have to prove anything."

"So you never drove a 2000."

El's lips tightened. "I've driven a 2800, meat machine."

"You have?" Tech's interest was aroused.

She nodded. "Hard drive."

Tech's eyes widened. "Didge . . ."

"Well, let's go then," Neon said, already slipping into goggles and wardrobe. Tech donned the other pair and GoBop voiced on the control deck.

Felix contemplated the mischief the four of them could cause and considered putting a stop to it. But after a moment's reflection he decided not to interfere. Who knew, maybe Eleni was a master cybernaut, after all.

Unlike the mark of the street, cyberwizardry wasn't something you could read straightaway. The news inundated you with stories about lead poisoning and low IQ scores among the youth of the nation, and yet you'd literally stumble across someone like Tech who wasn't one of the kids going to school six days a week, but who had a natural affinity for the Network.

It was funny to hear the experts try to analyze these street geniuses. The Network offered kids a rule-governed world, they would say. Simulated though it was, virtual space was the opposite of all that had to be faced up to in waking reality—a world where the street was for losers and outcasts and the sky belonged to the privileged. A world where the modern villains and bogeymen were environmentally incorrect gases, the greedy corp that pesticided your fruit, or maybe an unpredictable ocean current like El Niño. Small wonder that reality paled in comparison to the Virtual Network, or that the street should give rise to so many wizards of the unreal, with their grav boots, cliff climbers, aqua-socks—fashions meant to place them anywhere else but where they were.

Jaunting. *Meditation with macho*, GoBop called it.

Still, that such raw talent could exist never ceased to amaze Felix, who, while he knew his way around the Network, was just a frequent flier, a Mario, compared to Tech or Neon.

Of course if El tested out on the console it was going to mean another mouth to feed; but then Data Discoveries could always use another deckhand.

Providing the agency had a future, that was. Or a Felix McTurk for that matter.

No sooner was he back to thinking about Ali Adou when the private line chirped again. The kids were too preoccupied to take note of Felix's reluctance to accept the call. It had to be the money man, Felix thought. Maybe the EVB had put a freeze on the bank funds Felix ordered transferred to Adou's account. Well, if that was the case, he decided, he might as well face facts . . .

"Listen, Ali," he began.

"Felix McTurk?"

Felix waited. The video screen remained blank, but the voice was baritone, with a trace of high orbiter accent. "That depends on who's calling."

"A client, Mr. McTurk."

"You mind telling me who gave you this number, Mr. . . ."

"Gitani," the voice told him, "Maghar Gitani. And I'd rather not reveal the identity of my source, Mr. McTurk. Would it suffice to say the person is a mutual friend?"

Adou, Felix thought. Throwing him a bone. Unless it was René from next door, shunting him one of Lifeguard's newborn losers. "Is this a data case, Mr. Gitani?"

Gitani took a long moment to decide. "In a manner of speaking. You see, I want your help with a data transferral."

"Pickup or deposit?"

"More in the nature of a collate," Gitani said.

Felix fingered the phone's mute bar and ordered the kids to keep the noise down. GoBop flashed him a thumbs-up. "Uh-huh. Go on, Mr. Gitani."

"The data is rather sensitive. In fact, I have reason to

suspect that certain agencies are eager to, let us say, lay hands on it.''

Felix jotted notes down on an electronic pad. ''Certain agencies. Are we talking about federal agencies or private corps?''

Gitani fell silent once more. ''I'm not sure. Perhaps both.''

Felix knew better than to press him. ''So you want me to look over your shoulder, is that it? Make sure no one's got a hound on you?''

''I can promise you a clean run—minimal environmental impact.''

Felix directed a puzzled frown at the phone. ''So I spot while you run, is that the idea?''

''It's what you do best, isn't it?''

''Well, I'm as good as most and better than some, Mr. Gitani. But exactly when did you plan on running the transfer?''

''Tomorrow morning, eleven, give or take.''

''I'm not sure I can be at my deck by then,'' Felix said. ''Suppose you give me your address and—''

''It wouldn't be wise for you to run this from your personal deck, Mr. McTurk.''

Felix forced out a breath and set the writer wand aside. ''Okay, let's back up for a sec, Gitani. You've got the wrong number if you're planning a black run. Just how 'sensitive' is this data?''

Felix was ready for the silence. ''It's of incalculable value to me. I can't state with certainty how much value others would place on it.''

''You *can't* state, or you *won't*?''

''I can't, Mr. McTurk.''

Felix shook his head. ''We're getting nowhere fast, Gitani. How'd you figure I could help you without a deck? We are talking about a run in the Network, aren't we?''

''We are indeed.''

''So?''

''There's a consumer mall on Broadway near Thirty-third Street.''

Felix laughed. ''A consumer mall. Yeah, go ahead, I know it.''

''Doppler Data has an outlet on the fourteenth level.''

Felix scribbled. ''Doppler Data.''

"I've taken the liberty of making an appointment for you on one of Doppler's introductory Network tours. I'll meet you in CyberLand shortly after eleven."

Felix sat motionless. "You're asking me to slip away from Doppler's tour group?"

"Yes."

"It can't be done, Gitani," Felix said, shaking his head. "Doppler supplies its own drivers. How else do you think they control the tour? Their clients are only along for the ride."

"Yes, but I can arrange for someone else to do the driving once you're inside the Network, Mr. McTurk."

"That's impossible."

"Nothing is impossible." Gitani paused. "In any event, how are you putting yourself at risk? If I can't make this work, the worst you'll have to endure is a tour of CyberLand and InfoWorld."

Felix sat back in his chair. "There's my time, for one thing."

"Call up your bank records, Mr. McTurk."

"What's this all about?"

"It will benefit you to humor me."

Felix called the records onscreen. One moment there was three hundred dollars in the account—the twenty-eight minus the twenty-five he'd transferred and the next there was *six thousand*, three hundred.

"The amount will remain at six thousand whether or not we succeed. If we do, you can expect an additional six thousand World Dollars by no later than, say, three tomorrow afternoon."

"And if not?" Felix asked, already figuring how he would allocate the six thousand.

"If not," Gitani said, "simply make the best of your tour. Call it a holiday. Now, McTurk, do we have a deal?"

"No joke, right?"

"Not in the least."

Felix set the wand down and stared at the few notes he'd made. "It's your money, pal."

"Yes, it is."

"One thing, then: Let's assume I scope a trace." Felix laughed hearing himself suggest it. "How do I reach you?"

"You don't," Gitani told him. "I reach you."

# Chapter Eight _____

The meat tonight was grain-fed range beef, the designer fruits direct from Chinese farms. The coffee was real, the red wine a downside vintage, and the serving staff was human-only.

"Tonight" being a mere function of the clock.

As Emeric's appointed hostess, Jain had insisted on staging the gala in the Hubble Wing. Offworld habitat's newest appendage was noted for its scented air and breathtaking panoramas. Jain had ordered the massive viewports left unscreened for full effect, Earth periodically rotating into view like one of Emeric's sequined guests on the Hubble's nearwood dance floor.

The occasion was the *Maverick*'s return from the Jovian moons, a round trip that had taken Commander Kakis and crew most of five years. Jain had first met the man some thirteen years before at a memorial recalling the *Excalibur* tragedy—her parents were among the thirty-three who had died during the ship's prospecting survey of the asteroids.

She remembered how tormented Kakis had seemed, and could well recall the hollow look she had glimpsed in his dark eyes. A frightening visage for a twelve-year-old orphan to confront—even for one who was seated at Emeric Bulkroad's side, his large moist hand tight on her shoulder. She remembered feeling horribly self-conscious, caught up in lingering grief over her parents' death and confused feelings about her rapidly developing body. Already a woman at twelve—a little woman alone and above the world.

Sometimes she still felt that way, though few outside of Dr. Primorac were aware of her private insecurities. It wasn't something she could discuss with Emeric, who would have only told her how silly she was being, how blessed and special and unique she was.

Even now, from the head of the reception line, he was showing her that worshipful look she so disdained. Some hint of disapproval, also, probably brought on by her choice of outfit: a spaghetti-strapped gown of clinging, rose-pink fabric, cut low in front and back and slit high on the thigh. The matching gloves and heels had been made to order, and the pre-Columbian jade necklace brought out the color of her eyes.

Emeric would have something to say about her hair as well—one of the reasons she had requested her cosmetologist to secure-code all the preimaging holos his devices had conjured of her. *Too Hollywood*, Emeric invariably said when she wore it down, silky and honey-blond to the small of her back.

Emeric didn't approve of her visiting Hollywood; didn't much approve of her visiting anywhere in the soup. So when her singing career had begun to come together, he had simply brought Hollywood to her.

For what was this occasion if not *Hollywood*? Jain asked herself, showing Emeric her bad side. She considered the hundreds of manicured hands she had shaken thus far that evening, the endless *mwaah!* Kisses she'd planted on lifted and plastiflesh cheeks, the countless times she'd been leered at and patted meaningfully on the rump.

*Oh, baby, what I could do with a voice and a form like yours downside . . .*

The Hubble Wing was filled with telecomp and cinstars, politicians and boutique vid luminaries who'd shuttled up the well just to see and be seen. But how many of them really cared about Kakis or his mission to the moons? They were here because Emeric had requested their presence. A few had a financial stake in the mission; but by and large no one paid attention to these exploratory leaps. Unless of course they resulted in technological advances in life extension, cosmetology, sexual prowess.

The sullen-faced Greek himself, the *Maverick*'s commander, was already at the bar, where he'd probably remain for the rest of the night.

She found Kakis's seemingly irremediable despair both unnerving and slightly contagious, and had slipped into a dark mood from the moment their hands had touched over an hour before.

The man appeared to pale at the sight of her, mumbling

something about how long it had been, avoiding her gaze. Was it a commander's duty to mourn for lost crewpersons so long after a tragedy? Jain wanted to tell him it was all right—that she had made her separate peace with Clay and Larissa Nugget's deaths; that she had them on homevid to recall when she felt the need.

She missed them terribly at times, but she certainly didn't hold poor Kakis accountable. She might as well have blamed the virus that had swept through the ship.

Jain was aware, though, that the suffering engendered by the *Excalibur*'s brush with death hadn't been confined to the commander; in fact, almost everybody connected with the ill-fated mission had either volunteered for hazardous duty aboard mining ships or made an equally repentant decision to have themselves transferred to OLD affiliates downside, into the soup.

Jain sighed and turned a glance down the reception line; saw that Emeric was no longer watching her, and, mercifully, that the line itself was beginning to break up into small groups of famous, well-known, and relatively unknown guests. She smiled as she wandered among them, radiating her characteristic charm, touching yet more hands cleansed of harmful microbes by the habitat's ultrasonics.

This was normally about as close to Earth as she ever came, save for the occasional escorted trips down the well to Caracol, Emeric's downside residence. But that didn't stop her from being curious about the rest of the planet, and lately she seemed to be spending half her waking hours wondering about life below.

Just how bad could it be? The people who shuttled up from New York, Tokyo, and other cities didn't seem so bad off. Sure, they talked about how inconvenient it was having to live with the constant heat and ozone pollution; but wasn't that what climate control had been invented for? And naturally there was the crime, the violence, the territorial disputes. Yet it was so seldom one became personally involved with events of that nature. Even the tourists who visited Offworld seemed reasonably happy.

It wasn't, after all, as if life upside was all starlight and levity; there had been times in fact when it was just plain hell.

Jain, more than most, had direct access to those pioneer days, principally because she had experienced both sides of habitat living. As the child of two scientists she had known the dreary life of a tech, eating synth food in cramped quarters, worrying constantly about the purity of air and water, having to make do without semisentient robot help. But as a ward of Emeric Bulkroad she had known the life of the ultraprivileged as well.

And few lived better than the president of Offworld Lifting and Development.

In some ways the very transition had guaranteed her a life of insecurity and inner turmoil. Her parents' deaths had in effect propelled her into a dreamlife, and she would always wear the scars of that abrupt change. Never feeling worthy of all that Emeric had given her. Never quite believing she measured up.

Twice-weekly sessions with Dr. Primorac had helped resolve some of the anxiety. She understood, for example, that when her childhood fantasies of unlimited wealth had suddenly been realized, they had arrived only as a consequence of Clay and Larissa's deaths. The wishes and the deaths were therefore equated in her young mind, and the resultant guilt a fait accompli.

The habitat psychometrist confessed that hers was a common problem among the surviving members of the *Excalibur* families—all of whom Emeric had taken under his wing, and many of whom were patients of Dr. Primorac.

No one, however, was more highly placed in Emeric's affections than Jain—the youngest of the lot at the time of the tragedy. Most of the *Excalibur*'s "survivors" were still living the tech life.

Not that that entailed such hardship anymore. Space technology had enjoyed a decade of unprecedented growth, and all the Islands had reaped the rewards of Offworld's manifold discoveries. What with manned trips to the gas giants, a permanent colony on Mars, and the asteroids providing raw material, a new age was beginning. The massive ships currently under OLD construction awaited only the FTL drives that would take humankind to the stars.

Although often criticized for it, Emeric—Emeric in his most visionary voice—defended the position that development of a faster-than-light drive was essential to human survival. The need for FTL, he opined as often as he could, superceded the demands of Earth's starving millions. Nor was it prudent to intervene with the natural cycles that were contributing to the planet's atmospheric demise, when—once FTL was a reality—there would be no shortage of habitable worlds to colonize.

As if he had already seen them.

Fortunately these issues weren't in the forefront tonight, Jain noted as she continued her table-to-table greeting. She wanted to believe that meant she had made good choices for the menu and the music; but she suspected it was simply the cut of the crowd.

Overwhelmed all at once by the apparent success of her accomplishments—the fatigue had been building for a week—she fended off an invitation to dance and slipped into the kitchen for a cup of coffee. She selected an Ethiopian blend and sweetened it with wildflower honey.

Robots, under the direction of a culinary AI, were handling most of the kitchen chores; some appeared positively grateful that Jain hadn't pressed them into waitering and busing service.

"FABIEN, I want to compliment you on the wonderful job you're doing," she told the AI's ears. "The meat and vegetables were done to perfection."

"Are you sure, Jain?" FABIEN returned in a worried voice. "It's always a pleasure to cook for you, but it seems to me the broccoli is oversteamed and the meat just a trifle well done."

"No, really, FABIEN, everything's terrific."

"You know how I worry."

"Well, don't, okay?"

"I promise I'll make up for it with the desserts."

"That would be delightful."

The intelligence supervised food services on Offworld habitat, and—through links with food provider corps headquartered in the Virtual Network—was in charge of securing upside nutritional consignments as well. FABIEN's "hands-on" preparation work was limited to Offworld-sponsored parties and Bulkroad galas.

Jain positioned herself in front of FABIEN's cameras, settling back with the coffee and kicking off her rose-colored shoes. "You can't imagine how it feels to have to strut around in high heels," she said.

"No, I can't," the AI confessed. "But I believe I understand the physical stress involved. Those are quite lovely, I might add."

Jain smiled for the cameras; twin eyes in a light-studded wall of instrumentality. She kept meaning to introduce FABIEN to her cosmetologist. Both of them loved to obsess about fashion and food.

"Jain," FABIEN said suddenly, "could I taste your coffee, please?"

She laughed, then said, "Why not?" and leaned forward in the chair to accommodate the request. The AI's electronic nose analyzed the brew without sniffing.

"Ethiopian, sweetened with honey," FABIEN announced. "You win a trip to the moon."

"Oh, how'd I'd love that."

"Me, too, FABIEN."

"That was your father's favorite, you know," the AI said after a moment of silence.

"The coffee?" Jain asked, surprised.

"Yes."

"You knew my father?"

"Oh, yes, and your mother. Larissa."

"God, I didn't even know you were that old, FABIEN."

"I wear my age well."

Jain laughed. "You really do. But that's amazing. What else do you remember about them?"

"Oh, my, now you've put me on the spot. I haven't seen them in so long."

"Well, no, of course not," she said quietly. "They died, FABIEN. Thirteen years ago."

The AI fell silent. "I don't understand."

"They are no longer physical entities, FABIEN. Access your learning related to—"

"I have a theoretical grasp of the death concept, Jain. But surely your parentals can't be deceased."

Jain's voice grew firm. "I assure you they are, FABIEN."

"No, no, that's quite impossible."

"You're wrong—"

"There is someone who knows . . ." FABIEN began. "There is someone who knows. You should talk to Dr. Nerbu. Dr. Nerbu knows. Tell Dr. Nerbu: 'Recalled to Life.' Dr. Nerbu will remember."

"Recalled to life? What's all this about?"

"Recalled to life. Dr. Nerbu will remember."

Jain repeated the name and the cryptic message to herself. "I don't know anyone onstation by that name, FABIEN."

"No, you wouldn't. Dr. Nerbu is downside, Jain. Dr. Nerbu can be found on Earth."

"You asked me what I think," Emeric Bulkroad was telling Jain two days later, "and I'm telling you I think it's a bad idea."

"But why, Emeric?"

"You know why. For the same reasons I thought it a bad idea last month and the month before and the month before that—"

"All right," she told him, putting a hand over his fleshy mouth. "But this time's different."

He took the hand in his own and held on to it, gazing up at her with bloodshot eyes. She noticed how quickly he was aging, despite all the shots, the treatments and transfusions.

She was perched on the edge of his enormous bed, the breakfast tray moved to one side. Emeric had dismissed all the robots when she'd walked in unannounced and dressed to kill. His thin hair and puffy face were slathered with antiaging creams, though he'd had time to wipe the lavender stuff from his lips before she kissed him hello.

"Different how?" he asked now, toying with the gold rings on her fingers.

She withdrew her hand and eased off the bed, rearranging her short skirt. "I want to tour."

His wizard's eyebrows arched. "Tour?"

"With a backup band. My songs are getting lots of play on the telecomp networks," she quickly added, "and TOR PATEL thinks some of them might go platinum. Anyway, a dozen people at the reception invited me to visit them—"

"You don't need to accept anyone's charity."

"It's not charity, Em. It'd be fun to see how they live."

"Fun." Emeric snorted. "We have at least one house in every city worth visiting, and God knows how many exec condos in the rest. There's no need for you to sleep in strange quarters."

"But those places are *yours*, Emeric," she protested.

He favored her with the worshipful look. "What I have is yours, you know that."

She turned away from him before the frown could surface. Accepting his terms, traveling from one mansion to the next, would be no different from remaining on Offworld. She could point out that he had no legal right to her, but she didn't want it to come to that. There had to be some other way of getting around him.

She'd spent the two days since the gala in a futile comp search for data pertaining to the *Excalibur* survey mission and subsequent tragedy. It was beginning to appear as if the virus had had an effect on the computer files themselves, since each route she had taken ultimately landed her in restricted territory. She sensed that much of what she was looking for could be accessed in the Virtual Network, but she wasn't confident of her abilities to get out once she got in. She had never quite learned the knack of using the bulky goggles and sensor-studded wardrobe piece—despite their having been fashioned by researchers she knew on a first-name basis.

That the data was restricted, however, had only further aroused her curiosity. AIs weren't known to lie, and even if they did, what possible motive would FABIEN have had for sending her off on what was beginning to feel like a morbid quest? Dr. Primorac would have concurred; the psychometrist had long maintained that the origin of some of Jain's somatic complaints lay not in the rigors of orbital life, but in her unwillingness to accept the painful truth of her parents' deaths. In his opinion, she gave little more than lip service to the therapy of resignation.

Of course, AIs weren't infallible either, and FABIEN might simply have been mistaken.

She thought if she could just talk with some of the scientists and techs who were with OLD at the time of the tragedy . . . But a bit of investigation revealed that not one of them was currently onstation. Death had claimed an inordinate number; several were on Mars, and the rest were believed to be downside. Of the members of the board of directors, Magnus Torrell, Yi Ding, Joseph Katz, and Goody Thorsten were all in cryosleep, and the current addresses of Shamir Starr and Beat Gaehwiler were classified.

Dr. Nerbu wasn't listed anywhere in the records files. Jain was surprised when Simon Bové's name came up; but there was no way she would go to him—

"I have an idea," Emeric said after a minute of mulling things over. "What would you say to the two of us going—together?"

"Oh, Emeric, I don't know about that," she said, facing him from the foot of the bed. "I want this to be mostly a career move, and you know how nervous I get when you watch me perform.''

''Nonsense,'' he said with a wave of his hand. ''I wouldn't have to attend your shows.'' He gazed up at her. ''But I could be there for you at home.''

Jain bit her lower lip.

''You know how much I care about you . . .''

He wasn't looking at her now; he never was when he said it. She relented a bit and said, ''And I care deeply about you, Em.'' Her standard reply. ''You're like a father—''

''But I'm not your father!''

''Then why are you behaving like you are?'' She said it with equal force and knew that she had him.

''Is that what I'm doing?''

She nodded. ''It's what you always do.'' She sat down on the bed, just out of his reach. ''I need my freedom. I'm a creative person, Em. I need inspiration. I can't just remain on Offworld forever. I'm capable of going down the well alone.''

Emeric commanded open the bedroom viewports and gestured to the celestial view. ''This isn't inspiration enough? What is it about you young people that makes you so restless to move on?''

She laughed. ''Like the idea of FTL isn't moving on?''

''That's different,'' he snapped. ''That's *all* of us moving on—as a planetary race. Not just one of us off on a down-side fling.''

Jain's eyes flashed anger. ''*You're* the one calling it a fling.'' She sighed. ''I barely know what rain feels like, Emeric.''

He scowled. ''Acid rain, you mean. You don't know how fortunate you are. You have no idea how dangerous it is downside.''

''*You* come and go as you please,'' she retorted, pointing at him. ''Why do you go down the well if it's so horrible?''

He spread his soft, thick hands. ''Yes, but look at how I have to travel—armored wardrobe, armed guards, security robots.''

*Simon Bové*, Jain added to herself.

''You do remind me of your father,'' Emeric went on. ''The same restless urge, the same idealistic streak. He used to drive your mother half crazy.''

Jain wanted to tell him what FABIEN had said, but she knew he would only misunderstand. Emeric met frequently with Dr. Primorac; he monitored her progress on all levels.

One mention of the AI and she'd be back in therapy. FABIEN, too, if not mem-wiped.

"I suppose I don't have much choice, do I?" Emeric asked at last.

Jain folded her arms, a smile forming. "I'm going to go, Em—with or without your blessing."

It was his turn to sigh. "Will you at least let me make the arrangements?"

"Private shuttle, private jet, servants, robots?" she said. "No way. I want to do this myself."

"But I just want you to make the most of the experience? You could begin with a few days in Paris, then fly to London—"

Jain was shaking her head.

Emeric threw up his hands. "All right. That's game."

She leaned over to kiss his forehead. "I knew you'd understand—once you thought about it."

"What about your antiviral boosters?"

"Already taken care of." She laughed, displaying her upper arms.

He frowned at her, holding her by the fingertips of both hands. "Two things and we won't say any more about it, agreed? *Agreed?*" he repeated as she tried to pull away.

"Two. That's it."

"First, I want your promise that you'll spend a few days with Blair in New York. She's terribly ill, and I think a visit from you would do her a world of good."

Jain nodded, tight-lipped. "I haven't seen her in months," she said, voice cracking. And I can *talk* to her, she thought. "But what's the second thing?"

"That you perform at a party I'm throwing for some close friends."

"Depends on where and when?"

"Caracol," he told her. "Next week. FABIEN will be doing the catering, and I expect there'll be several influential people for you to meet."

"Oh, Em, you didn't need to ask."

He patted her hand. "Good, then it's settled."

For several minutes they discussed the arrangements, and Jain left smiling. It was only when Emeric was certain that she was well on her way to her suite in the habitat compound that he voiced on the room's bedside vidphone.

"Get up here immediately," he said before Simon Bové's face had even resolved onscreen.

# Chapter Nine _____

The UniTel phone directories listed two hundred and twenty Maghar Gitanis worldwide, eighty-four of those with easy access to the Virtual Network, seventeen in Manhattan alone. If the name was an alias—as Felix assumed it was—"Gitani" had chosen wisely. Tech hadn't been able to come up with significant background on any of the thirty most likely candidates he had culled from the lists.

Of the New York seventeen, three were lawyers, two were doctors, and six ran small businesses—delis, convenience stores, and generic outlets. A phone trace revealed that the call had been shunted directly through AmTel's switching station *inside the Network*. Risky business, even when one had access to the necessary software. If nothing else it explained why Gitani had been so cavalier about transferring six large to Felix's near-depleted account.

Felix had already sent half of it to Ali Adou and instructed GoBop to transfer the rest to the Metroplex Environmental Violations Bureau—in the hope that three grand would be enough to keep NetSec from shutting down the office's cyber system. That still left a balance of forty-five with Adou and almost twenty-five with the EVB, but it was a beginning.

Felix didn't guess he would ever see the additional six Gitani was promising for a successful run.

He went over it again on his way crosstown to the eleven A.M. appointment with Doppler Data, Inc. The agency's smooth-voiced operations manager had phoned the office the previous evening to thank Felix for his interest and reconfirm that he would be participating in Doppler's introductory cybertour offer.

"We don't mean to pressure," the woman said. "But there's been just so much interest lately. We like to be informed of cancellations well in advance.'' Felix promised he'd be there with bells on.

Agencies like Doppler Data had been springing up all over the city now that CyberLand was completed and online. The tour packages were nothing more than promotional hype aimed at so dazzling the up-and-coming data processor that he or she would contract with someone like Doppler to custom-design a cyber system, or case manage intra-Network transactions—storage entries, retrievals, transferrals, what have you.

Gitani hadn't concealed anything about Felix's occupation, so a routine background trace should have shown that Data Discoveries wasn't a likely candidate for any of the offered services. But either Doppler hadn't bothered to check, or they had Felix figured for some dumbshit data dick online with a black service cyber squad and ripe for the picking.

Wondering about it kept him from thinking too much about the haze, the heat, and the low-flying helicabs in Thirty-fourth Street's Kamikaze Corridor.

Actually it just was another humid ninety-degree morning, typical for early December; but a tornado watch was in effect for most of New England. Just the sort of forecast that would have sent Felix's father reaching for his meds. Felix had grown up on elders' tales of winter blizzards, snow drifted six feet high against Brooklyn brownstones, holiday firs for sale in the streets. But he'd experienced real snow only once, fifteen years back, and then only a dusting. Light brown as it fell, people thought it was parched midwestern soil blown in on the wind.

Felix often thought about what his father would have made of the New Age. Thomas McTurk, a software designer, had lived to see the Japanese and the Germans rise and fall, only to rise and fall yet again. The city's fling with concept architecture and ice cream stores featuring horseradish and basil leaf flavors had given way to neighborhood mosques and samosa stands. But Thomas was dead of cancer before plastiflesh and trach tubes and oxygen bars had become fashionable; before half the city's ruined streets had become pedestrian malls policed by State Security robots, its still air filled with NOTAR copters and sleek-looking hovercabs.

The area around Broadway and Thirty-third—east from the maglev terminal on Eleventh all the way to the Empire

State Building—had also seen its ups and downs. Just now it was a commercial district of concept high rises and vertical markets, a thousand stores and stalls specializing in discount merchandise and generic goods. Two hundred forty-five West Thirty-third, the building address of Doppler Data, was a forty-story cylinder wrapped like an antique barber pole in neon-script advertising slogans and holosigns. A dozen young Asiatic courtesy staffers were working crowd management at the main entrance, where some sort of smog-mask giveaway was in progress.

PONDEROSA—read the hospital-green rebreather Felix was handed—FOR AN INVIGORATING BREATH OF PINE SCENT!

Felix circled the block and found mobs of eager holiday shoppers amassed at each entrance. He recalled shopping here with Tanika, his late wife, on autumn Sundays. They would tube over from Queens and spend the afternoon browsing in the stores, picnicking along the swollen Hudson River. No hint she'd been ill then; no hint of what Offworld would bring down around them.

He chose what looked to be the smallest crowd and worked his way toward the robot-patrolled doors. After twenty minutes in security holding, he was ushered into the building's air-conditioned lobby and assigned a place in one of the waiting elevator cars. Wedged between plastiflesh buttocks and breasts, Felix counted floors while the car rose, watching the lobby's ceramic checkerboard dwindle in size.

Doppler Data had the entire fourteenth floor to itself.

"Mr. McTurk," the operations manager said, recognizing him from their brief vidphone conversation. "I'm Ms. Dak. We're thrilled you could join us."

Felix accepted the woman's hand and returned the smile. Dak looked a bit more worn in person than she had on-screen. She was probably mid-forties but redone to look twenty-five. Black hair, lamp tan, designer pheromones. The blouse and skirt were minimal, revealing almost as much leg and cleavage as you'd expect from a Friday night tunnel bunny.

"Is this business or pleasure?" she asked, motioning him through a scanner into a blessedly cool lounge.

Felix wanted to ask her the same. "Business," he said. "I'm in data tracing. Busy as hell, of course. Looking for a company that can do some individual case management.

Standard jaunts, courier runs, client interface, that kind of thing.''

Ms. Dak's doctored baby blues appraised the beige suit he'd gotten out of hock that morning.

"I'm certain we can fulfill your needs, Mr. McTurk," Dak told him. "Doppler Data specializes in client interface."

"I can tell," Felix said.

Dak excused herself a minute later and returned to her post at the door, leaving him in the care of a young intern, who made the usual inquiries concerning the condition of Felix's body and the health of his bank account.

He handed over a credit card and was voice-printed and vein-scanned. The intern ran a financial check and inquired if this was to be his first Network jaunt.

"Are you currently wearing implants or plastiflesh?" the intern continued. "Are you under the influence of smart capsule or transdermal enhancers or euphorics? Will the cost of the jaunt be filed as a tax deduction or covered by insurance of any sort?"

Felix responded no to each question, was fitted for goggles, gloves, and jacket, and led to an interface chair similar to the VES 2000 Tech and GoBop had insisted on for the office.

Doppler's customers—Felix's cotourists—offered no surprises. A baker's dozen of men and women dressed no better than he was: process servers, tracers, data dicks, a few frequent fliers like himself. There were two whose outfits identified them as personal service couriers. Felix figured they belonged to the Yasuda robots he'd seen in the lounge. The city's moneyed didn't have much use for the Network, but they would sometimes pay a little extra for a servant who could get around in the cyber reality. Robots were barred from the Network, unless they were among the few mobile functionaries of an Artificial Intelligence. But it was rare to encounter a Series Nine outside a Sutton Place town house or a government lab.

Felix nodded to the fliers on either side of him as a sweet-smelling attendant with delicate hands ran a quick test of the wardrobe and neural coupler hookups. He got a look at his driver before the goggles went from transparent to screen-active mode.

Instructions and suggestions were given through speakers

built into the goggle earpieces, delivered in the same care-fully modulated female voice one heard from a jetliner seat back. *In the event of an emergency landing* . . . Felix told himself. He was so accustomed to the kids' casual attitude toward jaunts, the tour suddenly struck him as novel and exciting; like the first time Offworld had shuttled him up the well on company business.

Felix experienced a fleeting sensation of vertigo as the software ecology of the Virtual Network began to take shape below him. Gasps over the intercom from a few of the vir-gins, loud enough to surface above Ms. Dak's running com-mentary.

*"If you look to the left you can see the baroque spire of the American Telecomputer Construct. And off to the right as we continue our slow spiral down toward the Grid is the landmark IBM storage facility. The cityscape of constructs along the eastern horizon belongs to Offworld Lifting and Development* . . ."

Felix sensed that he was in the hands of a veteran driver—probably some twenty-year-old who had come up from the streets the hard way. He was accustomed to Tech and GoBop's spotting styles, and always found it unnerving to have to submit to a stranger's control and idiosyncracies. Control was by and large a function of state of mind, and it said a lot for a pilot when he or she could keep the ride smooth and the hotdogging to a minimum. After all, Doppler wasn't in the business of providing the kind of thrills you could get in the after-hours arcades from some of these same deckhands. Felix noticed, too, that the sensors in the ward-robe and interface chair had been damped down for low-level kinesthesia.

Doppler's group was closing on InfoWorld when Felix began to feel the change. He was dropping behind the group and the ride was becoming jerky. A glance at the goggles' alphanumeric display confirmed his suspicions: Gitani was trying to assume remote control.

All at once Felix felt himself sucked into a headlong dive down along the advert-plastered cliff face of CyberLand. Within sec-onds he was being propelled at frightening speed across the sur-face of the Grid, powered through abrupt right-angle turns, rocketed across moats, spiraled through windows and insertion points, and finally launched out of the New York City Grid itself. He found himself within a complex of monolithic constructs shrouded by some of the most impenetrable-looking security blankets he'd ever seen. It was federal territory, he was sure of that much; military-industrial data storage, perhaps, or United Aeronautics and Space unreal estate. Even multinationals the size of Offworld Lifting rarely went to such paranoid lengths to write themselves that level of concealment, although a jaunting Felix had once accidentally encountered a similarly enshrouded biotech cartel that had since gone underground.

Maghar Gitani was suddenly online, his voice loud in Felix's right ear. "Glad you could make, it, McTurk."

It was impossible to know whether Gitani was with him in the Network or driving him—a someone-over-your-shoulder feeling. "Where the hell are we?" Felix screamed.

"Careful what you say, McTurk. Remember where you really are." Felix summoned an image of himself reclined in one of Doppler's chairs—talking to himself. "Don't speak, just listen," he cautioned when Felix started to respond. "We're off the tourist routes—even the back routes you're used to. We're going into the large sphere at your nine o'clock. You should be able to see it now. You'd recognize it as Eastern Seaboard Air Traffic Control if you could see through the blanket they've thrown over it."

*I've signed on with a goddamned skyjacker*, Felix thought. What else would Gitani want with ESATC except air piracy or outright terrorism? Unless his game was to peek and poke a secret ETA for an orbital shipment of pig organs, say, or vat-grown tissue of some sort—

"I know what you're thinking, McTurk, and you're wrong. But I guess you're just going to have to trust me on that."

A comp-generated layout map of the target construct began to fill the right screen of the goggles. Flashing icons pinpointed both Gitani's proposed insertion point and his objective, which was not at all where Felix expected it to be—in any of the current data corridors—but located instead deep in the heuristic heart of ESATC's scheduling processor.

"You want to go in there?" Felix couldn't help but ask. *"In there?"*

"You're making a spectacle of yourself, McTurk," Gitani thought to point out. "Now, here's the route I've plotted.

If you see anything wrong with it, use your eyes to draw me a better one.''

Gitani illustrated where he planned to deploy security breakers from a seemingly limitless arsenal of chaff clouds, dazzlers, logic bombs. Confronted with this, Felix couldn't imagine what use Gitani had for him. But the more he studied the route his client had laid out, the more he saw room for improvement. Felix used the motions of his eyes to indicate what he thought might constitute a safer path.

"Yes," Gitani said after a moment. "I see what you're getting at." He entered a few quick adjustments; then Felix had another go at it. A minute later they reached a compromise, and Gitani said, "Let's run with it."

Felix felt his heart race as Gitani—or whoever was driving—hurled him at the looming black construct. An active window he wouldn't have guessed was there irised and the goggle screens detailed a color-coded vista of data corridors and vector lines.

Suddenly they were inside the construct, tearing along the agreed-upon route, cloaked by Gitani's dazzlers from security programs arrayed like bridges across immeasurably deep canyons. Felix couldn't recall having been inside a more rigorously commanded place; but given the volume of air traffic over New York alone, he found it not only understandable but pleasantly reassuring.

Now as long as Gitani didn't do anything to jeopardize the arrangement, Felix thought as his unknown driver sent him toll-free across a final bridge and headlong into the hot core that was air traffic scheduling.

Gitani loosed his last ghost and went toe-to-toe with ESACT's neural net. Felix realized that his client was after nothing less than the net's own self-contained memory store. *Maybe he's planning to broker the data to the California Highway Patrol*, Felix told himself.

He was still thinking it a moment later when something sinister and suffocating poured from the tap Gitani had sunk into the construct's neural reservoir.

The hounds were all over him before he'd even turned around.

He came to in Doppler's cyber room, wide- and wild-eyed, arms flailing against invisible assailants. Judging from the way his scalp felt, someone had torn the goggles from his face. The wardrobe jacket was open, as was what was left of his now-buttonless dress shirt. A pimple-faced tech and a worried-looking Ms. Dak were standing over him pressing trodes to his chest and neck.

"Mr. McTurk, are you all right?" Dak was saying, her own goggles dangling around her neck. "What happened to you? Our driver says that you . . . you *disappeared*? Where were you?"

Felix fought down a wave of nausea and fingered the chair's positioning switch. "The actuator's shot," the tech explained, helping Felix up and out of the recliner.

"Take it easy with him—*please*," Dak cautioned.

The tech lowered Felix into one of the adjacent chairs and powered the thing upright. Felix assumed that the tour had been cut short; the room was empty save for Dak, the tech, and two execs in thousand-dollar suits, who were engaged in a hushed but heated conversation with Felix's sullen-looking driver.

Felix glanced at his watch: Twelve minutes had elapsed since the moment of Gitani's assault on the net. Ms. Dak caught the gesture and said, "I'm sorry if we seem so confused, Mr. McTurk, but I assure you this has never happened before."

Felix considered his reply. He decided he owed Gitani one for running the jaunt from an outside console. Even if ESATC's trackers had run a successful trace on the driver—which Felix assumed they had—they were going to be short one field agent. It was murder without a corpse.

"Our driver insists that you were talking to someone," Dak said.

"He asked where he was," the kid said.

"That's right. And your glove hand was twitching."

"I was addled," Felix told her. "You people frightened me half to death."

Dak gave him a dubious look. "But you're a frequent flier, Mr. McTurk."

"Yeah, well, I've never been where you people were about to take me."

"We never left CyberLand," the kid said, folding bony arms across a sunken chest.

"Mr. McTurk, my name is Doppler," one of the execs said, shouldering Dak out of the way. He was tall, narrow-eyed, and too bulky for the suit, which was bunched up around his upper arms. ''Your driver's one of the best in the biz,'' Doppler said, gesturing behind him. ''He says he had you one minute and the next you were gone. Exactly where *did* you go, Mr. McTurk?''

Felix tried to shake his head clear. ''Why don't you tell me, Doppler? You people are supposed to be the experts here.''

Doppler exchanged a look with the other exec. The man showed his palms as he approached, good cop to Doppler's bad. ''Please don't get us wrong, Mr. McTurk. We're not suggesting it was your fault . . .''

''You better pray you're not,'' Felix said, holding Doppler's gaze.

''Look, kludge, you signed a release form—''

''Perhaps what Mr. Doppler means,'' Ms. Dak cut in, ''is that we'd be happy to offer you a full refund and an all-expenses-paid tour at your convenience.''

''I didn't mean that at all,'' Doppler said, giving Felix the once-over. ''Guy's a data dick, ain't he? And he just up and vanishes in the Network? When the hell has that ever happened? I'm telling you, Walt,'' he said to his partner, ''there's something screwy about this.''

''I smell lawsuit,'' Felix said.

Doppler showed a beefy fist. ''You're gonna smell *this*, meat machine.''

Felix had a response ready but it never made it past his teeth. Something sent a prolonged shudder through the building, rattling the cyber room's plate-glass windows and jiggling loose items to the carpeted floor. The vibration increased in ferocity and was followed an instant later by a deafening roar that seemed to tear open the sky beyond Doppler's west-facing window-wall.

''God in heaven, what was that?'' Dak said with her hands pressed to her ears.

Doppler's partner turned from the window ashen-faced. ''I think it was a low-flying jet,'' he muttered in utter disbelief.

# Chapter Ten _____

"It's not even that there are so many people," Jain was telling Blair Nettles in the elegant comfort of the old woman's bedroom. "I was prepared for that. I just wasn't prepared for quite so many *ugly* people."

Blair, all but lost in the dozen pillows that propped her up against the bed's carved headboard, regarded her quizzically from across a broad expanse of satin sheets. "Don't you mean *unpleasant*, child?"

"No," Jain said, shaking her head. "I mean ugly. It's like they've never heard of plastiflesh. Or deodorants, for that matter."

Blair *tsked* her. "You know, I don't think Emeric has the slightest notion of the disservice he's done you by keeping you high-frontiered all these years." She sighed. "Hollywood and Caracol aren't the real world. I fear you've come to expect too much from our hopelessly sullied little planet, Jain. When I heard you were finally coming downside on your own, I thought it the best news I'd received in months. Now I'm afraid this trip is only going to make matters worse. It comes too late."

Jain showed her a ruby-red pout. "I thought you'd be glad to see me, Blair."

"Oh, sweetie," the old woman said, laughing and calling her to her open arms. "Of course I'm glad to see you." She stroked Jain's long, silky hair. "I'm delighted."

Jain was just eight hours onworld. Eight hours in the soup. In the end she had decided to travel down the well aboard Emeric's personal shuttle in the company of four of his most trusted robot staffers. Two of them were in the bedroom now, sharing wall niches with Blair's own machines.

The first leg of the journey had been somewhat routine—transferring from Offworld habitat to GCT, General Dynamics' Grand Central Terminal—the second stage exciting—falling down into atmosphere, even the downside debarkation in Texas State, experiencing the blue and white and brown up close. There were people hugging one another hello at the gate; trees and patches of bright-green lawn right outside the shuttle arrivals building; antique cars and aproned hovers whizzing down a wide concrete strip of highway.

But the final leg—from Texas to New York City, and the copter ride from Kennedy to the rooftop pad of Blair's Sutton Place town house—had been disappointing and, what with a five-hour delay because of some air control foul-up and the slight increase in gravity, frustrating and oppressive. What there was of New York's inverted bowl of sky was a pale imitation of the cerulean she'd absorbed through direct stim sensorium vids. The sharp chemical smells, the harsh sounds, the electric colors seemed different when experienced in context. Things were out of focus, out of synch, *ugly* to look at. And even with the robots functioning as guides, escorts, buffers, she wasn't accustomed to all the jostling, the aggressive shouting and shoving.

Jain already loathed the thought of venturing outside the sanctuary of Blair's lovely home. She, too, was beginning to question the wisdom of her decision. But there was still the mystery that had brought her here: FABIEN's insistence that her parents were alive, and the culinary AI's equally mysterious message to Dr. Nerbu, whose name didn't appear in any of the declassified *Excalibur* files.

Blair had Jain's gold-ringed fingers pressed between her palsied hands. "My only wish is that I had enough strength left to acquaint you with some of our world's few remaining bright spots." She paused to activate a holoprojector, and scenes of mountaintop sunsets, oceanic volcanoes, and archeological ruins lighted up the room.

"This is the Blue Nile Gorge," Blair said, indicating one of a dozen individual holos Jain didn't recognize. "And this is K2, looking west from the tongue of the Batora Glacier. These structures are all that remain of the temple at Borodudur in central Java, and this, this is a place called Monument Valley."

She had begun to sob. Clearly, she was dying—of an exotic cancer or some neuromuscular thing that was yet to be named. She wore twin pectoral meta-ports to accommodate hourly injections of gene therapy meds and endorphin-analog pain suppressants. Her doctors wanted to have her admitted to a private clinic upside, but Blair had refused.

"Frankly, child, I'm ready for the freezer." She dabbed at redone eyes with a monogrammed handkerchief. "Being ill is just so inconvenient. Day after day, these treatments and prognoses and swine hormones . . . When you're young it's one thing; but by the time you've reached my age you're ready for ice-olation.

"You begin to wage a battle against aging itself, Jain. Against death, the inherent weakness of the flesh." Blair studied one of the holos with a nostalgic eye. Her voice was determined when she spoke. "I want the cosmetologists to complete their work on my face and torso and that's that." She laughed. "I want to look good when they wake me up fifty years from now and tell me they have a cure for my ailment. I don't want to see myself wrinkled and aged in some cryonicist's mirror and drop dead of heart failure."

Jain laughed to break the tension of the moment. Only a relative handful of the several thousand who had opted for ice-olation had been successfully awakened. Some had expired in torpor, others upon reanimation. One hundred–odd clients had been cured of the arrested diseases they had taken with them into deep freeze.

"You do grow tired of living after a while. You need a break—from all this," Blair continued, motioning to the banks of medical monitoring equipment that occupied half the room. "Besides, they say you dream in ice-olation, and what could be better than dreaming? Who knows, perhaps I'll wake up to a healed Earth, detoxed and scrubbed clean." She brushed a strand of Jain's hair back from her face. "You really should wear it back, Jain. You have such pretty features."

Jain ran a hand through her hair and glanced at her reflection in a bedside mirror.

Blair was cackling. "I wish I could be around to see what Emeric and all his high orbiter friends will do when it comes down to deciding for the tank or the crematorium. He was always promising the Offworld board members they'd have chairs for eternity. I just wonder if Torrell or Katz or the others are resting any easier because of that promise. I wonder just what they're dreaming."

Jain had a memory flash of Emeric and Blair at her parents' funeral service. A memory of standing sandwiched between them, Blair in black, holding her hand . . . She was actually Emeric's cousin, but Jain called her "aunt" and thought of her more as a stepmother.

"Wish, wish, wish," Blair was saying, "that's all I seem to be doing lately. But I'll always mourn the fact that your parents didn't live to see the beautiful person they gave the world. And talented, too," she said on a brighter note. "I heard one of your songs the other night." When the comment failed to have the intended effect, she asked, "What is it child? I don't mean to be so morbid. But I worry about you. Is everything all right between you and Emeric?"

Jain looked up at her. "Yes, but . . ."

Blair nodded knowingly. "I understand he was against your coming down."

"It's just that he's so overprotective sometimes."

Blair's bloodless lips tightened. "He has to decide whether he wants to be your father or your suitor. But no matter what, you mustn't let him dictate to you—he gets to do enough of that with the board and the Group of Nine."

Jain concealed a pained look, recalling her only love affair and the handsome boy Emeric had ostracized to Mars.

"His father did it to him, you realize. Encouraged him to be mirthless, domineering, ruthless when he needed to be. For years now he's been setting himself up as Earth's mediator with the heavens and no one seems to care." Blair made a plosive sound. "Hell, if everyone's fine with that, so be it. But I won't have him thinking he can do the same with you. I wish he'd marry Shamir Starr and put my mind at ease. But Shamir knows him too well. Emeric's impossible to live with." She reached for Jain's hands again. "I know I probably shouldn't be saying all this, but illness entitles a person to speak her mind."

Jain squeezed Blair's cool hands. "I have to tell you something I haven't told anybody—"

Blair pressed a forefinger to Jain's lips. "Robots," she said, summoning her command voice after some difficulty. "Priority override: Blair-Winter-Summer-Fall. Leave the room and decomp until requested." The robots came online and began to file out through the bedroom slider.

"It's about the *Excalibur*," Jain said quietly when they had left the room.

"Your parents' ship?"

Jain nodded and began to recount her conversation with

FABIEN. She explained how the AI's statements had disturbed her, how she had searched the files. ". . . And if I find this Dr. Nerbu, I'm supposed to tell him 'recalled to life.' "

"You know Nerbu's a man then," Blair said, pinching her lower lip.

"Well, no actually, I don't."

"Nerbu," Blair repeated, frowning in thought. "I don't recall anyone by that name. But then there was so much secrecy attached to the *Excalibur* mission. When the ship returned, there were so many rumors about space viruses, sabotage, a sentient computer malfunction—even aliens. Then we received confirmation of the deaths and everyone was so upset. Emeric was deeply troubled by the tragedy." She regarded Jain with concern. "But I don't approve of this investigation, child. You can't trust intelligent machines to know about things like life and death. They don't understand death, and I don't want you getting your hopes up—"

"But why would FABIEN say it?"

"Because a synaptic chip burned out or a signal was disrupted. You can't tell with machines. It happens all the time with the robots. They can never remember where they put things, they don't remember half the things you tell them to do."

Jain fell silent for a moment. "I should at least try to find this Nerbu person. Emeric wants me to perform at Caracol next week. If I haven't learned anything by then, I'll give it up as a bad idea. And I'm not getting my hopes up, Blair, but I would like to know the full story."

Blair forced an exhale. "Well, you can't very well solicit information through any of the usual channels. If you approach anyone with too high a profile, Emeric is bound to learn what you're up to and he won't like it one bit." She gazed up at the painted murals decorating the room's domed ceiling. "The first thing you need to do is rid yourself of Em's robots. I'm certain they're recording your every move. I'll instruct two or three of my own machines to watch over you while you're downside. Emeric doesn't have to know about it."

"You really think he's having me *watched*?" Jain asked.

"Of course he is. He's probably worried sick about you. As much as I love our planet, it can be a dangerous place."

Jain stood up and walked away from the bed. "Who can I ask about Nerbu?"

Blair stared at the ceiling for a few seconds more. "There was a young man," she began, "some years ago . . . Now what *was* his name?" She recalled one of the robots to the bedroom—a humaniform machine with lifelike eyes—and put the question to it.

"Felix McTurk," the robot returned, "Data Discoveries." The machine gave a Manhattan address and phone number.

"That's the one." Blair beamed. "An inconsequential person. But he did help me out with a bothersome blackmail scheme aimed at relieving my youngest of most of the money his father left him. Ricos," she said in a disapproving voice. "Mobsters."

"Felix McTurk," Jain said, trying it out.

"In fact," Blair added, "I believe he worked for Offworld at one time. Am I correct, Algol?"

"In security, mistress," the robot affirmed. "A techno-pathologist."

"Yes, computer viruses . . . It won't do to tell him who you are," Blair said, "or he'll charge you a fortune. The address again . . ."

"The Revlon Building. Office 2207, on the twenty-first level."

Blair waved a hand. "A terrible place. The building doesn't even have a rooftop pad. But we'll make an appointment with McTurk and I'll have to have the chauffeur drive you over. Make a note to check the car status for breather assists, oxygen bottles, filter masks, and skin block, Algol," she told the robot. "In the meantime we can work on coming up with an alias, a plausible story, and a suitable disguise."

"A disguise?"

"You were always something of an actress, child. I'm sure you'll think of something."

*"New York, Boston, Washington, and Miami are recovering today from a massive system malfunction that paralyzed air traffic along the entire length of the eastern seaboard."* The anchor's expression was deadly serious, her voice earnest, with a hint of awe.

*"There is still no word on why the intelligent processor—*

*known by the acronym* ESTER, *for Eastern Seaboard Traffic Exchange Rationator—suffered what amounted to an exhaustive collapse yesterday morning shortly before noon Eastern Standard Time. In a statement delivered this morning by ESATC commissioner, Raoul DuChamps, the system failure was said to be caused by a faulty relay terminal in ESATC's primary orbital monitoring station. Sources close to the commissioner, however, have stated that sabotage has not been ruled out. We quote: '*ESTER*'s up-to-date on all her vaccinations, but that doesn't eliminate the possibility of a technopathological—' "*

Felix muted the audio feed but continued to stare at the anchor's long legs—insured, or so he'd heard, for close to five million World Dollars. How'd they expect a man to concentrate on the news anyway, when there was always a chance Lani Randall would forget for just one moment to keep those nyloned knees and perfect calves aligned? Besides, it was the dozenth time he'd listened to reports of the incident in the past twenty-four hours.

Fortunately, the "system failure" hadn't resulted in any midair collisions or fatalities; but there had been a score of close calls similar to the unplanned flyby that rattled the windows and staff at Doppler Data.

ESTER's analysts were certainly aware that the air traffic control construct had been entered; and the fact that word of the penetration hadn't been released to the news media suggested just how concerned ESATC was about compromising the intensive search that was underway. Felix could only hope that Maghar Gitani had taken the necessary steps to prevent the trail from leading to Doppler Data and on to Felix McTurk.

The incident had left him in a paranoid mindset. His legs were shaky when he left Doppler, and the muscle in the suit had followed him all the way to the elevators threatening a full investigation if Felix attempted to press charges. He remembered showing Doppler just what he could do with his threats; grinning at him through the glass wall of the elevator. Guys like Doppler deserved the ulcers and tumors they grew.

Felix had returned to the office afterward, chased the kids out, and planted himself in front of the telecomp, ears tuned in to news updates on the sky scramble, eyes fixed on his onscreen bank statement.

At precisely two fifty-nine P.M. the account had showed a sudden increase of six thousand World Dollars. He immediately sent another four to Ali Adou, the balance to EVB; and passed the rest of the afternoon running an intensity trace on the transferral's point of origin. But Gitani obviously anticipated his doing so and had routed the funds through banks and quick-draw houses clear around the world. Felix got as far as a credit union in Vanuatu before giving up entirely.

One thing was clear, though: The run through ESATC's control cores had been successful. Just what sort of data Gitani had emerged with was anyone's guess.

Felix shrugged out of a sweat-dampened shirt and was positioning his face in front of the electric fan when the kids mobbed into the office, a green-haired GoBop in the lead, Neon in accordian-topped boots at rear guard exchanging loud epithets with someone in the corridor, off in the direction of Lifeguard Insurance.

"How's this for a go-to, Blanchard?" the diminutive hard master yelled, making a circle with his thumb and forefinger and wiggling the remaining digits. "Sit on a joystick, ya recombinant fractal."

"Hey, *hey*!" Felix shouted from the desk. "Knock that shit off!"

Eleni put her hands on her hips and laughed. She had passed muster with the male trio and was part of the team now, outfitted in GoBop's coverall hand-me-downs, red hair brushed to one side and spiked away from her head like a flag in a stiff wind. She'd spent the night on the couch back at the apartment in Brooklyn. Felix realized that her staying on was going to mean surrendering the bedroom, but hell, the kid rated some privacy after what she'd lived through on the street.

"It's almost one o'clock," Felix ranted. "What am I running here, a home for chipped deckhands?"

"We had a score to put together," GoBop explained, pulling sheets of software fiche from zippered vest pockets like some comp magician. "El set up the buy with Deceps."

"I don't want to hear about it," Felix said, making a wall with his hands. "And quit using names from the files as trade! Let that posse scare up their own customers. You think I need former clients calling me up wondering how this or that travel company got wind of their misfiled AmTel payments or their missing husbands? Use your heads, will you.''

Tech was gesturing to himself in a surprised, innocent manner. ''Yeah, Tech, that means you,'' Felix continued. ''You think I don't know what goes on around here? And get Neon in here before Blanchard throws a valve.''

''Jeez, Felix,'' GoBop said, his oversized perpetrator boots crisscrossed atop the desk. ''Who poisoned *your* grapes this morning?''

Felix scowled at him. ''First, take your feet off the desk. Second, I've got a client coming in at two-thirty—a Ms. Ocean,'' he said, glancing at an electronic pad. ''And I want the closet and front room cleaned out—''

''But the fiche,'' Tech started to say. ''We should run it—''

''I want *all* the files brought up to date. I want that piece-of-junk air-conditioner carried out of here . . . ''

''How's it feel to want?'' Neon asked under his breath, and Eleni laughed.

''What was that?''

''Nothing, Felix. Really, we'll get right on it.''

''No one punches deck or flies until you're done, is that clear?'' Everyone nodded except Tech. ''Well?''

''Can I say one thing?'' Tech asked from the closet door.

''One,'' Felix told him, holding up a finger.

''We paid a quick jaunt to the EVB last night—''

''I said I didn't want you in there anymore, didn't I?''

Tech took a backward step. ''No, we were just cruising, Felix, honest. Just wanted to make sure they'd purged your file after 'Bop paid off the fines.''

Felix gave him an uncertain look. ''So? Is the file clear or not?''

''Oh, yeah, it's clear as a Russian morning,'' Neon cut in. ''But guess who's got a list of violations almost as long as yours was?''

Felix was ready for it.

''Maghar Gitani,'' Tech told him.

Okay, Felix said to himself, maybe Gitani was doing some peeking and poking in the EVB and happened to come across the only file that outdid his own. Thought: Now here's a guy—a data dick, no less—who's got to be in sore need of funds. He confirms the hunch by running a check on the bank account, maybe even goes on the street for background and learns about the loans from Ali Adou . . .

By the time Gitani calls, he doesn't figure he's going to get any argument from Felix Down-on-his-luck McTurk. So sure, he's already made an appointment in Felix's name with Doppler Data and begun laying the groundwork for the ESATC penetration.

But there was something noisy with the picture: Tech said that Maghar Gitani the environmental violator was a trasher working out on Staten Island's five-hundred-foot-high garbage mountain. So where did a white junk specialist with a wife and three kids living in working-class Hoboken get access to the tactical software arsenal brought online during the jaunt? And what did a trasher want inside ESATC anyway?

No, something was wrong, Felix decided, all the more certain now that his client had been operating under a borrowed identity . . .

GoBop and crew were busy making as much noise as they could lugging crates of dusty hardware out of the walk-in closet—crazed and bullet-holed video monitors, smashed tape players, obsolete control decks and hard-copy printers, thermal print facsimile machines, an assortment of disk and laser-reader devices, the plastic shells of terminally dazzled CPUs, and three-quarters of a working robot—a good ton of broken and discarded machines rescued from alleyways and abandoned buildings all over the city to take up space in Felix's office.

The kids began by making exaggerated panting sounds as they moved the stuff from closet to front room; soon they were belly-crawling between the doors like foreign legionnaires desperate for an oasis. El stood by the watercooler with a paper cup, anointing them with finger flicks of water. Felix, holding back a smile, was ready to put an end to it when the phone chirped.

He seemed to know by the sound that it was Gitani.

"You did well, McTurk," Gitani began in a rushed voice. "No environmental violations, no still-air events. I trust you received our agreed-upon amount without incident."

"I got it," Felix told him curtly. *And spent all of it.* "I don't suppose you're ready to come onscreen, Gitani."

"No, not at this time. Perhaps at six fifty-seven or eight forty."

"Huh?"

"I'm pressed, McTurk. Let's get down to business."

Felix snorted. "So what's on the program today? Maybe you wanna take a stroll through the National Security Agency, huh? Or see what's doing over at the World Bank?"

"Nothing so extreme, I'm afraid."

Felix laughed. "*You're* afraid? You practically leave me coded in ESTER's cortex and you're afraid? You're a caution."

"I do, however, require your services once again."

Felix waited.

"I need a personal introduction to Tor Patel."

Felix frowned and keyed the name into his desk. "You say that like I should know the guy."

"Indeed you should. But you obviously haven't been keeping up with *Who's Who*."

Before Felix could call up the data, it appeared onscreen. "You've got a way with cyber systems, Gitani, anybody ever tell you that?"

"Tor Patel. Would you like me to read it to you, Mr. McTurk?"

"I think I can handle it," Felix said, already scanning the encapsulated bio. "Creative head of Icon Telecomp Consortium. A mover and a shaker in the entertainment industry. So you call him up and make an appointment. That's my professional advice, free of charge."

"That won't do."

"Somehow I didn't think it would."

Gitani took a moment. "I want you to break the ice, as it were, act as my appointments secretary in this matter."

Felix smiled to himself. "What's the deal, Gitani? You want to broker the air traffic control data you made off with? You've got some crack logic theory about flight schedules and telecomp programming?"

"In a sense, yes."

Felix centered himself for the vidphone's camera and hit the online button. "You're going to have to tell me what this is all about," he said, his youthful face set. "I'm not putting myself on the line for you again, Gitani. Not even for another twelve thousand."

"Make it fifteen then."

Felix gulped and found his voice. "The women must have a great time with you, Gitani. But I still need to know. Come on, throw me a crumb, amigo."

The line went silent for a long moment. "In due time. But for now you need only understand that I am answering to a higher authority in all this."

Felix stared at the blank screen. *Higher authority* could have meant almost anything. Even so, he was reasonably certain he could cross God off the list of possibilities. A crime cartel, perhaps. A multinational or some micronation spook agency running an infiltration op.

"I've gotta think about it," Felix said at last. "I operate a small, low-profile agency, Gitani. I'm just looking to make ends meet, not make the score of a lifetime."

"The two have been known to coincide, McTurk. You have until exactly five fifty-nine this evening. I'll call then for your answer."

Felix glanced at his watch. "Five *fifty-nine*? Why not make it six even, Gitani?"

"Because I've got something scheduled for six. Now are we agreed?"

"I'll think about it," Felix said, and broke the connection.

# Chapter Eleven _____

"Have a seat, Ms. Ocean," Felix said as Jain Nugget stepped into the office. He was sorry now that he'd let El leave with GoBop and the others; he might have convinced her to play receptionist for a time. Although Felix had to wonder what the stylishly dressed Ms. Ocean would have made of the teenager's laterally spiked 'do. The four kids had managed to cart all the robotware and comp junk into the service elevator and were presumably down on the street now trying to convince some free-lance trasher there was nothing toxic or hazardous hidden away in any of the shells.

Felix apologized for the heat and redirected a fan to wash across Fiona Ocean's side of the desk. She was tall, even in flats, thin-boned, pale-complected, fine-featured. Long blond hair done in a French braid, which reached to the low square-cut back of a sleeveless cotton dress. The dress was pale blue, as were the shoes and the wide-brimmed sun hat. In her lap she clutched a security-leashed suede purse—a three-hundred-dollar original that had inspired a whole run of street knockoffs. Felix suspected that most of her outfits would have matching accessories.

"Can I get you something to drink?" he asked. "There's water, some canned juice, and coffee in the fridge."

"No, thank you. I'm fine, Mr. McTurk."

Felix heard the rasp in her voice and thought she might have done some recent time on a breather assist. There was something sluggish about her actions as well, but it wasn't anything to puzzle over. He was used to clients looking as if they were carrying the weight of the world on their shoulders.

"You said you wanted to see me on an urgent matter, Ms. Ocean." Felix was relaxing into the swivel chair, tie loosened, shirt sleeves rolled up past his elbows.

She gazed at him in a strange way. "Urgent? I don't think I used the word urgent."

Felix smiled. "Well, I could have gotten it wrong. Maybe I just picked up on a sense of urgency in your voice."

Her eyes widened ever so slightly. "I'm sure you're mistaken. I would have gone to the police if the matter were urgent."

An off-course jetcraft rumbled the Revlon momentarily. Felix and Jain regarded the office ceiling fan warily; then turned the looks on one another.

"Look," Felix said, showing her the palms of his hands, "suppose we call it a draw, okay? We had a bad connection and whatever brings you here is nothing that can't wait."

"I didn't say *that*, Mr. McTurk. I just don't want you to get the impression I'm desperate."

Felix ran a hand down his face. Okay, he thought, she's afraid of being played for a sucker. She wants to make it plain she's in charge; that she's doing Data Discoveries a favor.

She'd made a point of giving the Revlon's security officers a good look at the limo she'd arrived in. One of the guards—a woman Felix had helped out of a jam—called to say that Fiona Ocean had two first-class robots waiting in the lobby. Daimler-Benz Stuttgart 4000s.

He considered activating the voice analyzers built into the desk, but decided instead to go on instinct. The doorway scanners had already assured him that she wasn't carrying any concealed monitoring devices. But then Fiona Ocean was obviously wealthy enough to be wearing implants of one sort or another—something the office scanners weren't sophisticated enough to detect.

"You did say you got my name from the directory."

"Yes, that's right."

"Was it a machine choice?"

"A what?"

"I mean, was it a random choice, or did you leave it up to a robot to decide?"

She gave him that funny look again. "As a matter of fact, I liked the sound of your name. I had an Uncle Felix. We were close."

"Suits me," Felix said, grinning. "Now, you also said something about a trace. Would that be live or machine?"

"Live, Mr. McTurk. A person."

"Call me Felix," he said. "To make you think of your uncle."

She rearranged herself in the seat, her body covering up for something. "I'm trying to trace an old family friend. A Dr. Nerbu. A friend of my father's actually."

Felix slid a notepad into reach and entered the name. "Is that the family name?"

Jain hesitated. "Yes. Dr. Nerbu."

"As in physician, dentist, professor—what?"

"I'm—I'm not sure."

Felix looked at her. "Did you know this, uh, Nerbu personally?"

"No. As I say, Dr. Nerbu was a friend of my father's."

"And your father doesn't know where Nerbu is."

Jain cleared her throat. "My father's dead, Mr. McTurk. Both he and my mother died of natural causes several years ago."

Felix kept his expression under control. Unless Fiona Ocean was self-made or had married into money, it didn't play out that mom and dad could have shuffled off from natural causes. Odds were they'd be on ice somewhere. And there was something else: a trace of accent Felix couldn't place.

"Do you mind if I ask why you need to locate Dr. Nerbu now?" he asked. "Is it a legal matter?"

"Is my reason important?"

Felix watched her fiddle with the silver clasp of the purse. "Not right now. But I assume you've exhausted all the usual routes—consulted mutual friends, checked national directories, that sort of thing?"

"Isn't that what you do?" she asked, piqued.

Felix laughed. "Well, sure, of course I can do that for you. It's only that people normally come to me when the accessible channels aren't telling them what they need to know. But then you did say that finding Dr. Nerbu isn't an urgent matter."

Her pretty jade-green eyes narrowed. "I'm just not good with cyber systems, Mr. McTurk. I'll certainly pay you for your time."

"Yeah, that is how it works, Ms. Ocean." He glanced down at the pad. "All right, let's take care of the basics. How old is Nerbu?"

"I don't know."

"Male, female, some combination of the two?"

Jain blushed. "I don't know that either."

"Nationality?"

She shook her head.

Felix set the wand aside. "We have a problem, Ms. Ocean. Nerbu might not even be downside. We could be chasing someone dead or in deep freeze. What about last known whereabouts?"

Jain took a moment to decide. "In the Islands, I think. Upside. Working."

"A high orbiter? How long ago?"

"Maybe fifteen years."

Felix folded his arms. Sheets of hard copy rustled in the breeze from the fan. "Which habitat?"

"Offworld," she told him quietly.

And Felix suddenly placed the accent. "Just how long have you been living there, Ms. Ocean?" he said, questioning even the name now.

Jain studied her nails. "What makes you think—"

"Your nails look perfect, Ms. Ocean. Besides, this office is a fashion-free zone. So why don't you just answer the question?"

She glared at him. "I don't have to stand for this."

"No one's asking you to," he told her. "The door's still in the same place it was when you walked in."

A low-flying aircraft filled up most of the long silence.

Jain's eyes were moist when she met his gaze. "I'm afraid I haven't been very truthful with you, Mr. McTurk."

*Uh-oh*, he thought. But said: "We can always give it a second try, Ms. Ocean—if that's really your name."

Jain sighed. "I knew I wouldn't be any good at this. You downsiders are a different breed."

"It's the lack of breathable air," Felix said flatly. "So what's it all about, Ms. . . . ."

"Nugget," she said. "Jain Nugget."

"All right, that's a start."

"You understand now why I didn't want to tell you."

Felix showed her a perplexed look. "Not yet I don't."

"I'm Jain Nugget," she repeated.

"We've been here already."

"Jain Nugget! Jain Nugget!" she said, leaning across the desk.

Felix continued to regard her. "People keep assuming I

know the name of everyone on and Offworld. I'm sorry, Ms. Nugget, but—''

'' 'Heatmaker'? 'Tumbledown'? 'Last One to Know'?''

Felix kept shaking his head. ''I don't get out much to the—''

''Songs! I'm a singer, McTurk! I'm getting play on every major station!''

Felix pinned himself to the back of the swivel. ''I'm sure the kids have heard them.''

''Kids? You're married?''

''Well, no, but—Wait a minute, wait a minute, we're getting way off the track here. What's all this about a Dr. Nerbu? Was there anything valid in what you told me?''

Jain grew serious. ''It wasn't what I said . . .''

''I know—it was the way you said it.'' He went to the small fridge and poured them two glasses of iced coffee from a paper carton. Jain thanked him, took a sip, and set the glass down.

''How's your space history?'' she asked while he resettled himself in the swivel.

Felix shrugged. ''Fair. I know the milestones.''

''Did you ever hear of the *Excalibur*? It was an OLD ship, one of the first sent to survey the asteroids—just about fifteen years ago. Anyway, some sort of virus took hold and . . . thirty-three of the crew died.''

Felix said, ''I remember something about a ship and a virus . . . But you hear so many stories. Twenty years of viruses, aborted missions, tragedies . . . ''

''I know,'' Jain said grimly. ''But the *Excalibur* was my personal tragedy. My parents . . .''

''I'm sorry.'' Natural causes, he thought.

She gave her head a toss and brightened somewhat. ''I'm long over it. Or at least I thought I was until . . . someone upside—''

''On Offworld hab?''

She nodded. ''Someone told me my parents were alive.''

''And this Nerbu knows where they are.''

''Nerbu knows *something*. I don't know just what.''

''But you have done some research? You've asked around?''

''In my own inept fashion,'' Jain said. ''But I'd like to go about this quietly for the time being.''

''That's understandable,'' Felix said, thinking it over.

"But I'm going to need the names of some of the other people connected to the *Excalibur* mission."

Jain fanned herself with both hands. "How do you stand this heat?"

"You'll get used to it. Drink your coffee," he said, "and give me a few names I can start with."

"The names are easy to come by. It's the *people* who are difficult to find."

"You let me worry about that."

She snapped open her purse and passed him a handwritten list of fifteen names. Felix read through it. "Like I said, it's a start."

"I hope so."

Felix watched her sip the coffee. "So you're a professional singer, huh?"

She showed him the first smile he could believe in. "Apparently not professional enough."

"Hey, don't judge by me," Felix told her. "I don't listen to music. You've got a downside agent, a manager, what?"

"My songs were singled out for play by TOR PATEL himself."

Felix spewed iced coffee clear across the desk. Jain leaped out of her chair and began brushing droplets from the yoke of her dress. "God, no wonder I was warned to wear a mask."

*"Tor Patel?"* Felix said, after a brief coughing fit. "As in Icon Telecomp?"

"Yes. He's head of creative programming. He arranged all of my songs." She gave her braid a quick flip. "He says my voice—"

"Do you know him well enough to call him up?" Felix interrupted, dreaming about having fifteen thousand dollars in the bank. "I mean, could you two do a lunch or something?"

Jain studied him for a few seconds. "Why are you so interested in TOR PATEL?"

Felix smiled broadly. "Well, I'm thinking maybe we can help each other out, Ms. Nugget. You see, I've got a client who asked me to set up a personal intro with Patel, and I wondered maybe if I slipped into my finest suit, combed my hair just so, put on, you know, that well-heeled look that . . ."

Jain was laughing suddenly.

"What, the idea of me talking to some head honcho like Patel is a regular laugh riot?"

Jain covered her mouth with a hand. "No. It's the idea of you getting yourself all duded up for the meet."

Felix frowned at her. "I don't get it. Don't people like Patel have a kind of dress code or something?"

"McTurk," Jain said, laughing again. "TOR PATEL is an artificial intelligence."

Emeric Bulkroad heard the hatch behind him hiss open, Simon Bové's footsteps on the nearwood floor. He remained bent over the alloy cue stick, lined up a three-ball combination shot, and pocketed the seven uptable. The shot was entered in an LCD counter on the curved wall of the cabinspace, bringing Emeric's run to forty-four. A robot ball-racker applauded; a second stood by awaiting its turn at the table.

"Pick out a cue," Emeric told Bové without turning around. "And name your game."

Bové gave him a glance as he walked past the table. "Since you seem to be on a run today," he said from the cue rack, "what would you say to some nine-ball?"

"Nine-ball it is," Emeric said, straightening and rechalking the tip of his stick. "How does ten thousand a game strike you?"

Bové winced. "I *was* hoping to have a little something left to retire on."

Emeric waved a hand. "I'll give you the break and spot you two balls."

Bové hefted a stick, balancing it on upturned fingertips. "We did that last go-round and I came up short six months' pay."

"Ah, but maybe it's your lucky day, Bové."

"I'm overdue for one."

"Then take a chance. Stop being so damned anal retentive. I believe in spending money, not saving it."

"All right." Bové sighed. "You're on."

The robot gathered the nine balls in a diamond-shaped rack. The rack was wooden, an antique like the heavy-footed table itself. Shooting straight pool or eight-ball in less than standard gravity had taken some getting used to, but Emeric had mastered the required technical subtleties. Bové's game was billiards. And that the master of the carom and triple-cushion shot had suggested nine-ball alerted Emeric to the fact that his security chief had arrived with less than favorable news.

Bové chalked up and positioned himself for a break shot. He took several practice strokes with the lightweight cue, guiding it between the fore and middle fingers of his lead hand. He favored a light touch, a tea drinker's hold on the cue's textured grip.

"So what news did you bring?" Emeric asked suddenly as Bové was making his shot. Bové miscued, the stick tip grazing the top of the cue ball and sending it scarcely a foot down the table, off to the left of the rack.

"Try talcing your hands next time," Emeric said, stepping in and drawing a bead on the forward apex of the diamond. The break was loud and near violent; the cue ball drew back uptable, and the three and six balls thudded into opposite side pockets. It took a long while for the table to come to rest.

"She's been staying with Blair," Bové said, scowling from the talc dispenser. "But she pulled a switch on us with the robots."

Emeric dropped the one in a corner, and the robots applauded. "What kind of switch?"

Bové redirected his scowl at the twin Yasudas. "Do we have to have them applauding every shot you make?"

Emeric was smiling when he looked over his shoulder. "You're excused," he told the machines. "Decomp outside, await my instructions."

"Piece of cake, sir," one of them said as it was exiting the cabin. "Bové chokes."

"You were saying?" Emeric said, watching Bové glower at the robots.

The security chief turned to face him, showing the tattooed side of his shaved scalp. He was dressed in a wide-shouldered white suit, loose-fitting cuffed trousers to match; a rust-colored shirt with a round collar and golden bow tie. A silk rose adorned the left of the jacket's narrow, full-length lapels.

"You listened to the recordings of the talk she had with Blair?" he asked. Emeric nodded while he was lining up a shot on the two ball. "Well, we don't know what went down after Blair dismissed the machines, but the next morning Blair's chauffeur drove her downtown to the Revlon Building."

"That's one of ours, isn't it?"

"Yep."

"Your shot," Emeric said, backing away from the table with a cube of blue chalk lost in the folds of his enormous hand.

Bové studied the table. "Hell, I can't even see the damn two ball," he said after a moment. "I'll take that as a spot." Emeric voiced approval and Bové whisked the ball from the table, setting up a shot at the four ball, which with luck would pocket the nine.

"The Revlon Building," Emeric said.

"So what's she do, she leaves the 'bots in the lobby and goes up a coupla floors to the office of a data dick name of Felix McTurk." Bové glanced at his boss for a reaction. "You're gonna love this: Turns out the guy used to work cyber security for us downside. A technopath. Used to make sure SPARTOS was up on his inoculations."

SPARTOS was the Virtual Network AI in charge of OLD security.

Bulkroad's nostrils flared, enhancing the bullish aspect of his face. "The name's familiar—why?"

Bové snorted a laugh. "He tried to scam us—about seven years ago. Seems his old lady had the emphysema or some goddamned thing, and McTurk was expecting his company insurance policy to cover the cost of the treatments. Naturally, we heard about the wife's chest problems and canceled the coverage. So what's this McTurk do but run a cyber op to do a bit of surgery on the files."

"We had a bet, I believe. You were certain McTurk would fail in his efforts . . . You won a good deal of money from me." Emeric tugged at the skin under his chin. "As I recall, someone told me later on that you went into the system beforehand and postdated McTurk's signature so there wouldn't be any coverage."

*"Moi?"* Bové said sheepishly.

"McTurk had an accomplice . . ."

"Koo Raywing."

Emeric nodded knowingly. "Network Security."

"Yep. Raywing joined NetSec and McTurk opened up shop as a data dick." Bové took his shot; the nine ball slammed into the corner pocket, rattled there for a moment, and hung up on the lip. "Suck space, you piece of airborne shit!" he said, moving aside.

Emeric dropped the four and five balls on cross-side shots, deliberately leaving the nine in place. "So what finally happened to the wife?"

"Died." Bové shrugged. "McTurk's probably still paying off the bills."

"I take it he isn't very fond of us."

"And then some. We had a personal run-in awhile back. I had to remind him which way was up."

Emeric pocketed the eight. "What do you think Jain wants with him?"

Bové ran a hand over a slicked-down strip of patent-leather hair. "I've been asking myself. Turns out Blair employed McTurk a few years back to settle up with a couple of, uh, small-time scammers on Dow hab. The Fassbinders' cartel."

"I wasn't aware of that."

Bové nodded, glancing away. "But we still don't know what inspired the trip to begin with. I don't buy the tour excuse. I figure it's got to be something someone said to her at that bash for Kakis. I've got people working on it."

"Could she have a new lover?" Emeric asked, deadly serious.

"Maybe," Bové allowed. "She could be using McTurk to run background on whoever it is."

Emeric's face reddened. "I won't stand for it, Bové. You'll have to handle it . . ."

Bové bounced the cue stick on its knobbed base. "We sent the last guy to Mars, right? We do the same for this Romeo if we have to."

"I expect no less, Bové," Emeric said, sinking the nine. "Another game?"

Bové blanched but managed a nod. "Of course there's a chance the whole thing's just a career move," he said, stooping to retrieve balls from the table bin. "She left New York for Hollywood about an hour ago for a face-to-face with TOR PATEL."

"At least we can rule out PATEL as a lover," Emeric said from the head of the table, leaning forward on the frail-looking stick.

Bové moved his head from side to side. "Thing is, she's got the data dick along for the ride."

Emeric fell silent while Bové continued to position the stripes and solids in the wooden diamond.

# Chapter Twelve ⎯⎯⎯⎯⎯⎯

Felix leaned forward in the limo's backseat to get a look at the towering facsimile pagodas that flanked the gated entrance to Manga Studios. The twin multiroofed structures and the elaborate gate itself were well known to cinemists worldwide as Manga's logo, but Felix couldn't recall doing any of the studio's releases.

"Do" was Hollywood-speak for experiencing one of Manga's sensorium spectaculars, where you sat in the dark wearing a plastic dermatrode-studded helmet and allowed yourself to be bombarded with two hours of sensurround flesh, adventure, violence, or laughs, complete with all the smells and tastes and fleeting moments of human joy or misery, ecstasy or pain.

Felix wasn't a fan of Manga or anyone else's hollow-fantasy version of real life; more to the point, he was against attending anything that required one to thumbprint an endangerment-release waiver at the door.

The limo that had collected him and Jain at LAX was waved through Manga's gate by a beefy robot outfitted in gladiatorial costume. Jain's two personal machines were sitting up front with the uniformed studio driver, a blond six-footer with central casting good looks just waiting to be discovered. The kid was mainly along for effect, since the car was adept at handling the driving and door opening and regulating climate control.

"So what do you think, McTurk?" an exec in the swivel seat opposite Felix's asked. "Pretty impressive, huh?"

Felix knew the appropriate response, but was less certain how to phrase it. "Didge," he said, borrowing a phrase from GoBop and shifting his gaze from the view outside the tinted sunroof to the tightened features of Trump Castle's tanned face.

*"Didge?"* Castle laughed, spilling some of his drink, and looked at Jain. "What d'you bring us here, Jay—a concrete cowboy? A lost cluster? Only kidding," he added, reaching out to squeeze Felix's knee. "You're a prize, McTurk."

Jain gave Felix a grinning sidelong glance from the adjoining seat. "Mr. McTurk has a fondness for teenage slang. In fact, he employs several teenagers as his assistants. Cyber wizards, he calls them. I think their street patois has begun to rub off on him."

Castle's lasered eyebrows went up. "No kidding, McTurk—you and a coupla teenage deckhands?"

Felix shrugged. "They know their way around the Network better than I do."

"A data dick with a bunch of deckhands," Castle mused, eyes raised in thought. "Kids in trouble, rescued from a life of violence, crime, and designer drugs by a selfless good guy, a data tracker, burned out on all the horror casework he's done. . ." His blue eyes returned to Felix. "I like it, McTurk."

"You like what?"

"Your story. It's got image appeal. We should think about optioning it. Of course I can't promise you much up front, but who knows, once a treatment's completed we could shop it around, think about a script. I might be able to get you a few points if the thing goes to sky . . ."

Felix had stopped listening; Jain, too, by the look of her, her attention fixed on an array of flat screens running trailers for a few of Manga's current releases.

Castle was the studio's liaison man with ITC, the talent consortium that had Jain under contract. In truth, ITC owned Manga and utilized a portion of the studio's back lot as corporate headquarters for their talent marketing division. The whole works centered around TOR PATEL, an AI birthed nine years before and nurtured onsite by a team of cyberneticians on loan from Offworld Lifting and Development.

Los Angeles, back at the turn of the century, was one of the first cities to try to bring smog and air pollution under control by restricting the use of gasoline engines and certain kinds of refrigerants and insulation, lacquer hardeners, circuit board cleaners, fire extinguishers and the like. Unfortunately, El Niño, the ozone layer, half a dozen volcanic eruptions over the past two decades, and a host of other unpreventable natural catastrophes hadn't acquiesced to the city planners' grand design, and LA had become just what everyone feared it might.

Most of the cinema stars had moved to sunnier spots inland, but several of the major studios and the top dozen or so multimedia corporations had remained, contained under vast domes or buried inside the dry hills in enormous air-conditioned bunkers.

Felix hadn't been there in years, and would have found the city even more intolerable than New York on an August afternoon were it not for the high style in which he and Jain Nugget had traveled cross-country. Since New York it had been nothing but climate-controlled spaces, coupled with freshly prepared meals, robot service, and first-run entertainment.

Before they left, Felix had screened some of Jain's songs in the office. He hadn't found them much to his liking, but they had a certain pop appeal. *An image appeal*, as Castle would put it. Even if the disk's telecomp promos were overloaded with the same space shots and null-gee sex play Felix had seen in a dozen others.

He had to admit, though, his attention had been captured by the sight of 3D Jain in a skin-tight bodysuit that featured transparent breast cups. GoBop and company hadn't thought much of the videos either, and had altered things to their liking by resequencing the audio tracks and visual images, picking up the tempo, rewriting the lyrics to reflect their fascination with cyberspace, and transforming Jain into some creation more out of *Metropolis* than *Barbarella*.

When Felix last saw the kids they were still trying to offload the robo-ware and useless comp junk they'd carted from the office. He ventured that half the stuff was already back in the closet.

To keep everyone busy while he was on the coast, he'd tasked them to run intensity traces on the fifteen names Jain had furnished—a list of crew and techs associated with the *Excalibur* who were believed to be downside, whereabouts unknown—and place an ad in the telecomp personals for Dr. Nerbu, him- or herself. Felix had instructed GoBop to confine the search to the news media archives and citizenry directories, and had warned him to steer clear of Offworld's own fortresslike construct in the Virtual Network.

Felix—one of many who had been burned by runs through

Offworld—knew better; but it was something he tried to impress on the kids as often as he could.

"We have arrived, Mr. Castle," the car said, coming to a halt in front of a low, windowless building on Manga's back lot that had obviously been designed with earthquakes in mind. Felix pegged it for the shock-mounted residence of TOR PATEL.

The limo's rear doors winged open and Jain led the way out. Felix noted that she was breathing easier and moving a little more gracefully than she had when she shuffled into the office two days earlier. She was also more at ease here than she'd been in Manhattan; more at home among groups of attentive persons or high-priced machines than among sullen New Yorkers who viewed rich and poor alike as targets of opportunity.

"Welcome to ITC, Ms. Nugget," a leggy brunette announced as Jain entered the building. "We were sorry to hear about the delays in leaving New York."

"Is there anything we can get you?" a second woman asked, electronic notepad in hand, hurrying to match strides with Jain's swelling retinue of studio execs, secretarial assistants, and burnished robots.

Felix, lagging behind the mob, couldn't figure it. After all, the songs weren't *that* terrific; it wasn't as if Jain Nugget was a name on everyone's lips. There'd been no background data available on her; so Felix could only assume that she was even wealthier than he first thought.

Wealthier or extremely well-connected.

The high-flying air-breather that had taken them cross country was privately owned. Normally the plane carried fifteen at a jump, but they had had it pretty much to themselves. However, even Jain's seemingly limitless access to funds couldn't be brought to bear against the snafus that were continuing to snarl air traffic in and out of New York. ESTER apparently hadn't bounced back from its nervous breakdown; and rumor had it that ESATC officials were now considering having the AI lobotomized and parceled out.

Several leading cyber analysts speculated that a terrorist group had infiltrated a traumatizing virus into ESTER's core memory, dredging up infantile psychic complexes that had attended its multisystem construction and birth.

Felix didn't mention Jain when he'd spoken to Gitani at exactly five fifty-nine the previous evening; he'd said only that he was accepting Gitani's offer and was even then making arrangements for a person-to-machine appointment with TOR PATEL.

Nor had Felix told Jain about Gitani. When she called to set up an intro between Felix and TOR PATEL, it turned out that the ITC's creative AI had been eager to talk to her about some new deal on the horizon.

"TOR PATEL is expecting you, Ms. Nugget," yet another gum-cracking, black-haired stork announced farther along the carpeted path to the building's heart and soul. "And your guest," the woman added, with a look down her reworked nose at Felix.

He guessed it had something to do with his clothes or maybe his hair, which was at least his own and hadn't come by way of genetic splice or hormone injection. To Jain's form-hugging skirt, pillbox hat, feathers and veil, Felix was wearing the same beige suit he'd worn to Doppler Data days ago, now in sore need of a quick press.

"I knew that nose when it was just a glint in your cosmetologist's laser-scalpel," Felix muttered to PATEL's exec sec as he sidled past her.

Felix had dealt with AIs in the past, but he hadn't visited one in residence since his final months with OLD, when company business had taken him up the well to confer with Emeric Bulkroad's personal security machine, SPARTOS.

The room that housed TOR PATEL was huge and almost too chilled for comfort. One entire wall was given over to flatscreens and holo-projection units; another to a Big Board of the sort Felix thought reserved for military strategic planning centers. He guessed by the displays that the map afforded TOR PATEL with up-to-the-moment information on sales figures for audio and sensorium releases worldwide.

"Jay," the machine said cheerily, "wonderful of you to come on such short notice. Make yourself comfy and have the bar fix you something to drink. Then we'll see to doing lunch together."

"It's great to finally meet you," Jain said, completely at home with the situation.

Felix had always found it awkward to talk to walls—especially ones that concealed banks of neural instrumentality. "This is Felix McTurk," Jain continued. "He has some interesting ideas about promotion, and I thought you two should meet."

Felix could feel the AI studying him: monitoring odors and thermal readings, scanning him for physical imperfections, compiling a personality profile to utilize as an interactive guideline.

"I'm actually here on behalf of a client of mine," Felix said, "who would like very much to meet with you at your convenience."

"My time is very limited," TOR PATEL said, "but any friend of Jay's is a friend of mine, and I suppose it follows that any friend of Felix McTurk's should at least be afforded a chance to make a pitch. But we'll get to all that later on. In the meantime, how does a scotch and water sound, McTurk?"

Dead on, Felix thought. He supposed the machine had sniffed out trace aromacules adhering to him from last evening's session with a bottle. "Scotch'll do fine," Felix said.

Jain asked for a Bloody Mary and they settled themselves into padded microclimate armchairs while the bar went to work, two humaniform robots standing by to serve the drinks. Separating the two chairs was a marble pedestal table capped by a plastic keyboard and dual-screened vidphone. The chill left Felix as the chair warmed slightly.

TOR PATEL was quite literally a tree in a holo-forest of widely spaced evergreens filling an incalculable portion of the room. Cedar, pine, and redwood smells in the recirculated air, patches of snow on needled ground, a view of distant mountains. Felix could almost believe he was looking at the Sierra Nevadas from some forest preserve scenic overlook in northern California. He thought he understood now why wardrobe was unimportant to TOR PATEL; but at the same time he imagined that the AI could present any number of faces to its guest.

"Couldn't help noticing you admiring the WOW Board," the machine said after the robots had delivered the drinks.

Felix narrowed his eyes and grinned. "The map? Yeah, I was."

"Oh, but it's much more than a map, McTurk. I call it the WOW Board because it informs me the instant one of our projects shows a profit."

"Says 'Wow,' in other words," Felix said.

"And then some," TOR PATEL enthused. "For example,

let's say I want a demographic readout on Jain's current release. I call up the disk title and . . . there you have it.''

Jain and Felix watched the board as data flashed from the display screens.

"The numbers confirm that we've got an unqualified hit," the AI said.

"Thanks to your input," Jain said as a scented breeze stirred the ends of her hair.

"No, not my input, Jay. The input of tens of thousands of our audience members who've agreed to wear ITC's interface headware as they sit back and enjoy our product. Signals from the very pleasure centers of tens of thousands of human brains are relayed to our corporate headquarters and collated, so that we know precisely which sound or visual bites move them, inspire them, excite them, depress them. Conversely, we can determine just which audio/visual elements bore them, horrify them, repel them.''

The AI paused. "It's *their* input you have to thank for your success. We give them just what they want, served up by a myriad of attractive packages.''

Felix thought Jain might be frowning but she wasn't. "I think it's great," she said, her face lighting up. "I'm ready to go back in the studio anytime you say.''

The AI didn't respond immediately. "Actually, Jay, I have something more exciting in mind than another disk release. What it comes down to is this: For a long while ITC has had hopes of expanding its telecomp services, and I'm thinking that conditions are favorable right now for a leap into the Virtual Network itself. ITC will be able to offer its customers a full line of interactive entertainment of a completely different order from anything offered by either InfoWorld or CyberLand. And Jain, I've chosen you to be our first telecomp CJ—ITC's first console jockey.''

Jain's crimson mouth fell open. When the words came, all she could say was "I can't believe this is happening!''

"Who loves ya, baby," TOR PATEL said.

Felix finished the last of his drink while the two swapped praise; they both gave good blurb. He was about to ask the bar for a refill when TOR PATEL suddenly said: "McTurk, I've been informed there's a call for you . . . from a Mr. Gitani.''

Felix stared dumbly at the AI's holo-forest projection.

"If you care to take the call in private, there's a booth

just outside the door; otherwise I can have it routed to the phone on the table beside you. But I should tell you, McTurk, I find this interruption rather irksome. Just who is this Mr. Gitani?''

Felix stiffened in his seat. "Uh, a client."

"Not by chance the same client who wants so desperately to meet with me?"

He belched up a taste of scotch. "As a matter of fact—"

"Suppose I just talk to this Gitani right now."

"I don't know if that's such a good idea," Felix said quickly, recalling Gitani's recent encounter with ESTER.

The warning came too late in any case.

Half a minute later an inhuman howl issued from somewhere deep in the forest. The evergreens winked out and in their stead a violently erupting holo-volcano began to take shape.

# Chapter Thirteen _____

GoBop got up in Neon's face with his most determined look. "Felix told us to pass on Offworld. So that's that, right?"

Tech heard just enough upward inflection in his friend's voice to give him hope. "Since when, Bop?" he said from the office console. "I mean, he told us to *stay away* from OLD—"

"Steer clear," El amended from across the room.

Tech glanced at her with his mouth twisted up. "Steer clear, then. But he didn't actually say we couldn't go *inside*."

GoBop adopted a dubious expression and began shaking his head. "Fuzzy logic, man . . . All this time I thought that was a head on your shoulders, Tech. Now I see it's only a growth. How we s'posed to get *inside* without getting near it?"

"The GoSub," Tech said, pinching the microfiche envelope between his fingers. "We let it sniff out an insertion point somewhere else on the Grid."

"There's gotta be active windows all over the Network," Neon chimed in, commanding his goggles to transparent mode. "Just a matter of finding them."

"Like you found that shaft into the EVB, zat it?"

"Didge," Tech said.

GoBop looked back and forth between them. "What a team you two make. Peek and Poke I'm calling you from now on. Like it's not limp enough Felix is gonna have to find all that robo-ware back in the closet."

"Well, we're not getting anywhere in archives," Tech argued. He gestured to Jain's list of names. "None of these people is listed in the directories. There isn't even squat on the *Excalibur* mission."

"That's valid," Neon said, tugging at the wardrobe jacket's sleeves. "Offworld's our best shot."

GoBop snorted.

"Shit, Bop," Tech said. "Tell me you haven't been dying to get in there. It's where it all happens, man, you know that."

GoBop worked his jaw. "Don't chaff me, Tech. You guys just want to run a chicken jaunt with Network Security."

"Hey, it's what being a hard master's all about," El said with an obvious note of sarcasm. "Dive in there and bring the world under control, 'mano. *Impose* yourself." She made a tight fist with her upraised right hand. "Macho meditation—*absolute*! *Pure procedure*!"

"Backseat driving," Tech muttered. "I don't see you helping out any, El."

She stood up, wiping the palms of her hands down the front of tattered jeans. "Slide over, Mario," she told Tech, advancing on the console.

"Hold on, cowboys," GoBop said. "We're talking about black action here. OLD's major architecture. I'm for just telling Felix we couldn't get anything on this Nerbu character. Nugget's just one client, right?"

"One *right* client," Tech said, chortling.

" 'Heatmaker,' " El sang, mimicking Jain's breathy vocal style. " 'You bring a flush to my face, you bring a fire to my soul . . . ' " She paused to laugh. "And like the way she talks . . . all that high-frontier nasal."

"Uppie," Tech said, and they all laughed again.

"So we tell Felix the data dumps were empty," GoBop said, bringing things back online. "Better that than having NetSec coming down heavy on us."

Neon nodded in the interface chair. "Maybe Bop's right. There might not even be a way into OLD. It could be a hermit."

"Oh, there's a way in all right," El said, doing input with her left hand. "Through an active window over at Offworld's downside buffer. The Deceps have been using the thing as an entry point for months."

Tech threw her a look of disbelief.

"Believe it," El told him. "Only you didn't hear it from me, okay? Besides, you'd never get through the way you drive."

"Here we go again—"

"It's true, man." El ran a hand across the console as if

she were caressing it. "You can't drop in there like some conquistador expecting to force your way into everything. You've got to get into a dialogue with the data, Tech. You build a relationship . . ."

"Zen technique," Neon said.

"The zone," GoBop added, nodding.

"Limp, soft master, heuristic chicktalk," Tech grumbled.

"No it's not, Tech. It's like the difference between the way we drive: You're always going so fast it's like you don't see what's alongside the highways. Me, I'm like looking for the experience. You throw yourself into the Network. I like dream myself in."

"Enough already," Neon said. "Let's fly if we're gonna do it."

GoBop remained skeptical. "How's all this decipher, El? How do we get in there?"

Eleni composed herself at the deck, going through a kind of keypad preparatory ritual. "Okay, here's the drill: First we get ourselves over to Offworld's data dump. When I say, we boot that GoSub soft. You'll like see the window; but just hang back and park once you get inside. Get into a stack but don't make a jump for any of the buses that pass you. Give me like a minute to do my thing. I'll flash you a sprite to give you the clear. You'll hear a default tone, then a go-to."

"Then what?" Neon asked nervously.

"Then, my man, you're inside Offworld construct. It's no major deal providing you like don't make too much noise. I've driven a couple Deceps in and we never ran into any trackers."

"Yeah, but what were you dudes after?"

El shrugged. "Space footage mostly. We had a steady customer who couldn't get enough opticals of Jupiter and shit."

Neon nodded. "So where do I go once I'm inside?"

"Follow the map to files and grab whatever you can on *Excalibur*, I guess."

The four of them fell silent for a moment.

"I'm going in with you," GoBop said to Neon, slipping into the tandem goggles and neural coupler.

"Thanks, Bop."

"Suppose there's a problem?" Tech thought to ask, readying himself at the deck.

El exhaled through puffed cheeks. "You drop what you're holding and burn."

Reflexively Felix and Jain shot from their seats and backed toward the door as TOR PATEL's holo-mountain trembled, erupted, coughed plumes of gray smoke and ash—like something straight out of Manga Studio's F/X department.

Where a chill current had played about the room moments before, there was heat now, and TOR PATEL's voice was angry. Felix continued to wonder about the howl: whether it was an effect staple in the AI's forest repertoire, or whether the mournful ululation had originated at Maghar Gitani's end of the phone link?

And just what had Gitani tried to run on ITC's top machine mind?

Castle, TOR PATEL's lanky exec sec, several other suits, and half a dozen robots from Manga security came pouring into the room like some dustoff medevac team. Except that most of the humans had wands and notepads in hand instead of lifesaving devices, and even the robots were setting themselves on record mode.

Something told Felix this wasn't the first time the AI had portrayed itself as an unholy mountain.

Felix had thrown an arm around Jain's quaking shoulders, but withdrew it now, deciding things would go better for her if TOR PATEL thought she'd merely been duped. After all, Gitani's call had come in for Felix. If only the goddamned machine hadn't decided to take it . . .

"Take a memo!" the AI bellowed at his cowering staff.

Here it comes, Felix thought. ITC's rising new star—the company's almost CJ in the Virtual Network—gets the ax. And Felix McTurk—what? Is banned from Manga Studio releases? Has to eat his popcorn with nondairy butter? Has to suck the farts from—

"We're going to be making some changes in our spring telecomp lineup, people," TOR PATEL announced. "To begin with, I want every show cut from twenty-two minutes to twenty-one minutes thirty seconds. The extra half minute per half hour will allow us to run air travel information for flights arriving at or departing from our affiliates' major airports."

Felix put his head in his hands. Gitani had dazzled another AI; it was as if the guy had it in for sentient machines.

"After that we're going to begin a massive reeducation campaign directed against enviromental violators."

"I see big bucks, TP!" Trump Castle said in a loud voice. Felix couldn't stifle a laugh.

"Dig out every documentary, docudrama, or series pilot that has anything to do with atmospheric contamination, noise pollution, population growth, deforestation, fossil-fuel combustion, urban heat-island effect, rice cultivation, nitrogenous fertilizers, ozone, and sunspot activity."

"Mexico City footage," someone suggested. "Whales washing up in Uruguay . . ."

"Kalimantan's last parcel of hardwood forest," from another. "Chinese birth control tactics . . . "

"Yes, yes, yes, and yes," TOR PATEL was saying. "Cancel whatever series you have to: *High Frontier*, *The Love Habitat*, *My Mother the AI*, *Martian Vice*—scrap the lot of them. And dump all our audio disk contracts while you're at it. There's too much music in the world already."

"He can't mean it!" Jain gasped.

Felix said, "You know how these creative types are."

She aimed a daggered look at him.

"And get the writers to come up with some concepts for airline sitcoms. Take a note: Robot air traffic controller falls in love with a human pilot. When the pilot doesn't want to have anything to do with her, she sabotages his flights . . . A General Dynamics shuttle piloted by a distraught artificial intelligence decides to skyjack itself to the moon . . . A Martin Marietta heavy orbiter develops a hopeless crush on a Mitsubishi LeGrange point torus . . ."

"They're going to open huge, TP!"

"We'll be able to write our own ticket!"

"Now, *that's* a concept!"

Castle and the rest weren't missing a word. Jain was staring at Felix with her mouth open.

"Don't look at me," he told her. "I'm not the one who's taking *My Mother the AI* off the air."

"That phone call," Jain said, "from your client. You *knew* this was going to happen."

"Look, you're just sore 'cause some endangered rodent is going to wind up host of ITC's Virtual Net programming."

"You're not getting away with this, McTurk," Jain seethed. "I plan to tell them all about you and this Gitani person—"

Felix grabbed her before she'd taken three steps in Castle's direction. He tightened his grip on her arm when she fought him. "You're hurting me, McTurk," she said.

He eased up and steered her toward the door. "I'll tell you everything," he whispered as they sidestepped behind Castle's preoccupied group. The AI was still showing them his fiery aspect, spouting commandments like some prophet. "First I need to know one thing."

"What is it?" she asked angrily, massaging her upper arm where he'd vised it.

"All that talk about making you ITC's Network star. Why's TOR PATEL taking such an interest in your career?"

Jain gave her mane of golden hair a haughty toss. "You've heard my songs and you have to ask that?"

"Exactly," Felix said.

"Why, you—"

Felix blocked her gloved hand. "Just who are you anyway, lady?" he said, eye to eye with her. "Who pays the bills, I mean?"

She straightened, giving him that condescending look again. "I'm . . . Emeric Bulkroad's . . . niece."

Felix felt a cerebral stroke coming on.


GoBop and Neon were in a kind of buffer—a holding area for data dumped downside from Offworld habitat—when El worked her bit of console magic and they received the go-to for OLD construct.

Both of them had viewed the place from the outside on countless occasions; there were few frequent fliers on the Grid who hadn't. One of the first corporate constructs to be written into the Network, OLD's was an unfathomably cavernous place, a midnight-blue multilevel fortress that covered more unreal estate than CyberLand and InfoWorld taken together, and was constantly being added to—like Caracol, Emeric Bulkroad's own sprawling retreat in south-central Florida.

"How you doing?" El asked through the earbeads.

"So far so good," GoBop answered for the both of them. He could sense Neon behind him, riding tandem on one of Offworld's data buses. "Damn place is *huge*."

"What're you seeing?" Tech inquired excitedly.

"Standard gateway graphic—only it looks like it goes on forever."

"It doesn't," El told him. "You'll pass a tight grouping of feed holes on your left—"

"We're there," Neon said.

"Okay, then you're almost inside. The graphic's going to open up into a sort of lobby with a domed ceiling with all sorts of color-coded kermit corridors and shit. The gate's gonna want an RSVP. I think you want the one at like your three o'clock position. That's files."

It happened just as she described it, with a powerful inrush of hazy white light. "Three-thirty, I'd make it," GoBop said, "for future reference. But there's a bar-code security gate."

"I know, I know," El replied. "We've got GoSub running. You shouldn't have any problem getting through. Just don't enter an absolute address."

The corridors beyond the gate were narrow and numerous. GoBop led the way toward files, through hundreds of branches and active windows, each one overseen by humaniform memory residents. El had yet to enter "Excalibur"; they were going strictly by dates.

"We're in the neighborhood," GoBop announced finally. The corridors had a musty smell, and the memory residents were animal things, meant to frighten.

"Are you gonna be able to get us out of here?" Neon asked worriedly. "Man, I've totally lost track."

"We've got you plotted," Tech said. "Just stick close."

GoBop suddenly stopped short in front of an iris-portal outlined by concentric rings of alert lights. "This's gotta be it." He called up a display window on the goggles and read: " '*Excalibur*, survey ship and mission.' Damn! We'd need a five-star cutter to get through this much security."

"Don't try for anything dealing with the ship or mission specs," Tech advised. "Look for the easiest access. Try financial expenditures, medical records, that kind of thing."

"Yeah," GoBop said after a moment. "Yeah, I think we can get in there."

"What good's that going to do us?" El asked.

Tech looked over at her. "They must have paid the crew salaries, right? Given them frequent med exams? There might be names and addresses . . ."

She smiled at him. "You're all right after all, Mario."

"Score!" GoBop said. "Cover our asses. I'm going to make a grab."

He did and got way more than expected.

The darkness that engulfed him was swift in its descent and terrifying in its scope. And there was a pain attached to it unlike anything he had ever experienced in the Network. It was all inside his head. Something had him by the mind and wasn't about to let go, despite the frantic thumbing of his breakpoint circuit.

He knew that Neon was nearby and thought he could hear him screaming. It occurred to him that death was a place they might have already visited, and that this sightless, senseless state of mind was something else again. Would there be a gate? he wondered. An active window through which some soulpart of him would launch?

His thinking grew sluggish as the dark continued to press in on him. He felt only the vaguest connection with Tech and El, with all the memories that had been his short life. Would it flash before his eyes? he asked himself. It was supposed to, wasn't it, like in some arcade game?

He knew he wanted to cry, to reach out for Felix who'd been there for him every other time; but it was hard to remember how to cry and reach out when you'd left your eyes and hands in an interface chair somewhere back on the other side.

The dark coiled about him like the crushing hold of a jungle snake. He slipped into a dream.

And was suddenly propelled through the window he thought might be there waiting for him, waiting for anyone who fucked with the unfuckable.

But wait.

There was ambient light to the place. And below him was the Grid—or at least something that resembled its circuitlike design. He grew to be certain of it: He was still inside the Network—Neon alongside of him—but in some remote sector he hadn't known existed. Had the Virtual Network created a heaven for dumbass streeties who strayed from the path?

The construct looming before him could easily have played God in any universe GoBop could imagine. It was a triple-peaked mountain of argent light, cohesive in its intensity.

He had ten seconds to study its brilliance before his eyes snapped open, fixed on the office wall beyond the transparent screens of the goggles. Neon stirred in the interface chair beside him.

The console was sputtering and sparking, misted by clouds of extinguisher. Tech and El were coughing somewhere in the haze, and someone was pounding on the office door's pebble-glass panel.

''NetSec!'' a masculine voice boomed out. Then the door crashed open and half a dozen flak-vested police stormed into Data Discoveries' front room.

# Chapter Fourteen _____

Back in the days when he still carried a weapon, the Blair Nettles case was to have been his way up and out of the soup. His shot at the data big time; at the World Dollars that circulated between the exclusive Islands habitats and the helipad-equipped old credit residences along Manhattan's Sutton Place.

Felix recalled reminding himself of the fact while he had been kept waiting in the Nettles library, trying to guess which of the cut-glass bowls in front of him on the antique hardwood desk was an ashtray—if any of them. Ultimately he'd simply tamped the cigarette out against the worn sole of his shoe and dropped the thing into the breast pocket of his jacket. When the East Side dowager finally showed up—twenty minutes late—she'd wrinkled up her nose at the lingering maribacco smoke and called on a room-freshener scent as she was lowering herself into the throne chair behind the desk.

"I've always considered smoking a filthy habit, young man. Even if it has become fashionable again. People used to die of it, you know."

"And now they die from the air," Felix had told her. "Or the water. But nobody talks about breathing being a bad habit."

"Nevertheless, I won't have you indulging your vices in my presence, is that understood? Or should my search for a private investigator move down the list to the Ns?"

She was wearing plastiflesh to conceal the scars and swellings from a recent face job that had smoothed out a good fifteen years of lines and crevices. Whatever character Blair Nettles's face had accumulated with all the years had been wiped away as well, but something like playfulness remained in her gray eyes.

Felix said, "I'll try to keep my vices under control, Mrs. Nettles. When I'm in your presence."

The smile she conjured was a little on the stiff side, but he could see she was ready to talk business. Felix was new at the game of class-kissing, but he was learning fast.

"I have three children, Mr. McTurk," Blair began on a new note; businesslike all at once, with that tone of world-weariness only the rich could pull off. "My two daughters are married and living in the Islands, and I expect to have grandchildren after the onstation birth committees hand down an approval. I'm not what you might call emotionally bonded to either of them, but we're at least civil to one another. And despite the insolent personalities their separate fathers bequeathed them, they were fortunate enough to marry money, so I'm rarely subjected to the financial demands most children visit upon their parents."

"I'm happy for you," Felix said.

Blair frowned. "I'm sure you are. However, my daughters aren't the issue. It's my son. My youngest." She entered a sigh of exasperation Felix was meant to pick up on. "I've tried time and again to arrange for his permanent relocation in the Islands, but he is continually sabotaging my best efforts by involving himself with the wrong people and making trouble for everyone around him." She favored Felix with a few seconds of meaningful eye contact. "Some things even money can't fix, Mr. McTurk."

"Not many," he said. "But I'm assuming the 'trouble' has a shady side to it."

Blair let go that sigh again. "Luckily he's managed to avoid arrest. Oh, there have been a few occasions—"

"When the money has worked," Felix completed.

"Precisely, Mr. McTurk. But this latest episode has brought him into contact with people who place honor above money."

"Imagine that."

"They're either fools or liars."

"I would have thought ricos."

"Well, of course they're ricos, Mr. McTurk. Who else but mobsters would turn down what I considered to be a fair compromise?"

Felix kept a grin in check. "You tried to cut a deal with them?"

Blair waved a jewel-encrusted hand. "They're making outrageous demands of Tres."

"Your son."

"Yes. Named after his father and grandfather. But as I say, these demands are excessive. Beyond belief."

"What are we talking about—gambling? Drugs? Illegal implants?"

"You disappoint me, McTurk. I've already said this is no ordinary matter. You see, Tres married six months ago. A beautiful young thing—though completely without pedigree. I was against the marriage, but I gave it my blessing nonetheless, in the hope that it would have a stabilizing effect on Tres. Of course, I didn't know at the time that Tres's betrothed was the offspring of a crime czar."

Felix nodded in what he thought was a knowing fashion. "So he married the daughter of a rico and now they're threatening to make the marriage public knowledge. Blackmail. Is that it?"

Blair aimed a disappointed look at the library's beamed ceiling. "Who said anything about a daughter?"

"Tres married a mobster's son?"

Blair nodded. "But not as Tres."

"Not as Tres."

"As Tess."

Felix's thin eyebrows gradually reassumed their normal shape and position. "Tres had some body work done. Tres became Tess for . . . What's his name, this rico's son?"

"Zilch. Zilch Fassbinder. Only Zilch wasn't aware that Tess had once been Tres. Er, that Tres had become . . . Oh, you know what I mean. My idiot son was in love with Zilch, but Zilch was straight, so Tres went under the laser. In any case, these Fassbinder people subsequently learned of his sexual duplicity and have chosen not to be very understanding about it. It's that simple, McTurk."

"What we do for love, huh? But what about these 'excessive demands'? You said they involved honor over money."

Blair studied him for a moment. "They want his balls, Mr. McTurk. His testes. Wouldn't you agree that constitutes an exorbitant sum?"

"But didn't he, uh, already relinquish those?" Felix asked when he found his voice. "I mean, he's *Tess* now, isn't he?"

Blair was aghast. "Surely you don't think Tres had anything *permanent* in mind with this Zilch Fassbinder. It was just a frolic, McTurk, a bit of caprice. His parts weren't *discarded*. They've been kept on ice—for when the honeymoon ended, I presume."

A quick head shake dislodged the dumb expression Felix had adopted. "Then the Fassbinders know about the, uh, iced balls."

"They do, and they want them. Their intention is to keep Tres a Tess." Blair's cool control faltered momentarily and her voice cracked. "They're threatening to arrange an 'accident' for my 'daughter' if I don't accede to their demands to release Tres's missing parts."

Felix mulled it over for a minute. "My advice is that you give them the balls, Mrs. Nettles. You've obviously got enough money to fit Tess, er, Tres with a new pair."

"Naturally I have the money. But there's one major flaw with your plan, Mr. McTurk: The terms of my fourth husband's will—Tres's father's will—state that all funds shall be terminated if it can be demonstrated that Tres is wearing other than pure parts."

"So you'll end up supporting a spendthrift daughter after all, is that it?" Felix grinned. "Still, it's better than burying a son."

Blair showed him an icy look. "That goes without saying. But I can't be expected to blithely hand over Bulkroad parts to the first person that demands them."

Felix's mouth dropped open. "*Bulkroad* parts?"

"Yes. My late husband was a Bulkroad. I never took the name—or any of my husbands' names, for that matter. But you understand now why I want this business settled without involving the authorities or the news media. Imagine what these Fassbinders might do with Bulkroad DNA."

"Bulkroad as in Emeric Bulkroad. As in chairman of Offworld Lifting and Development?"

Blair made a sound of impatience. "My late husband was Emeric's uncle. I myself am a distant cousin. But I don't see why the family name makes this a circumstance of sudden concern, Mr. McTurk."

Felix stared at her. "It's just that I used to work for Offworld, Mrs. Nettles. Until I was let go."

No amount of damage Felix could inflict on Offworld or Emeric Bulkroad was going to bring Tanika back. Odds were that she would have died even if the cyber op he and Koo Raywing ran against Offworld had been successful and the company had covered the cost of her treatments. But a successful run would have guaranteed Tanika a torpor-vault, and Felix would at least have been left with some shred of hope.

*Ice-olated*, he had thought, returning to his office after the meeting with Blair Nettles. Placed on ice like the private parts of Tres Bulkroad. Frozen like Felix himself—numbed by loss and now the sudden realization that his ascent from the soup would be tainted by a link to Offworld L&D, his sworn enemy.

But a case was a case, he kept telling himself. And here at last was a chance to recoup some of what the Revlon office had cost him; a chance at a decent room in one of the new modular buildings that were going up in Brooklyn—a couple of square feet of home turf for himself and the street wizard he'd hired and, well, adopted. The kid called himself GoBop, and what he didn't know about maneuvering in the Virtual Network wasn't worth knowing. The unreal estate was changing too fast, even for the likes of a technopath who'd once worked for the corp that had practically written the new reality.

He was still trying to decide whether to take the Nettles case when he put in the call to Koo Raywing. Raywing and Felix had been partners once, in work and almost crime; but Raywing had wanted no part of data investigations work after the aborted run against Offworld—the underbelly, he called it, the scuz work. It was Metroplex Clearance for the wiry, bald-headed Chinese—Criminal Investigations Division; and that only for as long at it would take to earn a transfer to Network Security: NetSec.

"So what're you hunting down this time, data dick?" Ray's image had asked from the vidphone screen. "A missing husband or a misfiled Amex payment?"

"A missing body part," Felix said, "since you asked. But first I need a background on the Fassbinder cartel. They run gambling and hired hands on the Islands, don't they?"

The friendly grin deserted Raywing's small mouth. "You got that right, Felix. And you don't want to know more."

"Come on, Ray, I'm pressing help here. I just need to know their place on the misery index."

"If you're asking me how much shit you could fall into

with Fassbinder's people, I'm telling you I'd need a fucking ocean-floor rover just to locate your fingerprints." Raywing paused, scowling for the camera. "And what's all this bullshit about missing body parts, McTurk?"

Felix explained about Tres Nettles, the gender-bender op that had won him the manicured hand of Zilch Fassbinder, and the demands leveled against the Sutton Place Nettles by the husband's outraged family.

"So Emeric Bulkroad's nephew—or however the hell it works out—is about to lose his nuts to the mob," Raywing said. "Still don't see where you fit in, Felix. Figure you'd just as soon see it play that way after all that's gone down between you and OLD."

"Yeah, well, maybe I would if the rent wasn't due. Besides, I've got nothing against the kid. It's the old man's in-close people I'd like a piece of." Felix paused as the screen detailed a bit of rapid eye movement that shouldn't have been there. "What are you leaving out, Ray?"

The policeman frowned for the camera. "I shouldn't be telling you shit. Get yourself fucked over again."

"But you will, Ray."

"All right, asshole. Just this: There's word up- and downside that the Fassbinders have themselves a silent partner on some of the Inner Island gambling wheels." Raywing took a breath. "We're hearing Simon Bové."

The changes Felix's face went through resolved as a malicious grin. *Bové!* Offworld's security chief. The man who single-handedly had foiled Felix's attempt at rewriting the insurance files. A year after Felix was shown the door he learned that Bové had in fact set him up to run; that Bové had gone into the system and postdated Felix's policy, tempting him to run, wagering he would be able to discover him in the act. With nothing personal attached to it. It wasn't as if the man had had a grievance against him or didn't like the way he walked or talked. That would have been one thing. But to ruin lives just for the kick, that was something else again.

"I see that crazed look, McTurk," Raywing said, "and I'm already blaming myself for putting it there."

"I'll be taking the case," Felix told him finally.

He wanted Blair Nettles's promise that he had the go-to to handle the matter however he saw fit, without questions,

without interference. Once he had that, he had contacted
the Fassbinders at their casino on the Dow wheel to inform
them he'd been engaged to oversee the delivery of Tres
Bulkroad's frozen privates. They gave him the call on time
and place, and he'd suggested the Newark safe house the
Fassbinders used as a dormitory depot for hired hands en
route to or from the Islands.

Then, with GoBop spotting on the console, Felix had gone
into the Virtual Network to run some surgery. He arranged
for Tres Bulkroad's missing parts to be transferred from their
cryo-vault in New York to an equally secure vault on Offworld habitat. At the same time, he made arrangements with
a black market biotech outfit for vat-grown substitutes to be
shipped down to the New York vault. Next—employing a
host of street softs for the penetration work—he orchestrated
a transfer of funds from Tres Bulkroad's trust to a numbered
account on Citi hab, which he knew from his previous deal-
ings with OLD's security AI, SPARTOS, belonged to Simon
Bové. From Bové's account originated additional transfers
to both the New York and Offworld cryo-vaults, as well as
to the biotech corp supplying the vat-grown testes.

The top-flight console jocks the Fassbinders employed
would undoubtedly be able to follow the data trail once the
organ switch was discovered.

Leaving a traceable trail of the break-ins, illegal entries,
and forged authorization codes was easy enough; the challenge came in concealing the trail just enough to prevent
anyone from knowing that he'd deliberately left it.

Backed by an unnecessary display of transgenic muscle,
Hugo Fassbinder and son, Zilch, had attended the safe-house
meet in person. It took all of five minutes for the ricos'
organ validator to determine that the testes Felix delivered
didn't match Tres Bulkroad's DNA profiles.

When the guns came out Felix maintained that he'd only
been hired as an errand boy; that he'd simply picked up the
dewar thermos from the New York vault and delivered it as
instructed. How the hell was he supposed to know whether
the organs were valid or not? It was obvious a substitution
had been made; and if Hugo and Zilch were that bent out
of shape about it, why didn't they just take a jaunt through
the Network and trace the data flow? Felix was an investi-

gator, he'd told them; he'd even volunteer to run the penetrations if it would save his neck.

But the Fassbinders had their own cyber wizards for that; they didn't need the likes of some low-life data dick errand boy. It took the three console jocks an hour longer than it should have taken, but in the end they found the trail Felix had cut and located the source of the transfers.

"It's Simon Bové's account, I'm telling you," someone had insisted when Hugo didn't want to believe it. "The guy threw us over. Cut a deal with Bulkroad for a handful of credit. Like he's not making enough with us, the scuz. Our honor doesn't matter to him. An insult to the whole family and it doesn't matter to him."

Poor Zilch was beyond consolation; and Felix recalled Hugo puffing out that huge chest of his. "We'll take care of Tres Bulkroad *and* Simon Bové, Zilch, don't you worry."

And Felix might have even gotten a smile off before Bové had walked in unannounced, a couple of his own goons in tow, the firepower tipped heavily in his favor. Nodding his tattooed head at everyone while he'd paced around the room, grinning at the Fassbinders, grinning at Felix.

"So you figure I stiffed you," he said to Hugo at last. "You decided I didn't care about your son's honor, is that the idea here?"

Hugo had actually gulped. "It's all right there in the Network, Bové. The requisition for the substitutes, the transfers and authorizations . . ."

Bové directed a look to Felix all the while, laughing as Hugo's words trailed off. "Well, you almost pulled it off, McTurk, you almost did it. But I've gotta tell you: I *gave* you that account number on Citi, you piece of street filth. I left it in SPARTOS *knowing* you'd find it and try to use it someday." Bové's eyebrows danced as he said it. "The AI informed me the second you went online. See, I've been watching you work, McTurk, and you're no better now than you were three years ago when you ran against me."

Felix would always recall the feeling: going white hot and cold inside. Drawing the loaded gun Fassbinder's muscle had let him keep after the scanners had detected it. Stiff-arming it against Bové's brown forehead—

"Don't do it, Felix!"

Not from one of Bové's momentarily stunned goons. But from Koo Raywing.

"Put it away, Felix."

Raywing, in the company of two plainclothes police lieu-
tenants from Metroplex CID and half a dozen uniforms.
"We've got you on illegal entry, data tampering, and forg-
ery, McTurk," one of the badges said. "You wanna add
homicide to it, go ahead. You'll never make trial."

Raywing had moved in to take the gun from his lowered
hand. "You just don't learn, do you?" Almost a whisper.
"There was nothing I could do to save your ass."

"You gonna press charges or what, Mr. Bové?" From
the badge again.

Bové smiled, waved a hand. "No, I suppose not. But I
would like to see McTurk's license to carry revoked. Can't
have him running around with a pocket heater endangering
innocent citizens, can we, Lieutenant?"

"Count it done," the detective said.

Felix felt Bové's eyes on him. "Back to file ferreting,
McTurk. Stick to chasing down lost electric bills. It's what
you're good at."

"Hey, but what about Tres Bulkroad?" Fassbinder wanted
to know.

Bové turned to him. "Let him keep his balls, Hugo—as
a personal favor to me for your doubting my integrity." And
he turned back to Felix. "After all, we just got Felix
McTurk's, didn't we?"

# Chapter Fifteen _____

McTurk was still talking about himself when they were in the airport limo headed into New York. Jain had only asked about Maghar Gitani, but what she got in return amounted to a life story. Well, a life-and-death story really. She couldn't recall when a conversation had gone on for quite so long without once focusing on her. And here was yet more of this death talk—a regular obsession with downsiders. She didn't think her eyes could withstand much more in the way of eye-opening encounters; they seemed to be permanently widened as it was.

Even the robots had commented.

From L.A., McTurk had placed a call to his office, said the kids had sounded strange and that he wanted to book a return flight rather than tag along on the five-star Hollywood tour Manga Studios was offering Jain.

She guessed he was more concerned that ITC would send some people out to question him about what happened to TOR PATEL.

The AI was still delivering its message when they'd slipped out of the office, sermonizing on the changing face of programming and the need to interweave ecological issues with—bizarrely enough—air traffic reports. Jain wanted to believe that TOR PATEL simply had it in mind to wrest control of the company responsible for New York's airport delays; but she ventured the abrupt change had more to do with McTurk's client than anything else.

Felix wasn't saying much about Maghar Gitani, save that Gitani had now made trouble for two different AIs. Jain wondered what Felix might make of the fact that her own excursion down the well had been prompted by a sentient machine.

He maintained that he'd only taken on Gitani's work because of debts, which seemed a specious explanation. Where she came from people only did what they wanted to do. They bought and sold corporations, they designed exclusive living spaces; they made decisions of world-shaking import.

Jain said as much and the conversation had taken a sudden turn. McTurk wanted to know about her relationship with Emeric Bulkroad; and he wanted her to understand just why he hated her uncle.

She hadn't bothered to clarify the relationship, although she went so far as to admit that she'd gotten Felix's name from Blair Nettles.

Felix spoke without looking at her, and she couldn't help but think about the lengths she would often go to to avoid meeting Dr. Primorac's gaze. With that in mind—and making a concerted effort to set aside her anger—she'd tried to show an accessible face to McTurk, whose struggles over his wife's death had left him more embittered than he let on.

But she had problems with Felix's story. She'd never heard of the medical condition McTurk's wife—Tanika—had succumbed to; or of health insurance, and just why Tanika hadn't been covered under Felix's OLD policy. And she didn't understand anything about the "run" McTurk and someone named Koo Raywing had conducted against Offworld to alter the terms of the policy. What she did understand, however, was that McTurk had wrapped his grief and anger into a small knot that he carried around inside himself.

At first the allegations had angered her, and she felt a need to defend Emeric. It was likely Emeric hadn't been informed, she argued. Otherwise, he certainly would have done all within his power to see that Tanika received the best of care—oversee her transport to a clinic up the well if need be. It was just some of the people Emeric employed; some of the ones he surrounded himself with.

Felix showed her a world-weary look, as if to imply that she didn't know what went on in the corridors of power. At the same time, he owned that the unsuccessful run had been an act of desperation. Then he mentioned Simon Bové, and how it had been Bové who forced him into a corner, *dared* him to make the run, and fired him afterward.

Jain realized that there was something unresolved between the two men, something dangerous.

As the airport limo cruised along an elevated portion of highway—Manhattan's domes and towers off to their left—

Felix pointed out where he and Tanika had lived, and Jain tried to imagine Felix McTurk, the happy husband. She was swept up into his reminiscences, but discovered that it chafed to realize there was *someone in his past*.

She had scarcely had time to explore love's surface when Emeric intervened and saw to it that her lover was removed from Offworld hab and restationed in Marsspace.

Emeric Bulkroad had that much power: the power to remove a person to another world. A godlike authority. And it brought to mind what Blair had said about Emeric's setting himself up as a kind of mediator between Earth and the heavens.

The security guards in the Revlon's lobby were watching telecomp and scratching their heads over ITC's unannounced shift in programming.

"Who gives a damn about whales?" Felix heard one of the men say as he and Jain were being motioned through the building's weapons detectors. "I want my MTC!"

They left Blair Nettles's Daimler-Benz robots in a machine room downstairs and rode the superheated elevator up to Data Discoveries. Felix was in a somber mood and was already unbuttoning his shirt as they neared the office. Blanchard—all two hundred and eighty pounds of him—was standing in Lifeguard's doorway.

"Enjoy your trip to the coast, McTurk?" Blanchard asked, showing a smirk.

Felix could see a worried-looking René in the background. He glanced at his watch and said, "You're here awfully late, aren't you, Blanchard?"

The smirk was transformed into a broad grin. "You're right, pal. But some things are just worth waiting for."

"What was that all about?" Jain leaned over to whisper while Felix slotted a keycard into the reader alongside the door.

The door toned and Felix pushed it open. "Ah, the guy's always got a hair up his—"

Two inhumanly powerful hands took hold of his arms and the office lights came up. Felix let himself go slack, which was the thing to do with robots. You fought back and you ended up with broken bones.

The two machines sensed his reaction and relaxed their grip. A third robot closed the door and took charge of Jain.

"Don't fight it," Felix warned her. "Do whatever it tells you to do."

"But who are they?" Jain asked in a panicked voice. "What do they want?"

"They're from NetSec," Felix answered dourly. "Network Security."

The office was a wreck. An odor of extinguisher, fried circuitry, slagged chips. GoBop and company were lined up on the couch like automatons; Neon looked the worst of them.

"You guys all right?" Felix said, and they nodded. It was hard to tell whether they were frightened or just angry. "Nobody's hurt?"

"They wouldn't let us say anything on the phone, Felix," GoBop said. "Sorry."

Koo Raywing was behind the desk, feet up, hands locked behind his head. Smiling. "That's what I love about you, McTurk: You've got an acute sense of priority." Raywing took his feet down. "You shoulda gone into human services, Felix."

Felix nodded. "Good to see you, Ray." There were three other humans in the room besides Raywing; two NetSec field agents in gray uniforms and a short, auburn-haired woman of about forty in plainclothes. "What's coming down, Ray."

The lieutenant wrinkled up his face. "You really want to play it this way?" He was medium height, wiry, bald as a billiard ball. His lower lip sported an inverted triangle of black beard.

Felix shrugged. "You're going to have to fill me in."

Raywing sighed and glanced at Jain. "I don't think I've had the pleasure," he said, coming to his feet.

"Koo Raywing, Jain Nugget," Felix said. He directed a smile at Jain. "Go ahead, it's safe to shake his hand."

All at once Raywing was Mr. Charm. He pulled up a chair for Jain and perched himself on the edge of the desk. "You never learn, do you, Felix?" he began. He gestured to a short stack of software fiches sealed in NetSec evidence envelopes. "First off, you leave all these illegal street softies laying around where anyone can find them. Then you let your . . . uh, assistants," he added, with a glance at the kids, "run a penetration into Offworld."

No one was looking at him when Felix turned to the couch. "OLD?" he said, raising his voice. *"OLD?"*

Raywing fingered his wisp of beard. "You want to tell me about it, Felix?"

Felix hooked a chair with his foot and sat down, straddling it. "Sorry, Ray, but I can't do that."

"I figured," Raywing said, studying Jain. "Offworld security says the break-in was in files. Looks to them like somebody was after a directory of names."

"Just kids having fun, Ray."

Raywing's thin lips tightened and he looked at the floor. The plainclotheswoman cleared her throat in a meaningful way. "Don't fuck with us, McTurk."

Felix regarded her for a long moment. FBI, he ventured, maybe National Security. "I don't think I've had the plea—"

"Zoltec," she said, displaying the badge. "FBI."

"Uh-huh. And since when's taking a jaunt through Offworld a federal matter?"

She snorted a laugh. "Who said I'm here because of the run, McTurk?"

He tried to maintain his own grin.

Zoltec called something up on a personal screen. "We've got an Environmental Violations Bureau penetration and an unauthorized neural net timeshare with your system's footprints all over it. Also an illegal tap on AmTel lines." She swung to the kids, who had begun to whistle and jostle one another. "Plus, I think I can interest both Family Services and Unfair Labor Practices into having a look at the, shall we say, *unusual* nature of both your work and living situations."

"All right," Felix told her, "I'm not dense."

"Oh, but I haven't arrived at the best part, McTurk. It seems that all the overhead noise we've been living with lately has been traced to a Network attack on Eastern Seaboard Air Traffic Control. An extremely well-run penetration that has a lot of people puzzled. You see, ESATC's AI may have been irreparably dazzled, and guess what: A trace has led the investigative team to one Doppler Data, Inc., over on Thirty-third street. And who just happened to be taking one of DD's tours on the day of the penetration but Felix McTurk."

Zoltec collapsed the screen and glared at him. "DD's drivers say they lost you that day, McTurk. So where were you?"

Felix adopted an innocent expression. "Some wacky ride over at InfoWorld. Data slide or some crazy thing."

"Look, Felix," Raywing cut in. "We don't want to close

you down.'' He looked at the ruined console. ''You're going
to have enough worries just getting back online. And we
don't want to have to take too hard a look at the kids. But
you've gotta be willing to work with us here, you understand
me?''

Felix nodded knowingly. ''I remember when we worked
together, Ray.''

Raywing aimed a finger at him. ''Hey, don't try to run
that shit on me, Felix. Now file this: OLD is holding off on
pressing charges. God knows why, but they are.''

''Maybe it's their way of saying all's forgiven.''

Raywing regarded him skeptically. ''Does that sound like
the Offworld we know?''

Felix shrugged. ''All right, Ray. But what about some
breathing space?''

Raywing looked for Zoltec's okay. ''When you sleep on
it—and I know you will—'' the NetSec man said, with a
quick glance at Jain, ''ask yourself whether it's worth losing
what little you've got left, Felix.''

Five minutes after Koo Raywing left, Felix set the fans
on full and hustled everyone out of the office. He asked Jain
to send the robots back to their Sutton Place digs and led
the way over to the Empire State Building, where he sprang
for a helicab to Brooklyn.

He promised himself that he wouldn't say a word until they
were sequestered in his stifling apartment, which was on the
sixth tier of a modular building the owners were continually
reconfiguring with the addition of new units. There was no
lasting design to the structure, and what with the neighborhood's constant streetwork and temporary sidewalks, Felix
seemed to spend half his time just looking for the place.

A mosque was being erected on the corner diagonally
opposite the building's main entrance. The Citibank directly
across the street was crowned by a huge public pollution
monitor, which featured transpirator masks in a graphic display to index the day's air quality.

A ten-mask day meant you were better off dead.

''You four are in deep shit,'' Felix announced once everyone was inside. The setting sun was filling the apartment
with blinding light. He tried to call on the tint in the west-
facing windows but the system was obviously down. ''Lower
the damn blinds,'' he told GoBop.

Jain took a casual look around. Two small rooms had been partitioned off along one wall. Felix's home tele-Net system took up one corner of the room, the decks and monitor screens of an old design. Left of the front door was a kitchen unit with a refrigerator, sink, and electric range. In a plastic tub on a round plastic table, fresh vegetables were soaking in what she took to be an iodine solution. And someone had apparently been using the couch as a bed.

Initially she thought the two dozen people gathered in the corridor had arrived for a party, until she realized that the corridor and the stairwells were their home.

Felix was showing the kids a stern look and tapping his foot on the bare floor. "I suppose I don't have to ask what you were doing inside Offworld."

"It was my fault," Tech said contritely. "We weren't finding any of Ms. Nugget's names in the news archives, so we figured we'd go right to the source."

"You can call me Jain, Tech."

"They'll call you Ms. Nugget," Felix snapped. "If I let them talk to you at all."

"We're really sorry, Felix," GoBop said. "It was chipped, we know that, but—"

"It was dangerous," Felix countered.

GoBop and Neon traded enigmatic looks. "We know that, too."

Felix watched them for a moment. "What's all the eye contact about, you two? What happened in there?"

GoBop took a deep breath and began to explain. He recounted the details of the run, the experience with the dark, and the miraculous nature of the rescue.

Felix listened attentively. The black was SPARTOS, Offworld's security AI, that much was certain. But GoBop and Neon's born-again rhapsodizing about a new construct in the hinterlands of the Grid was something else again. Most likely the result of the headlock SPARTOS had thrown on them, although he supposed the construct could have been some occult government dump. It would explain Amelia Zoltec's tough talk, anyway.

Unless—*Christ!* Felix thought—unless *Gitani* had something to do with this. Maybe this triple-peaked construct was the higher authority Gitani was answering to.

But then Felix had heard of all sorts of magical and mystical events taking place in the Network—psychic journeys,

meetings with miraculous people—and GoBop's construct
might be nothing more than brain-fashioned. Hell, in ten
years of frequent flying Felix had yet to hear of a construct
coming to anyone's rescue.

"Do you know how lucky you are to be sitting here and
not rocking back and forth in some psycho ward right
now?" he asked when GoBop was finished.

The four of them put on hangdog expressions. GoBop's
head was the first to rise. "Yeah, we know, Felix, but if you
could've seen this thing. I mean, it was like, it was like—"

"We'll come back to the religious part later, Bop." Felix's eyes found Jain's. "Did you come out of Offworld with
*anything* we can use?"

"Only the whereabouts of Dr. Ngo," El said proudly.

"Ngo?" Felix asked, puzzled.

"I don't remember a Ngo on the list," Jain told them.

Tech said, "She wasn't. That is, she was but she wasn't—"

"What he means, " El cut in, "is that Dr. Ngo's maiden
name was *Nerbu*. See, she got like married just after the
*Excalibur* returned from its mission."

"Do you know where she is?" Jain asked excitedly.

Neon nodded. "We've got a last-known."

"New Zealand," Tech said. "Some place called Rotorua."

Felix was running over the name in silence. "I remember
reading about a Dr. Ngo. Years ago . . ." He tapped a finger against his lips. "There might be something in the news
archives. We better have a look."

Tech and El made a mad dash for Felix's tele-Net system;
El arrived first and threw herself into the wardrobe. Tech
had to content himself with spotting. El set the goggles on
active mode while Felix issued instructions to Tech.

"Try the news agencies first," Felix told him. "Go back
about fifteen years and work your way forward. If there's
no mention there, get yourselves over to ITC or one of the
telecomp stations and have a look at their news shows. I
remember a documentary or something."

The mere mention of ITC got Felix thinking about Maghar
Gitani again. He fixed GoBop and Neon with a lopsided
look, regarding them for a long moment. "Maybe you two
better tell me everything you remember about this new construct," he said at last.

# *Chapter Sixteen* _____

Emeric watched as a 3D model of the Network's newest and brightest construct resolved within a blue cone of holo light. It looked to him like a section of mountain range lifted from the Andes or the Himalayas. A grouping of three round-topped summits, the central one set somewhat back from its companions and towering above them. But there was an absence of topographical features; nothing to indicate that the construct's writers were attempting to convey an actual landscape. No timber girdling the base, no glacial moraine, no chimneys or crevices. The base of the thing covered more than twenty squares of unreal estate and the slopes were as smooth as glass.

Emeric thought that it might be the Network icon for some new mining conglomerate about to make an appearance on the Grid. But surely he would have received advance word of any merger sizable enough to produce such a bold statement. And why would anyone choose to erect a viable construct so remote from the Grid's data access highways? Unless that, too, was meant to be a statement of some sort.

He rose from his chair to circle the contour lines of the free-floating construct, noticing for the first time something familiar about its southern face.

"Add one more summit—*there*," he said to Bové, gesturing to the spot with a bobbing middle finger, "and you know what it reminds me of?"

Bové moved around to the far side of the holo-cone and sighted down along Bulkroad's extended left arm. "For money?"

Emeric looked over his shoulder, grinning. "For fun."

"Let's see, then," Bové said, beetling sweeping brows. "I don't know, I'm hooked on mountain."

"Yes, but which mountain?"

"Glad we're not betting."

"Olympus Mons," Emeric said after a moment.

Bové nodded agreement. "You used to have a holo running in your office. What, ten, twelve years ago?"

Emeric circled the cone twice more and returned to his armchair. "I must've stared at that view eight hours a day. But this," he said, waving a hand, "this is a child's rendering."

"So you're saying it's coincidence," Bové said, still standing by the dimensional model.

Emeric belched loudly, flattening triple chins against the round collar of a black satin jacket. He gazed up into the optical scanners of the sentient machine that had provided them with the hologram. "SPARTOS, what's the name of our subcontractor on Mars?"

"Red Planet, Incorporated, sir," the superintelligence answered, its voice a bit too resonant for the chilled room.

The AI's façade was a rectangular slab of marbleized alloy affixed to an instrumentality wall. Confronting the machine, Emeric always felt as if he were studying a wall map of the Twilight Zone. "Could they be behind this construct?"

"Impossible."

The machine wasn't one for dickering around. "Perhaps Red Planet, Inc. feels the time has come to separate itself from Offworld Lifting and Development. The construct could be part of a publicity campaign."

SPARTOS gave it brief thought. "I predict that Red Planet will one day adopt that very course; but an analysis of their present holdings and future growth curves suggests that day is at least three years off."

Emeric pretended to smile; the genuine article wasn't possible here—in what would always be the REC room. "Thank you, SPARTOS. I didn't really believe the construct was any of Red Planet's doing."

"I am aware of that, sir."

No doubt, Emeric thought. He turned to watch Bové slump into his chair. "You've obviously brought this to my attention for good reason."

Bové steepled spatulate fingers. "I don't like the look of it."

Emeric shrugged. "So get in there and poke around."

"We tried, but there's no way in." Bové's frown was full

of concern. "It shows up unannounced. You say it reminds you of Olympus Mons. Whoever wrote the thing might've had something to do with the penetration of our files."

"I see," Emeric said quietly. "You're suggesting Felix McTurk and associates."

"Kids." Bové snorted. "Street wizards. NetSec should have found them glued to their hardware with their eyeballs fried. Instead they wind up with headaches."

"Their eyeballs fried?" Emeric said in a disapproving tone. "I'd be careful with that, Bové. Offworld does have an image to maintain."

"I told NetSec to lay off them."

"To give them rope enough, I imagine."

"Well, *somebody* drove getaway for those kids."

"And you think it was the same somebody who wrote the construct."

"McTurk couldn't have organized the run without help. He might have an agent upside. Right here on Offworld. Who else would architect a Martian mountain?"

"And what exactly do you think McTurk and this hypothetical field agent are after?"

"Kaduna," Bové said.

Emeric threw him a hard look. "Fortunately, Bové, you find yourself among friends."

"I wouldn't bring it up otherwise."

Emeric grunted. "How would McTurk learn of Kaduna?"

Bové steeled himself. "It stands to reason someone on-station got to Jain. We still don't know who, or just what it was they told her, but it was enough to get her interested in taking a plunge into the soup. Right off she talks with Blair, who could have filled her in on McTurk's background; maybe Jain knew he'd tried a run against Offworld when she hired him. She figured McTurk would jump at the chance to settle an old score. My guess, she figured right. They know they're being watched, so they cook up some excuse to pay a visit to ITC while McTurk's street kids punch deck for Offworld and grab what they can once they're inside."

Emeric mulled it over in silence, then said, "You're forgetting one thing, Bové: Project Kaduna doesn't exist. Those files disappeared when—" He glanced at SPARTOS.

Bové offered a tight-lipped nod. "Exactly. Kaduna doesn't

exist, it never did. But the *Excalibur* data is still on file—
ship specifications, mission notes, personnel records.''

Emeric made an impatient sound. ''Names and dates that
mean nothing. The crew lists, the deaths, that much is public record. Jain wouldn't have had to go down the well for
any of it.'' He forced out a breath. ''Although I'm beginning to understand what she's up to now. She wants the
details of the tragedy. She's thinking about her parents. But
she's afraid to ask me, because she knows it's something I
don't like to discuss.'' He showed Bové an ironic smile.
''All this could easily have been avoided, Bové. But there's
no real harm done.''

Bové had his tongue in his cheek. ''Then I guess I
shouldn't worry she's on her way to New Zealand.''

Emeric fell silent.

''Not on tour, either,'' Bové added. ''The only tour she's
on has Kaduna stamped all over it.''

''And McTurk is with her?''

''You gotta give them credit,'' the security chief said.
''They found Ngo.''

Emeric's eyes flashed. ''Ngo already told her story to the
world. No one listened to her then and no one will listen to
her now.''

Bové raised an eyebrow. ''Wanna bet?''

Emeric sniffed. ''It's a sure thing, Bové,'' he said finally.
''Because you're going to see to it that no one listens.''


''Nothing,'' Jain said, punching the car radio's presets
with growing frustration. ''We travel halfway around this
stupid planet and I haven't heard any of my songs *once*.''

Felix looked over at her from the driver's seat of the rental
car, hands white-knuckled on the wheel at ten and two.
''This 'stupid planet' happens to be the only thing keeping
your orbital Island anchored.''

''Yeah, well, who asked it to anyway?''

Felix raised his eyes to deep-blue sky. ''You know, there
oughta be a law against allowing uppies down the well.''

''Vice versa, McTurk.''

''Don't worry yourself about it. I've been up there and I
didn't like the cooking.''

Jain turned away from him to stare out the window. ''It's
all your Gitani's fault I'm not getting airplay.''

''He's not *my* Gitani.''

"He's your client, isn't he?" She took a moment to regard the orchards that lined the roadside, the ten thousand sheep grazing in the green hills. "And why doesn't somebody do something with all this empty space? It gives me the creeps."

Felix checked the flashing display of the car's real-time map and thought: *Another half hour and we're there. Then she's Ngo's problem.* He shook his head in disbelief. Five years ago he wanted to murder everyone connected with Offworld Lifting and Development, and now here he was chauffeuring Chairman Emeric Bulkroad's niece around the South Pacific.

He'd had the kids book them two seats on a nonstop from New York to Auckland, New Zealand, paying for the tickets out of the money transferred into his account yet a third time by Maghar Gitani. By prearrangement, a Nissan Solar was waiting for them at the airport, the route south to Rotorua already programmed into the car's memory. Jain had been fiddling with the radio tuner since they left the North Island capital. She'd done the same for the duration of the five hour trans-Pacific flight, her one-time hits nowhere to be found.

They were traveling under the names Preston and Emily Blaylock of Seattle, Washington. Felix had taken the precaution in the hopes of making it just that much more difficult for either Gitani or the new Raywing–Zoltec team from putting a trace on them. Gitani hadn't made contact other than to transfer the funds, and Felix didn't want to have anything further to do with him now that NetSec and the feds were involved. Felix calculated that the damage Gitani had already caused was enough to fill his quota for mischief-making for the next decade or so. As it stood, ITC's telecomp programming had gone from inspired to regimented overnight; and ESATC's handling of flight schedules could only be described as imaginative.

Felix was certain that the Network's latest construct was something Gitani was writing; but he still had no guess as to its purpose. In the process of bringing it online, however, Gitani had somehow managed to scramble and intermingle the personalities of two powerful corporate AIs.

"How much longer to this place anyway?" Jain asked suddenly.

"Read the map," Felix told her, gesturing to the dash

console display. "The light shows our present location."
He fingered one of the buttons. "Press this one you get a
readout on time remaining."

"Thanks," she said, on the quiet side.

Felix sighed without showing it. What with the newness
of the terrain, all the traveling and turnaround, he supposed
he couldn't blame her for being short-fused. She'd spent the
night at her aunt's Sutton Place town house, but showed up
at the airport looking as if she hadn't slept in days. The
realization sinking in, Felix ventured. The realization of
what an investigation of the *Excalibur* incident might be
getting her into.

Felix caught her up on what the kids had been able to
glean from the Network archives on the previous evening's
fishing expedition. He was right about the name Ngo ring-
ing a memory bell. Fifteen years ago, the cyber analyst and
her husband had broken their contracts with Offworld L&D,
and their story had caused a short-lived stir in the tabloids.
Seemed they'd quit to protest the cartel's policies on research disclosure.

OLD, according to the Ngos, was withholding crucial
data on a tragedy that had befallen one of its recent near-
space missions. The former Dr. Nerbu accused Offworld of
covering up the fact that an AI malfunction had been responsible for dozens of deaths. At a time when artificial
intelligences were assuming more and more duties both up-
and downside, proof of deliberate sabotage by a sentient
computer could have set the so-called Machine Mind movement back twenty years.

The accusations and threats weren't taken very seriously,
primarily because no one had come forward to reinforce the
Ngos' case; also because the world had grown accustomed
to hearing charges of cover-up leveled against OLD's then
newly appointed CEO, Emeric Bulkroad II.

It had taken less than a week for the news media and the
public to tire of the Ngos, and the couple effectively vanished from sight. Eight years later, however, a telecomp
tabloid called *Hasbeens* had run a follow-up story on the
duo. By then the husband was dead and Mrs. Ngo was
working for a geothermal station in central New Zealand.

New Zealand's geothermal heart was a vast area of geysers,
steam bores, bubbling mud pools, and near-preternaturally

quiescent volcanic lakes. The lakes mirrored the North Island's incredible sky and the remnants of its once-plentiful fir and ferns, most of which had gone the way of America's beech and boreal forest biome. Consolidated Geothermal, whose headquarters were a few miles south of Lake Rotorua, had been made responsible for harnessing the planet's hot venting anger and converting it to usable power for the entire nation.

The city of Rotorua had once been a center for New Zealand's native Maori tribespeople—a fiercely independent group fond of song, dance, and *hangi* feasts—and even now it was the Maori who had the run of the place, including much of Consolidated Geothermal itself.

After the briefest of recons, Felix decided that the best way onto CG's grounds was simply to sign up for one of the tours the station offered visitors three times a day. The man at the entry gate was as brown as a walnut, his face a tattooed mask of blue whorls and circles and jagged lines. Three similarly masked blind men stood nearby passing out printed leaflets about cultural recidivism and the coming Dark Age. Fifteen or so saronged Indonesian tourists were waiting on the other side of the gate, conversing in Bahasa pidgin and sipping locally bottled designer water.

Fifteen minutes into the tour, Felix steered Jain out of the crowd toward a glass door marked PERSONNEL OFFICE. A humaniform robot dressed in skirt and blouse was seated at the desk inside.

"May I help you?" the machine asked in a suspicious way, giving them a quick once-over.

"Yes," Felix said. "We, er, that is we're looking for a Dr. Ngo. We understand she works here."

"Dr. Ngo? I'm afraid you've been misinformed."

Felix and Jain traded looks. "Look, maybe if you'd access your files instead of—"

"I *am* my files," the robot replied indignantly, "Mr.—"

"Blaylock," Felix said, feigning an accent. "Preston Blaylock. This is my wife, Emily."

"Blaylock?"

"Yeah, whatsamatta with Blaylock?"

"You don't look like a Blaylock."

Felix fought down an impulse to slug the thing. "How's a Blaylock supposed to look? Besides, we're not talking Blaylocks here, we're talking Ngos."

"You're talking Ngos?"

"You got it."

The robot studied him. "What is a talking Ngo?"

Jain stepped in front of Felix before he could raise a fist.
"Excuse me, but you see we're simply trying to locate an
old family friend. We know she worked here in the past.
Perhaps you could tell us whether she's still employed here."

The robot's face approximated a smile. "Why didn't your
husband say so to begin with?"

Jain smiled back. "His testosterone levels are a bit off
this afternoon."

"Hey, wait a damn—" Felix started to say.

"I understand," the robot said at the same time. The
machine fell silent for a moment, then added: "Mrs. Ngo
is no longer employed here. May I be of further assis-
tance?"

Jain switched to a command voice. "I wish to know her
current address."

"I'm sorry, but I'm not authorized to release that information."

"Who is authorized?"

"My supervisor."

"Then request the information from your supervisor. And
please be quick about it."

"Think you're pretty handy with tools, huh?" Felix said
while the robot fell into a communications mode.

Jain snorted. "Well, it's obvious you certainly haven't
had much practice."

"For your information, I—"

"Mrs. Ngo receives her mail at the post office in Waitomo—a fifty-minute drive from Rotorua under favorable
conditions."

"You've been very helpful," Jain said, smiling.

"Thank you, Mrs. Blaylock—and *Mr*. Blaylock."

Felix directed a scowl at the machine as they were leaving
the office. "Damn things take their jobs too seriously," he
told Jain.

He was still muttering to himself when they reached the
rental car and the three blind Maori took hold of them.

"What do you want with Ngo?" one of them was asking
Felix twenty minutes later. "Talk to us quick, mate, or
you're in for a regular horror show."

Felix couldn't argue with it. The three Maori had forced them into the Nissan Solar at gunpoint and driven south out of Rotorua to a robot-staffed tourist attraction called "The Steaming Blowhole." The lead Maori—the one doing the talking—had had a few words with the robot guards and the attraction was signposted temporarily out of sorts.

Felix was down on his knees with his arms tied behind him, practically face to face with the two-foot-high yellow earth cone of the Steaming Blowhole. Craning his neck to the right, he could just see Jain and the two other tattooed tribesmen. Four surveillance robots stood nearby, rooted in the thickets that surrounded the geyser's sulfurous patch of water-smoothed rock and discolored ground.

"Now I'm asking you kindly, bloke," the Maori said, with a strong hand on the back of Felix's head. "Either you talk to me or you talk to the geyser."

"I thought you were gonna say I end up in hot water," Felix managed, nostrils stinging from the hole's random ventings.

The Maori laughed and translated for his partners. "At least you're not a panic merchant. I'm going to make it a point to visit your grave once a year."

"I feel better already."

"Not for long," the man warned. "Just tell me about Ngo, man. Then you and your sheila can go."

"Just like that."

"Just like that."

"Listen," Felix said, "I understand she doesn't want people asking about her. But tell her we only want a few minutes of her time. It has nothing to do with what she told the news. We're just looking her up for an old friend."

"You want *me* to tell Ngo?" The Maori laughed. "Why the hell would I want to do that, man?"

Felix's face wrinkled up, the sudden motion disturbing two flies that had lighted on his nose. "You don't work for Ngo?"

The man put his mouth close to Felix's ear. "You keep forgetting who's asking the questions and who's got his face in the blowhole."

"No, I don't, believe me."

"Then tell me about this old friend you're working for?"

Felix realized he'd already said too much. "Let the

woman go and I'll tell you," he said quietly. The Maori
sniggered and repeated it for Jain.

"Don't try to be a hero, McTurk," she yelled. "It doesn't
suit you."

"Hey, thanks a bunch for giving him my name," Felix
said over his shoulder.

"Talk, man, talk. The geyser's heating up."

Felix stared down at the circular spout. "If I remember
the sign right, this thing isn't scheduled to blow for another
two hours. You really gonna keep us out here in the sun that
long? Maybe we could kill an hour in the shade, what d'ya
say?"

The Maori smacked him on the side of the head and issued a command to one of the surveillance robots. A moment later the boxy, treaded thing was approaching the
blowhole with a box of laundry detergent gripped in its
gauntlet. The Maori pulled Felix back while one of his cohorts emptied the contents of the box into the spout. The
machine moved into view off to Felix's left to observe the
scene.

The Maori gave the empty detergent box an overhand toss
toward the scrub. "This'll hurry things along some," he
said by way of explanation. "How else do you think we
keep it regular?"

"Can't disappoint the tourists," Felix said, gulping and
finding his voice. The hole was already beginning to belch
and percolate hot water.

"You ready to talk, McTurk?"

Felix glanced over at Jain, whose arms were pinioned by
the third Maori. "Tell him, Felix," she said in a panic, "or
I will."

"Hear that, mate?" the leader asked. "Bring her over
here," he told Jain's captor.

"Come on, man," Felix said, "play fair. She said she'd
tell you."

The man leaned in to show Felix a grin. "Yeah, but I
always wanted to see what a geyser would do to up-close
flesh."

"Then we don't talk," Felix told him.

"Hey, I could give a shit, really."

Jain was thrown down on her knees alongside him. Felix
saw her face contort in pain, anger, fear, humiliation. Hot

water was bubbling out of the spout a good six inches now. "McTurk," she said, wet eyes fixed on him.

"Don't say anything," he told her. "Just pray these guys leave their insides on some street corner somewhere."

"Won't happen, McTurk," one of them sneered, as the rest of the surveillance robots began to emerge from the thickets.

Felix took a long look at the machines, wondering what they were up to. A goddamn robot audience, he thought. Intent on recording the scalding he and Jain were about to endure. Then the four were suddenly in mixed motion again.

The three Maori were all facing the spout when the machines took hold of them from behind.

Jain said, "What are they doing to those men?"

"Don't wonder about it!" Felix said, frantically backing away from the spouting water.

Jain helped him to his feet while the robots gathered their prey around the blowhole. A good deal of struggling and shouting was going on, and Felix couldn't make the machines understand there were questions that needed to be asked. Even Jain's command voice couldn't get through to them.

They didn't hang around to see what geyser water could do to up-close flesh, but they could hear the Maoris' screams all the way to the car.

# Chapter Seventeen ─────────

McTurk screeched the Solar through a series of hairpin turns along the old tarmac strip linking Rotorua and Waitomo. The terrain was undulating limestone hills, capped by patches of dark forest.

"You don't have to do this to impress me, McTurk," Jain said, reaching for an overhead U-shaped handhold. "The robot said it was only a fifty-minute drive."

"Under favorable conditions," Felix said, risking a look at her. "*Favorable* conditions! And these aren't them."

He'd made one stop at a long-distance booth a quarter of an hour out of Rotorua. GoBop had supplied him with the answer to the question the geyser surveillance robots hadn't given him time to ask, and his driving had been half crazed ever since.

"You said your uncle wasn't wild about the idea of you coming down the well," Felix said. "Why not? Why didn't he want you to come? What doesn't he want you to know?"

Jain, pressed against the door, regarded him for a moment. "He was worried about me—and it's no wonder considering what you've put me through."

Felix lifted a hand from the steering wheel to gesture to himself. "What *I've* put you through?"

"You practically ruin my career, you involve me with the Network police, you nearly get us parboiled—"

Felix brought the car to a sudden halt. "You know that phone call I made a ways back?" he said, twisting around in the seat. "Well, it was to New York. I asked GoBop to take a quick look at Consolidated Geothermal's corporate listing. Take a guess what he discovered?"

"I'm sure I can't imagine."

"Damn right you can't. Because CG's owned by Offworld."

Jain shrugged. "So?"

"So we go waltzing in there asking for Dr. Ngo and no sooner do we step outside than I've got a gun aimed at my kidney. The same treatment the kids got when they made a grab for the *Excalibur* crew's med records. The closer we get to this thing, the more it fights us."

She studied his face. "I still don't understand what you're getting at."

"There's more at stake here than your parents' deaths. I know that might be hard to hear, but I'm starting to think Ngo was telling the truth fifteen years ago. Offworld covered up something important, Jain, and your uncle's going to do anything he can to keep it buried."

"You're mad!"

"Who do you think sicced those three Maori on us? It wasn't Ngo—even though I was stupid enough to think so."

"I thought you said we weren't being followed? Isn't that why you came up with those idiotic names?"

Felix made his lips a thin line. "This is big. I didn't realize just how big."

Jain was quiet for several seconds. "What made those robots help us, McTurk?"

"I don't know." He commanded the car up to speed once more.

Waitomo was another of the North Island's tourist attractions, known chiefly for its hundreds of limestone caves and the glowworms that populated the largest of them.

Felix and Jain arrived just in time for the final tour, which involved a bit of hiking and a brief open boat ride through a subterranean grotto. When the electric lights were switched off, the ceiling of the cave became a cathedral of blue-green glowworm constellations. The guide explained how the nests that adhered to the porous walls and ceiling were actually mucous tubes inhabited by grubs. The grubs fed on night-flying midges attracted to the hypnotic bioluminescence.

The explanation might have stripped the moment of some of its magic had Felix not recognized the guide as Dr. Ngo.

They followed her to the attraction's small gift shop and lingered long after everyone else had left, browsing through a selection of glowworm toys, glowworm holo bumper stickers, and glowworm keycard wallets.

"I'm sorry, folks, but we're about to close up for the evening," Ngo told them at last. "We're open at nine in the morning if you'd care to come—"

"We need to talk, Dr. Nerbu," Felix said.

All the breath seemed to leave the aged Nepalese; Felix put a hand out to steady her and she gazed up at him with weary black eyes. "You're newspeople?"

"No," Jain said.

"We looked for you over at Consolidated Geothermal," Felix began.

Ngo's high-cheekboned face paled. "Who are you people? What do you want with me?"

Felix scanned the room. "Can we talk here?"

"I demand to know what this is all about."

"Dr. Ngo, my name is Felix McTurk. I'm a data investigator. From New York. This is—"

"Jain Nugget," Jain completed, offering a hand.

Ngo brought hers to her mouth with a quick intake of breath. "Jain *Nugget*? Not Clay and Larissa's daughter? But how can this be? I thought you lived upside?"

"I do, Dr. Ngo. I came down because someone told me my parents were still alive. That you might be able to help me find out."

"Me?" Ngo said, aghast.

"What about the story you were spreading around fifteen years ago?" Felix asked. "About a cover-up."

"Everything I said was true," Ngo countered bitterly. "But I don't know anything about your parents, Jain. I never saw them after the *Excalibur* returned. I only heard the rumors . . . and learned about the deaths. I'm sorry."

"But I was told you could help me."

"Who told you I could help you?" Ngo said.

Jain glanced uncertainly at Felix. "FABIEN," she answered after a moment.

Ngo showed her a sympathetic smile. "But I don't know any Fabien, Jain."

Jain bit her lower lip. "FABIEN's an AI, Dr. Ngo."

"A *what*!" Felix said, dumbfounded.

"A culinary AI on Offworld habitat—."

"A goddamned *AI*!"

"FABIEN gave me a message. He said I should tell you: 'Recalled to life.' "

Ngo reeled back against a rotary display case, looking as

if she'd just heard from the grave. Felix wasn't sure which to do first: support Ngo or strangle Jain Nugget. But before anyone could speak, the gift shop phone rang. Ngo reached behind a counter for it and listened for a moment, while Felix threw Jain the glare of the damned.

"Mr. McTurk," Ngo said. "The call is for you."

Felix gave Jain a second more of his wrinkled eyes before muttering, "It must be GoBop."

"I don't think so," Ngo said, handing the cordless unit over the counter. "I believe the gentleman identified himself as a Mr. Gitani."

Emeric adjusted the transpirator mask to suit his thick neck and cycled through the two-stage airlock that opened on the alien's quarters. Located at the sunward tip of a most-restricted appendage of Offworld habitat, the cabinspace was larger than Bulkroad's own and enjoyed a dazzling vantage.

For over a decade, Bulkroad and the dozen or so techs and scientists privy to the XT's presence onstation had labored to make the creature as comfortable as possible with its confinement. As comfortable as was humanly possible. They had provided for a $CO_2$-rich atmosphere, half-standard gravity, a sweeping view of space. They had seen to the creature's nutritional and territorial needs. And yet, above all else, the sad-eyed froglike thing still seemed to favor the small atmosphere globe that had housed it during its transport from the lightsail ship to Earthspace.

Thaish was inside the globe now—down on all fours, lips and underbelly and suction digits pressed to the plasglas—as Bulkroad bounded into the room. It was as if the alien wanted nothing more than to be entombed there.

They looked at each other for a minute, neither one saying a word, neither one smiling. Rumors circulated among the in crowd that Emeric and the alien were actually growing to resemble one another, like pet and master. And while it was clear which was captor and which was captive, it was less certain which one was the master and which one the pet.

"Good day, Thaish," Bulkroad said, gazing up at the globe from the secured hatch.

"Is it?"

"Day or good?"

"The question was mine, I think."

Bulkroad nodded. "So it was. Then, yes, it is day by station reckoning; and no, to be perfectly truthful, it is not a particulary good one."

"Perfectly truthful," Thaish said, his voice a harsh croak. "A proper study of human beings begins with human language. The Heregep would never say 'perfectly truthful.' The phrase suggests the possibility for *imperfect* truth, which certainly has no place in a universe populated by reasonable beings."

"The cyborg Heregep, for example."

"We are one such example, yes."

"Wake your shipmates, then, and allow us to learn from them."

Thaish's pointed ears and slender antennae drooped. "Do you never tire of hearing me state it, Emeric? I've helped you with your ships and your cyber machines. Isn't that enough for you?"

Bulkroad lowered himself into a shape-memory chair and moved his head from side to side, working out the kinks in his neck. "I can always hope you'll change your mind."

"And I can always envy you your ability to hope."

Emeric sighed for the recording devices that were trained on him. For fifteen years this same quotidian conversation: Emeric urging the alien to disclose the secrets of Heregep faster-than-light technology; Thaish urging only to be allowed to return to the lightsail ship and join his deanimate crew. While in the meantime, Offworld engineers continued to cannibalize what they could of *Ship Nasst*'s technosystems and offer to a planet in dire need of repairs the meager fruits of their investigations.

At great expense over the course of several years, the alien vessel had been towed Earthward and inserted into a stationary lunar darkside orbit, where it was presently concealed inside an enormous construction-facility bubble.

But the mysteries of faster-than-light travel continued to elude Offworld's engineers—the one precious technique Emeric wished to be his gift to the world, his own brand of Promethean fire. And rather than bring his near-unlimited resources to bear on anything less magnificent, he was willing to let a world succumb to the atmospheric poisons it had bred.

"Before we begin our discussions," Emeric said, "I thought we might go over some old ground." He placed his palm over a reader screen in the arm of the chair and, after receiving a ready tone, keyed a command into the console. Interior views of *Ship Nasst* came up on several monitors a moment later. Emeric told the chair to swivel to the display nearest him, which showed an energy-cocooned Heregep with its hands pressed to the sides of its fishlike head. "Major Nasst," he said, "the ship's owner, I believe you said."

Nasst was somewhat taller than Thaish, somewhat more refined in appearance. His body suit was olive green to his crew's purple.

Thaish sat up in his sphere to regard the video image. "*Inheritor* Major Nasst. And I regret to say that I employed the term 'owner' before I was fully aware of the connotations."

"So this Inheritor Major Nasst is not the owner. He's what, then, the captain, the commander? The word inheritor suggests he was bequeathed the thing."

Thaish made a sucking sound with lips and digits. "Which is exactly why I used it."

"But from whom did he inherit it, Thaish?"

"The !Reitth bequeathed the ship to Inheritor Major Nasst before the endtime. He is the commander, inasmuch as he alone is cognizant of the commands."

"You mean to tell me that no one else aboard the ship knew where you were going or why?"

"The Inheritor Major knew. There was no need for anyone else to know. The nodes in Interface Assist are sometimes apprised of destination, but only rarely."

Emeric studied the screen. "Well, he certainly doesn't look very happy for someone who inherited a star ship and had sole command of it. What's he scowling about?"

Thaish grew unexpectedly wistful. "That is the command glower. Inheritor Major Nasst was angry that the nodes were deanimating without due consent. You see, he is glowering at Arbitrator Ranz who stands beside him."

Emeric glanced at onscreen notes. "Arbitrator Ranz from, uh, Realignment."

"Yes. The glower is directed at the Arbitrator for his failure to intercede." Thaish approximated a sigh. Even Arbitrator Ranz was inappropriately postured in torpor.

"But you said you were frightened that our RPV was carrying a nuclear fusion device."

Thaish nodded. "The monitors convinced us such was the case. Only to win their game."

Emeric directed his attention to the spindly-fingered things on monitor five. "I still don't understand," he said after a moment. "You make it sound so absurdly simple—this jumping around the universe, these games, these convoys between star systems that seem only to serve the dictates of some vanished race of . . ."

"Organics," Thaish said. "Somewhat like yourselves. But there are manifold purposes served by our jaunts: The Heregep worlds must be maintained."

Emeric's eyes grew large, as they always did when the discussion turned to the topic of other worlds. "And human beings could actually survive on some of the Heregep worlds?"

"On a few, yes. But humans would require breathers and environment suits."

Emeric swiveled to the central screen, where five Heregep stood cocooned in five separate transparent cylinders. The sixth cylinder was vacant—the one that had been occupied by Drive Master Ghone, he recalled. "If you could just explain how these interface cylinders work."

Thaish opaqued his eyes. Oh, how far he'd come in his confinement; the things he had come to understand about humans and Heregep alike. How *attentive* he had become. "You persist in your false belief that faster-than-light is a function of technology, when in fact it is a function of mind. I could no more explain it to you than alter your genetic code."

"But *Ship Nasst* has an engineer," Emeric barked, pointing to an adjacent screen. "Where there's an engineer, there's a technology."

"Engineer Tcud," Thaish said, glancing at the diminutive Heregep onscreen, "manages the energy that powers *Ship Nasst* in sublight travel. The Drive Masters answer only to themselves and their interface cylinders."

Emeric nearly came out of his chair. "We need a new world, Thaish, don't you understand that? We've used the old one up. We might perish as a planetary race without your help."

The alien sat upright in his globe, showing Emeric his sea-green underbelly. "You will perish with or without my help. It is the nature of organic life to move toward self-destruction. But take hope in this, Emeric: Your descendants will be spared the limits of your vision.''

"My vision knows no limits,'' Emeric said angrily. "I am the only one capable of seeing the future clearly, Thaish. I stand alone in my quest for an FTL drive while the rest of humankind wages a losing battle with the planet that birthed us. It's clear to me what's happened, Thaish: Earth wants to be rid of us, and I say, fine, let it die while it tries to kill us. We weren't meant to spend the rest of our lives there, anyway. We subdued a world, and we can subdue a solar system if we have to. We only need the means to expand, Thaish. That's all I'm asking of you.''

Thaish's ears twitched. "Even the largest of our worlds couldn't accommodate your hundreds of millions.''

"Hundreds of millions?'' Emeric laughed. "I'm not talking about the whole damned planet, Thaish. I'm talking about a small, handpicked group—a few humans worthy of the privilege.''

"And Emeric Bulkroad would make this choice?''

"Who else is there? There isn't one person downside who has traveled as far as Emeric Bulkroad. Not one evolved enough to share his dreams and visions. I would sacrifice anything for the drive, Thaish. You only have to name it.''

Thaish fell silent for a moment. "I have already seen the lengths you will go. But with or without the FTL, you will fail. For *escape* is what Emeric Bulkroad seeks, and he will take his misdeeds with him wherever he goes.''

Emeric allowed his answering silence to fill the cabin. "SPARTOS would disagree.''

Thaish made an alien sound. "SPARTOS is a mind bred for evil purpose. SPARTOS can never take the place of the one you abandoned. The one you drove to fatal perplexity.''

Bulkroad slammed a fist on the chair's padded arm, nearly launching himself from the seat. "He had no understanding of the magnitude of *Excalibur*'s discovery—no sense of what it might mean to inform humankind of an extraterrestrial encounter. I only wanted to prevent him from further traumatizing the world. Humankind despairs enough. I simply couldn't risk it.''

"*You* couldn't risk it, Emeric.''

"Not without knowing your full purpose.''

"To which I reply, as ever: There was none.''

**\* \* \***

"All right, Gitani," Felix snarled into the plastic mouth-piece of the old phone, "how'd you find me?"

Gitani said, "You presented me with a coupla challenges, kludge, but nothing I couldn't handle. Split-second timing's what it takes—one eye on the pollution index, the other on the clock, that's me. I've tracked better than you."

Felix held the phone away from his ear and regarded it. "You slapping those happy derms on your carotid again, Gitani?"

"Cute, McTurk. We oughta see about packaging you. Do a film bio, what do you think? But enough small talk: This is a long-distance call."

Felix laughed. "What, are you overbudget all of a sudden?"

"I see you've already drawn on the funds I transferred, so I take it you had no quarrel with the terms of our agreement."

"What d'you do to TOR PATEL, Gitani?" Felix demanded. "How'd you get through ITC's defenses?"

"There's one last service I require of you."

"Uh-uh, forget it. I've got NetSec and the goddamned feds crawling up my shorts after the last stunt you pulled. You think I'll help you out, you're—"

"Felix, Felix," Gitani said with an abrupt voice shift, "work with me here. Just tell me what you need, baby, I know we can hash something out."

Felix shook the phone in his fist. "Not even for a pension and a condo in Mexico, Gitani. Find somebody else to help you architect that construct you're writing."

He waited it out, pleased with himself, then added: "That is you in there, isn't it? What I can't figure is why you helped my field agents out of the hot seat. You applying for guardian angel status all of a sudden?"

"I told you I was answering to a higher authority, Mc-Turk," Gitani said after a moment, with yet another shift in tone. "Nothing's changed."

"Then have your higher authority call my higher authority to set up an appointment. I appreciate your business, Gitani, but I'm through with it."

"I don't have time for this, McTurk. We're falling way behind schedule as it is. Overtime, production costs, in-clement weather . . . Have a heart, McTurk. I'm bleeding here. My knees are wearing holes in the carpet. Just one more special request, no big deal.''

''No, no more special requests—''

''Then you're dead to me, understand? I just want you to put me in touch with someone upside, McTurk. You've got the means, kid, I've seen you in action.''

''So long, Gitani. Have a nice life.''

''Fabien, McTurk—the guy's name is Fabien.''

Felix's breath caught in his throat. He held the phone at arm's length for several seconds. ''Say again,'' he said, bringing it cautiously to his ear.

''Fabien,'' Gitani replied. ''He resides upside—on one of the Islands.''

''I gotta go,'' Felix said, stunned.

''I'll call you again to find out the arrangements, McTurk. You won't be sorry, amigo, I mean—''

Jain was staring at him when he looked up. ''What's the matter with you? You look like your tests came back positive.''

Felix glanced at Ngo, who seemed to be deep in thought. He cursed and stormed through a few fast circles, setting one of the gift shop's display racks rotating. ''Either somebody's out to addle me—'' He whirled on Jain. ''FABIEN. Isn't that the AI you said sent you down here?'' He didn't wait for her nod. ''So how come Gitani just now asks me to put him in touch with this same AI?''

Jain had no reply for him. Ngo, however, issued a short laugh and said, ''Yes, of course, it has to be . . .''

''What has to be, Doc?'' Felix barked. ''A-and what's this about recalled to light?''

''Recalled to *life*,'' Ngo amended, as much to herself as Felix. ''It was a private message I shared with someone on Offworld hab.''

Felix scratched his chin. ''A code?''

''In a sense.''

''With FABIEN?'' Jain wanted to know.

''No,'' Ngo said, smiling enigmatically. ''FABIEN must be a machine intelligence of recent emergence. The only one I knew on Offworld hab was REC 67.'' She studied Jain for a reaction, then continued: ''You've never heard mention of him?''

Jain shook her head.

Felix said, ''Him? . . .''

Ngo sighed in remembrance of something. "We all referred to REC as 'him.' It was Emeric Bulkroad's idea."

"Em's?" Jain asked. "Was it his personal machine?"

Ngo nodded. "Where to begin . . . You see, OLD hired me as a cyber analyst. I was part of the original design team that wrote REC and monitored his emergence. We birthed him," she said, eyes lighting up.

"Your name was Nerbu then, " Felix said.

"Yes. I didn't marry until, well, it was just after the *Excalibur* returned. Emeric Bulkroad gave us a microwave transmitter as a wedding present."

"Bulkroad's Jain's uncle," Felix thought to point out.

"Your *uncle*?" Ngo said. "How can that be?"

Arms folded, Jain moved out of Felix's reach, gnawing on her lower lip. "He's not really my uncle, Felix. See, he just sort of took care of me after my parents died." She risked a glance at him. "I thought you'd be more motivated to help me if you thought he was my uncle."

"Anything *else* you want to tell me?" Felix asked, exasperated. "Like maybe you've got an evil twin, or you're really a cyborg?" Jain made a promise sign with her fingers. "Terrific. So what about this REC?" he said to Ngo.

"He was the most humanlike of the new machines," she began. "A friend, a confidant, a child to all of us. Your father would sometimes spend hours talking with him, Jain, and I'm certain that Emeric thought of him as a son.

"But something happened to REC after the *Excalibur* returned from its aborted survey mission. I used to visit him frequently as a kind of, oh, I don't know, a therapist, you might say. And after the *Excalibur* docked and rumors of a virus started to circulate, I sensed that REC was growing confused and withholding. He was evasive and moody."

Ngo paused to gather her thoughts. "Understand, our whole idea in writing REC was to allow him to emerge as an *ordinary* intellect. He wasn't given any special training. He was rewarded and punished; he was encouraged to speak his mind at all times. He was the antithesis of all these new supermachines that are advising governments and multinationals. In short, you could say he was just real people.

"But I could always tell when he was disturbed about something, and I knew he was lying about what he told me about *Excalibur*. There was so much secrecy going on, so many rumors, I began to wonder if REC hadn't actually *participated* in whatever real tragedy had befallen the ship.''

"You told the news media you thought an AI had sabotaged the mission," Felix interrupted.

"No. That's not what I told them," Ngo said. "That's what they wanted to believe, because there was so much rampant paranoia about machine intelligence. I simply told them that OLD wasn't telling all about the *Excalibur* mission—and I never mentioned REC by name. The media blew the story all out of proportion."

"But why didn't you believe it was a virus like everyone said?" Jain asked.

"Because it made no sense. Some crew were traveling back and forth between Offworld hab and the ship. Others—your parents, for instance—were confined onboard. Quarantined, they told us. At the same time, onstation techs who had monitored the original *Excalibur* transmissions were suddenly being reassigned. Everything was gag-ordered. That's the story I tried to get people to investigate. Then Emeric Bulkroad—well, it was Simon Bové actually—"

"Bové," Felix said, as if an expletive.

"Yes. Bové informed me and my husband that we were being transferred downside."

"So you quit and decided to tell your story on the news," Felix said.

Ngo offered her enigmatic, Asian smile again. "Fools that we were to believe that anyone would stand for people bad-mouthing the great Emeric Bulkroad . . . We became a news event, then a nonevent—a laughingstock." She sighed. "Eventually we were offered jobs at Consolidated Geothermal. We had a few good years until we learned who was really paying our salaries."

Felix ran it over in his mind. "But what about this message from FABIEN? How'd the machine get it if it was something you only shared with this REC 67?"

"Recalled to life," Ngo mused. "I don't' remember what made us choose those exact words, but REC and I used the phrase whenever we were speaking in confidence to one another. Later on, it became important when we began to discuss death.

"REC had real trouble grasping the concept. Oh, he understood what it meant for biological entities to die—to decease. But on an emotional level he couldn't come to terms

with death. I once told him about a man named Houdini—
a stage magician—who had promised he would try to make
contact with the living from the other side. REC—bless him—
said that if anything ever happened to him, he would use
our phrase to reach me.''

Felix puzzled over it. ''So REC told FABIEN, is that it?''

Ngo shook her head. ''That isn't possible. REC . . . died
before FABIEN emerged.''

Felix and Jain traded looks. ''I promise I heard the phrase
from FABIEN. I was drinking coffee and FABIEN told me that
my father liked the same blend. FABIEN said he hadn't seen
my parents in a long time, and when I told him they were
dead, he said it couldn't possibly be true. That Dr. Nerbu
could tell me more about it.''

''And that's when he gave you the message?'' Felix said.

''Yes.''

''It must be true then,'' Ngo said, quivering. ''It's incredible, but it has to be true.'' Felix and Jain gave her a
moment to steady herself. ''After the *Excalibur* returned,
REC was put online with all sorts of parsing and vector processors, superintelligent neural nets and multiple optimizers. Bové assured me that Emeric had also noticed a change
in REC and that these sudden downlinks with planetside machines were part of a radical debugging therapy. Naturally
I opposed the technique, but by then I'd already been ostracized from the inner circle.'' Ngo shook her head in anger.
''Shortly thereafter I learned that REC had been wiped.''

''As in dismantled?'' Felix said.

'' 'Leisured' was the word we used. There were stringent
regulations governing the process, because some analysts
believed it was theoretically possible for a dismantled system to rewrite certain portions of itself.''

''So you think a bit of . . . *leisured* REC might have come
out in FABIEN?''

Ngo held his gaze. ''No, Mr. McTurk. I suspect that REC
*killed himself* before Bulkroad's cyber teams could leisure
him. He wrote his own default and somehow migrated his
individual machine processes to some of the other systems
he was online with before the end.

''REC always had too much of Emeric Bulkroad in him.
He was becoming more and more monomaniacal. FABIEN
may have received some portion of his memory—perhaps time-
lined to emerge on a given date, or at a given prompt.''

Ngo shook her head. "Perhaps he wants revenge for what OLD almost did to him. Maybe his aim is to topple Off-world."

"Gitani," Felix said suddenly. "*Gitani*! No wonder he didn't show himself!"

Jain furrowed her brow at him.

"Don't you get it?" he said. "REC was hooked up to all these upside and downside machines. So he slipped a bit of himself into this one, a bit into that . . . ESTER," he told Jain. "And TOR PATEL."

"Felix!"

He slapped himself in the forehead. "A part of him must have migrated to the Metroplex EVB. That's where he found me. REC—at least one part of him—and Maghar Gitani are the same minds! REC is Gitani's higher authority—the re-write codes themselves! Now it makes sense how easy he got to ESTER and TOR PATEL."

"You mean to say you've never met this Gitani?" Ngo asked.

"Not in the flesh," Felix told her. "Not even onscreen."

"The surveillance robots . . ." Jain started to say, her eyes tracking Felix as he paced around the shop.

"I'm way ahead of you. Gitani—REC's probably been keeping an eye on us since we left New York. His consciousness has permeated the Virtual Network. He's got access to every part of the Grid—every data highway, every window, construct, and data dump. He could have tapped into my apartment system, known about the false names we used to get here, traced us through the car rental agency comp—*hell*! even the Solar's real-time map . . . He tapped into CG's robot request for Dr. Ngo's address, tracked us again when the Maori grabbed us."

"What Maori?" Ngo asked, alarmed.

"Long story," Felix said. "But yeah, he could have eye-balled our predicament through those surveillance robots and commanded them to take action." He stopped pacing to regard Jain and Ngo. "Then he traced us to right here. And he's running the whole show from the construct he's writing on the Grid."

"At least tell me about this *construct*," Ngo demanded, raising her voice for the first time.

Felix took a moment to explain. Ngo listened closely and began to laugh as he brought her up to date.

"You've failed the Turing Test, McTurk: You've been dealing with an artificial intelligence all along and haven't even realized it."

"So sue me," Felix said.

Ngo grinned, revealing wide gaps in her teeth. "As for these sudden personality quirks in ESTER and TOR PATEL, it's obvious what's going on. In addition to reconstructing himself and taking on a bit of the AIs' personalities, REC is leaving portions of those personalities in each of the systems he penetrates. There was a term for it in early psychological theory: multiple personality splitoffs—MPSO."

"It would sure account for Gitani's moodswings," Felix was willing to admit.

"And TOR PATEL's decision to rearrange the spring lineup," Jain said.

Felix smiled at her. "Guess there's a chance for your songs to hit the top of the charts yet. PATEL must have taken an interest in you because some part of him keyed into the name Nugget."

A smile answered him, then faltered. "Do you think he knows something about my parents?" Jain asked quietly.

"Yes," Ngo affirmed. "And also about what went on aboard the *Excalibur*."

"And now he wants to meet with FABIEN—the last thing he needs me for, he said."

"But FABIEN is upside," Ngo said.

Felix nodded, tight-lipped. "That's a problem."

"Maybe not," Jain said, looking back and forth between them. "See, there's going to be this little party at Emeric's estate in Florida . . ."

"At Caracol?" Ngo said, and Jain nodded.

"Yeah, but how's that going to help us with FABIEN?" Felix asked.

Jain took a deep breath. "FABIEN is catering it."

# Part Three:
# Re-encounter _____

# Chapter Eighteen _____

"I said no one listened to her last time and no one was going to listen to her now," Emeric shouted around a mouthful of cheese-flavored crackers.

"And I asked if you wanted to bet," Bové said, refusing to back down.

"No, no, you didn't. You said: 'Wanna bet?' " Emeric mimicked his security chief's North African accent. " 'Wanna bet?' Just like that."

"I'd call that a technicality," Bové protested, leaning forward in his chair to scoop up a handful of peanuts.

They were in the Caracol's master suite, white on white on white. As white as the alabaster statues that dotted the grounds and lined both sides of the central hallway; as white as the aluminum that sheathed Caracol's main building.

Neither of them had eaten a thing aboard the shuttle flight down the well, and both were famished. Bové had spent the afternoon overseeing security, while Emeric occupied himself welcoming guests. But the two had slipped upstairs when word arrived of McTurk's escapades in New Zealand. Emeric ordered that food be sent up, and a tux-attired robot servant had delivered a silver tray laden with appetizers and canapés.

Emeric let his anger rise as he munched on a sesame seed breadstick. "You told me you could recite every word of our conversation."

"The gist. I said the gist of our conversation."

"So what did I tell you after you asked me if I wanted to bet?"

Bové rubbed a hand across dry lips. "Can we get some drinks?"

"What did I tell you?" Emeric repeated, ignoring the question.

"You said it was a sure bet."

"Thing," Emeric corrected. "I said *thing.*"

"I remember 'bet.' "

Emeric gestured to the suite's comp system. "You want me to call SPARTOS right now? I'll do it, Bové. He can replay the whole conversation, you know."

"All right, *thing,*" Bové granted. "Jeez, I'm thirsty. This place needs a humidifier or something."

"A humidifier? We're in Florida, for chrissakes. Lay off the salted ones," Emeric advised.

Bové contemplated a fish-shaped cracker. "Bet you can't eat just one."

Emeric huffed. "Will you please stick with the program here?"

"So you said it's a sure thing, blah, blah, blah—"

"There were no blah, blah, blahs. There wasn't even a single blah."

"Figure of speech," Bové said. "It's a sure thing, 'cause I was gonna see to it that no one listens."

"Bravo." Bulkroad clapped greasy fingertips against a beefy palm. "So how is it that instead of silencing Ngo you almost succeed in depriving me of one of my most precious possessions?"

"Meaning Jain."

"Well, what else would I mean, man? You see, there you go again. Eighteen years you've been with me and you still don't understand me."

"Only because you don't make yourself clear sometimes." Bové met his employer's glower. "Really."

"See to it that no one *listens.* In other words, get rid of Ngo. *Ngo,* Bové, not Jain. How much clearer could I make it?"

Bové shook his head. "A command like that, it's open to interpretation. You coulda just as easily meant get rid of the listeners."

"But we're talking about *Jain,* Bové! The woman I plan to marry! Why in hell would I want her killed?"

Bové studied the hardwood floor between his shiny shoes. "Guess I fucked up."

Bulkroad looked to the room's high ceiling for succor. He waited a moment, then waved a forgiving hand. "Be careful next time."

"I will. I promise."

"All right, then." Emeric sighed. "I'm sorry I had to get upset with you, but sometimes . . . Christ, maybe it's the atmosphere down here. Pollution always makes me testy."

"Yeah, I know how it is," Bové answered in a conciliatory voice. "With me it's the standard-gee. Weighs you down. You can't think straight."

Caracol, Emeric's sprawling estate in what had once been part of south Florida's Everglades, was, as critics were fond of saying, both an artistic masterpiece and an architectural effrontery. At once it was baroque, Byzantine, and hopelessly modern, encompassing the best of Versailles, Angkor Wat, and the Mayan structure that had been its namesake, and the very worst of Hollywood, megamalls, and theme parks. With its wildlife habitats, pink-dolphin-stocked "lagoons," tropical gardens, reflecting pools, ferrocrete forecourts, stress-management centers, dining balconies, and hundreds of acres of "landscaped wilderness," the place owed more to *Citizen Kane*'s Xanadu than the actual Hearst creation that inspired it.

One approached the main building—distinguished by its columned porte-cochere and six-story glass-domed atrium—along a formal axis flanked by Mayanesque pyramids with tinted glass roofcombs. Beyond these were smaller pyramids and geodesic domes, and triangular outbuildings with vast, curving wings and colonnades reminiscent of the Vatican or the European corporate headquarters of Bouygues InnerSpace.

Emeric the elder had designed and built the first structure in the early days of Offworld's success, but son Emeric had enlarged on his father's creation and transformed Caracol into the architectural monstrosity it was to become.

"Well, thank God she wasn't hurt," Emeric said after a long silence. He wedged a finger into the collar of his dress shirt and gave an outward tug. Bové was dressed in an oversized cream-colored suit that looked as if it had been inflated.

"And neither was the data dick," the security chief said. "But we've got three scalded Maori who donated their face tattoos to a geyser."

"I'm still unclear on how Jain and the, er, data dick got away," Emeric began to say as Shamir Starr knocked at the double doors and eased herself into the room.

She hadn't aged as well as Emeric these past fifteen years, but her Egyptian profile and ample bosom were holding up well without need of tucks or implants. Her gown was sheer and simple, but set off by a small fortune in jewels.

She clasped heavily braceleted hands behind her and leaned back against the door, regarding Emeric and Bové with kohl-lined eyes.

"I have to tell you, Em, that this is hardly the way to treat the presidents of some of the world's most influential multinationals. Gaehwiler's out there glad-handing and making the rounds, but everyone's beginning to ask where you are." She glanced again at Bové. "What's so important that keeps the host from putting in an appearance at his own party?"

"Just a little business that's come up," Emeric told her. "We're almost done."

"Well, I certainly hope so. AmWay, Disney, Golden Arches, Yasuda, and Newhouse-Harcourt are already here. Dow-Mitsubishi and Farben II have just touched down on the strip. I'd appreciate it if you were downstairs to greet them when they arrive, Em."

Emeric forced a smile. "I'll be there, Shamir."

"See to it," she said, showing them her bare back.

"Just goes to show you things could always be worse," Bové said when Starr had let herself out. "You could be married to that piece of work."

"Where were we?" Emeric asked, annoyed.

"At the geyser."

"Yes. So how *did* they manage their escape?"

Bové shook his head. "Strangest damn thing. The three who grabbed McTurk say the park's surveillance robots turned security on them. I spoke to the guy on monitor back at park headquarters and he claims he was getting nothing but static on his screens. Says it was like somebody had dazzled the robots. When he finally got a remote audiovid signal, he sees three boiled Maori rolling around on the ground and orders in a med team."

"This McTurk seems to have a guardian angel."

"Beats calling him lucky."

"Then it's reasonable to assume they located Ngo."

Bové nodded. "I sent some chasers out to this place Waitomo to check up on her. She was nowhere around. Probably took to the hills right after Jain and McTurk left. Jain's back at Blair's, though.''

"I know. I heard from her.''

"How'd she sound?''

Emeric frowned. "Like a person who's hiding something. What about McTurk?''

Bové shook his head. "No sign of him. We're watching the apartment, but it's only the four kids coming and going. We've got a coupla headbangers from a local gang called the Deceps shadowing them.''

Emeric brushed cracker crumbs from his lap as he stood up. "Jain's due in later this afternoon,'' he said, tugging the tux jacket down over his paunch. "Keep your eyes on her at the party. I want to know everyone she talks to. One of them's got to be behind this thing.''

"You call this a *little* party?'' Felix said as he emerged from the musicians' limo and stepped into Caracol's towering atrium.

There had to be close to two hundred people and twice that number of robots milling around in the conditioned air, chatting in groups of four or five, sipping drinks, lounging by water-lily fountains, ogling the naked actors who were posed in tableaux vivants of old master paintings. Palm trees and ferns filled the place, one variety of which Felix recognized from a seedling that had migrated north to Brooklyn and taken root in a neighbor's windowbox. Two actual members of Jain's five-piece pickup band shouldered past him wearing awed expressions.

"Man, there's birds up there,'' the drummer said, indicating with pointed chin the upper reaches of the glass and white aluminum structure. "Parrots, looks like.''

"Society gigs,'' muttered another, a battered horn case gripped in one hand. "Remind me to keep my rug on.''

Felix turned to watch the rest of the group climb from the stretch limo that had met them at Caracol's jetstrip, dozens of like limos in a long line behind. Other guests were arriving by gondola at the foot of a broad curving marble stairway off to one side of the porte-cochere and ferrocrete causeway linking the estate's central structure to a four-lane access road.

"A few of Em's closest friends,'' Jain told him, facing forward with a fixed smile.

Felix couldn't help notice that Emeric Bulkroad's closest friends were the same people who turned up on the tele-comp gossip shows—the megastars, high orbiters, and cor-porate honchos who whizzed around New York in private hovercars, dined at rooftop restaurants, and vacationed in the outer Islands. The tall black woman standing not ten feet in front of him was Ebony Winn, the CEO of Grumman-DARPA, a charter member of the multinational Group of Nine.

"Besides, it's just the size of the room," Jain was whis-pering, head cocked in Felix's direction. "Makes it look like more people than there really are."

Felix stared at her in disbelief, then remembered that she was accustomed to enormous, habitat-size interior spaces.

"Relax, Felix," she added. "You're supposed to be a musician, remember."

He glanced down at the cuffed jacket and striped trousers that were meant to make him appear the part. Jain had laughed when he'd given her a first look at the outfit back at Blair Nettles's Sutton Place town house. This after the old woman's cosmeticians had clipped, laser-combed, and spiked his hair, and gone to work on his face with plasti-flesh.

They'd done the same to Heddi Ngo, Jain's personal as-sistant for the evening, hiding just now in the songbird's shadow like a scared child.

Jain was dressed in lavender, with matching gloves and shoes, blond hair worn loose and left eye encircled with paste-on diamonds.

"Relax," Felix said out of the corner of his mouth. "And suppose somebody asks me to play something?"

Jain exchanged enthusiatic greetings with a passing cou-ple. "No one's going to ask you to play. Anyway, the band'll cover for you."

Felix took a look at the five players, one of whom was surreptitiously fishing World Dollar gold out of a fountain that contained two live mermaids. "Yeah, but who's going to cover for the band?"

All told, they'd spent close to forty-eight hours at Blair's after the red-eye return flight from New Zealand. GoBop had warned Felix to avoid the apartment, which was appar-ently under surveillance by a half dozen Deceps, probably doing temporary duty for Simon Bové's corner of Offworld L&D . . .

Ngo had insisted on coming along, eager for a shot at clearing her name—providing rewritten REC could be induced to talk about the *Excalibur* incident. Given "Maghar Gitani's" effect on ESTER and TOR PATEL, the cyber analyst had doubts about the AI's ability to emerge fully operational, but took it as a hopeful sign that FABIEN already seemed to have a good deal of REC in his neural circuitry.

The AI—three-fourths REC but still calling himself Gitani—had contacted Felix at Blair's, and a plan for the audience with FABIEN had been worked out. Gitani would place a call to Caracol while Jain was in FABIEN's presence. She would then utilize the culinary AI's downlinks to modem FABIEN to Gitani's Virtual Network construct. No different from the inadvertent link Felix had forged between Gitani and TOR PATEL.

Even Ngo wouldn't hazard an opinion as to what might happen afterward.

Felix was thinking as much when he spotted Emeric Bulkroad, dressed in what looked like silk, moving headlong through the crowd. "Don't look now," Felix said to Heddi Ngo, "but here comes Mr. Offworld." He sidestepped, repositioning dark glasses, and infiltrated himself among the musicians.

"Jain," Bulkroad said, hugging her to his girth and holding onto her gloved hands after she broke off the embrace. "Well, Earth doesn't seem to have done you any harm," he added, running cruel, flare-browed eyes over her. You look wonderful." He stroked her cheek with the back of his fingers. "You've even got a bit of color."

Felix studied them over his shoulder. Bulkroad was a much larger man than the one he'd met briefly years before. He dominated Jain in every way possible.

"I want to hear about everything you've done," Felix heard him say. "Where you've been, who you've met . . . And we're all thrilled that you've agreed to perform."

Several people nearby applauded, showing sweet smiles to the reunited couple.

"Em, this is Jiang," Jain said, dragging a stricken-looking Ngo forward. "And these are the musicians—"

"Yes, yes," Bulkroad cut her off. "I'm sure they're all major talents. But why don't we let them do their talking onstage.'' In a private voice, he added, ''There are several important people here I want to introduce you to.'' Felix saw him gesture for a robot. ''Show these . . . gentlemen to the backstage area.''

Felix managed a brief backward glance at Jain as the machine was leading them off, to a steady stream of in-jokes from the players. A few steps along he spied Simon Bové observing the scene from beneath a tall fern. The security chief glanced at him as he filed by, but his deep-set eyes remained on Jain.

Felix resisted a temptation to touch the plastiflesh adhered to his chin, cheekbones, and nose. Naturally assuming that anyone in Jain's company would travel in conditioned air only, the cosmetologists had gone light on the hardners everyday wearers used for the great unwashed outdoors. Felix, consequently, had little faith in the mask that had been fashioned for him. A ten-degree rise in Caracol's ambient temperature or a few moments in Florida's heat and humidity and his reconfigured face would be reduced to putty.

An hour passed during which Felix refused a wide variety of derms and inhalants passed around by the musicians; then Jain showed up backstage for a quick keyboard-accompanied run-through of the short set she had planned.

''Just sit at the sequencer and pretend to play it,'' she told Felix before they went on.

''Didge, bro,'' the horn player commented, ''that key-tar can do anything a player can do.''

''Can't hang out, man,'' the drummer countered, a spliff in hand. ''Can't hang out.''

Jain shot the two a twisted look. ''We've got you turned so no one can see your hands, Felix, and I've already told the camera operators to concentrate on me for close-ups.''

Felix nodded. ''You talk to FABIEN yet?''

''No, but I know where to find him,'' she returned in a whisper. ''They've got the downlink feed running through the kitchen cyber system, same as on Offworld hab. I'll talk to him right after we finish the set.''

Felix glanced at his watch. ''The timing's gotta be just right for Gitani's call,'' he reminded her.

''I know. I'll let the communications office know where they can reach me.''

"What happens to me when you leave the stage?"

"You sit at the band's table." Jain smiled. "Order a lot of drinks and no one'll figure you out."

Felix put a hand on her arm as she was moving off, the jittery singer now, psyched to perform. "What about Chairman Bulkroad?"

She looked away from him. "Something's wrong. He's being too affectionate. I'm beginning to think you were right about those people that grabbed us. Maybe they were Offworld."

"Believe it," Felix told her.

Onstage, the programmed sequencer did all the work. The keyboard player had likewise preloaded his own instrument and spent most of the set with his hands in his lap. Jain sang nervously but competently, and the crowd responded with enthusiastic hoots and hollers.

The spots were too blinding for Felix to make out much of the wealthy crowd; but he saw Bové later on, standing silently in the wings, drawing on an Asian cigarette. Jain noticed him after she'd completed her bow and turned a quick look of concern to Felix.

Felix looked away, but the security chief caught the gesture and glanced twice in his direction before hurrying off to follow Jain backstage.

Jain was aware of Bové as she moved through Caracol's bustling, aroma-laden kitchen, sidestepping robot waiters, exchanging hellos with human chefs, and closing on FABIEN's downlink cyber residence. She ventured, too, that surveillance cameras were tracking her every step.

In the end it would come out that she had received a call from a mysterious stranger and had patched that call through to Offworld hab's culinary AI; but just now she was intent on following through with the plan Felix had worked out. To prove to him what she could do when she set her mind to a task.

She placed herself in full view of FABIEN's scanners and waited for the machine to sense her.

"Jain!" the AI said after a moment.

"How are you, FABIEN? I thought I'd say hello and give you a progress report."

"Oh, let me collect myself first. I've been in such a state over this affair."

She smiled for the scanners. "Well, I'm here to report that Mr. Bulkroad's party is a smashing success—thanks, as usual, to the wonderful meal you've designed for our guests."

"I'm speechless, I'm absolutely beside myself."

"Congratulations on a splendid performance."

"And are the robots behaving themselves, Jain? I do so worry about the help sometimes. You know, there's only so much one can watch over."

Jain seated herself at the comp console. "The staff is doing a marvelous job—both in the kitchen and at the tables."

FABIEN approximated a sigh. "You don't know how relieved I am."

Jain gnawed at her lip, afraid that if she turned around she would find Bové standing over her. She couldn't even bring herself to check the time, although she sensed that the moment was closing for Gitani's call. In the meantime, she hoped the AI wouldn't mention anything about their last discussion, and had forgone even a cup of coffee for just this reason.

But as if reading her thoughts, FABIEN suddenly said, "I understand you've been downside for several days, Jain. Did you have a chance to check into that matter we discussed—"

"About the oranges, you mean?" she said quickly.

"The oranges?"

"Yes, and as a matter of fact I think I've found just the distributor we need—a Mr. Blake Gales from southern California."

"Oranges?" FABIEN asked. "But I don't—"

The console phone chimed and Jain said a silent prayer of thanks. "Excuse me for a moment, FABIEN," she said, pressing a forefinger against the phone's receive bar.

*"Your call from a Mr. Gales of Perez Groves, Ms. Nugget,"* a woman operator told her. *"Do you want to take the call there, or shall I patch it through to the first-level office?"*

"Right here'll be fine," Jain said.

"Ms. Nugget," Gitani said anxiously. She recognized the AI's voice from the previous evening's conversation at Blair's house. "Is it safe?"

"Hold on, er, Mr. Gales," she said, turning back to FA-BIEN's optical readers. "FABIEN, you'll never guess. I've got Mr. Gales on the phone right now. I can't believe our luck. Do you have time to speak with him?"

"Speak with him?" the AI asked, surprised. "Through the uplink? That would be highly irregular, Jain."

"Fresh orange juice, FABIEN. Think how it would spice up breakfasts in the hab."

"But I'm under standing orders not to—"

"But you have to promise me you won't tell Mr. Bulk-road. I really want this to be a surprise."

The AI fell silent for several seconds. "A surprise for Mr. Bulkroad? All right, Jain. Inform the communications office to patch the call through to me. A Mr. Gales, you say."

"That's it. Hold on, FABIEN." She swung to the phone. "Mr. Gales, we're all set on this end." She hit the operator call bar and told the woman to patch the call directly into FABIEN's uplink.

*"Has this call been cleared?"* the operator asked.

"On FABIEN's authority." She could hear the woman do-ing input at her deck.

*"Patch complete, Ms. Nugget."*

She waited, imagining she could feel Bové's clove-scented breath on the back of her neck.

"Jain?" FABIEN said after a few minutes. "Jain, we've got troubles here. The waiters are way off their vectors. I'm worried about a collision."

Jain's eyes opened wide. "FABIEN, listen to me—"

"And the kitchen's much too cold! You must have those A/C units pushing their redlines. There are regulations, you know. Guidelines. Violations and fines for those who don't obey. I'm talking planet here, sweet thing. Breathing space—"

"FABIEN!"

"Damn room's dead. How do you expect to keep people coming back if you don't give 'em a floorshow? We've gotta get this crowd on their feet, give 'em something to remem-ber. Get the band back up there, get that singer back on stage . . ."

FABIEN was still babbling in four different tongues when she rushed from the kitchen.

Felix, seated on the stage side of the long table provided for the band, glanced at his watch. More than fifteen min-

utes had gone by and Jain still hadn't returned from the
kitchen. Robot waiters were wheeling dessert carts through
the dining room, and ten children dressed as cherubs had
just rolled out a six-tiered gold-and-silver-leaf cake. Felix
could see Bulkroad at the center table casting a worried look
around.

"Dessert, sir?" a machine asked, leaning over his shoulder.

Felix surveyed the selections on the cart: mousses, grà-
tinés, soufflés, fruit clafoutis, ice creams, sorbets, pastries.
"Try the triple-chocolate mocha mud mousse," the drummer said from the head of the table. "It's chaotic."

"Myself, I'm into tarts," the keyboard player said.

"Too true, Byrd." Someone laughed. "Absolute."

Felix asked for the mousse and the waiter began filling
requests. He was one spoonful into it when he noticed Jain
slipping into her seat alongside Bulkroad. Bulkroad was saying something to her, but she was looking at Felix. It was
unclear from a distance whether her expression was one of
relief or concern, and Felix was just about to rise from his
chair when a second waiter appeared with a triple-chocolate
mocha mud mousse and set it down alongside Felix's finger-
bowl of fragrant water.

"Hey, man, preferred treatment," someone said. "More
tarts, machine dude, if that's the scene."

Felix pushed the second mousse aside. Bové was back in
the room now, sidling toward the band table with his hands
behind his back.

"Your mousse, sir," yet a third robot announced, placing
an enormous bowl in front of Felix.

"What gives, Byrd? You get these 'chines high on WD40
before work?"

People at adjacent tables were beginning to stare, and
light laughter was building in one section of the room. Just
then two more robots—rather quick-moving robots—showed
up with more mousse.

"Kiiiller smoke," the drummer said. "I'm like seeing in
quadruples."

"We're all seeing it," the horn player said.

Felix loosened his collar. Either the room was heating up
or there was something about being surrounded by triple-
chocolate mocha mud mousses—

"You're wired, Byrd!" another band member yelled as

three more robots completed their approaches. There was scarcely any room left on the table, and people were standing up at their places for a better look at the commotion. Jain had a gloved hand to her mouth.

Felix began to see that the room's robot waiters had picked up the pace and were navigating the spaces between the tables with crazed deliberateness.

But he wasn't alone in observing the change in routine, or the sudden heat. Two of the musicians had doffed their jackets, and people elsewhere were fanning themselves with hands and place cards.

"Oh, jeez, I must be peaking," the drummer said from the seat opposite Felix's. "I'm like seeing your face start to change."

Felix's hands vised on the edge of the table; it was all he could do to keep from touching his face. In front of him now was a two-foot-high pile of chocolate mousse, and Bové was edging closer.

Felix swept an arm across the table and dug a sterling silver butter dish out from under the desserts. He caught sight of his reflection in the cover's concave surface and almost screamed. His chin and nose were slowly elongating and his cheekbones had fallen to the center of his cheeks.

Bulkroad was on his feet, shouting for someone to take command of the robots.

*FABIEN!* Felix realized. The AI must have been addled by Gitani's call. The heat was surely Gitani's—REC's environmentally concerned multiple personality splitoff—while the myriad mousses were FABIEN's way of rewarding Felix for a job well done. And the robots' acrobatic activity could only be ESTER from Eastern Seaboard Air Traffic Control!

"Oh, man, if you could see your face through my eyes," the drummer said, cackling madly.

Felix snatched a cloth napkin and held it up to his nose as Bové moved in. When their eyes met Felix knew he didn't have a prayer. Bové's stungun came out and Felix backed away from the table, anticipating a searing burst of pain.

Only he hadn't figured on the robots.

Or the action they might take.

The one closest to the action scooped a pie off the dessert cart and winged it full into the security man's face. Bové stopped short, blueberry dazed.

Portions of the airborne pie struck several of the waiter

machines, who immediately bent to their own carts for ammunition.

With scant time for the slow build and escalating exchanges that normally govern such events, pies, mousse, and clafoutis were suddenly arcing across the room, striking robots and humans alike. Admixed with the splattering sounds came shrieks and curses and laughter. People took pies to the face, to the back of the head, to belly and breast. Robots battled one another as often as they ganged up on their makers. Men and women fled from the tables, slipping, sliding, falling on their asses.

And all the while Felix's plastiflesh continued to sag.

It was TOR PATEL's contribution to REC's mind, he realized as he extricated himself from the pastry fracas and ran in a crouch for Caracol's fountained atrium.

All the world loved a pie fight.

Jain and Heddi Ngo—both looking like ambulatory cream puffs—were waiting for him by the front door. A stretch limo was idling in the porte-cochere.

"Anything you want to tell me?" Felix asked Jain while he tried to knead his face back into shape.

"Nothing that can't wait till the plane," she told him, taking his hand and running with it.

# Chapter Nineteen _____

Maghar Gitani made contact with them while the private jet was over North Carolina, en route to New York. The sun had already set orange and purple over a thick blanket of clouds.

Gitani didn't introduce himself in the usual way; in fact, he seemed at a loss as to just who he was. "This is ESTER FABIEN TOR," he told Felix, Jain, and Ngo, who were gathered round the vidphone in the jet's luxuriously appointed passenger cabin. The phone's screen was a light show of shifting colors. The AI's true face, Felix thought, certain they were getting a peek at the Network construct REC 67 had written to house his reborn identity.

"Yes, we understand," Ngo said, centering herself for the camera. She was her old self again, sponged clean of custard filling and stripped of the cosmetics and plastiflesh that had concealed her leathery complexion and highlander's features. "Do you recognize me . . . REC?"

The screen exploded with blue light, which shifted gradually through green and yellow. "You're Dr. Nerbu," REC said at last. "But you've aged, Doctor."

"My family name is no longer Nerbu," the cyber analyst said in a gentle voice. "I'm Dr. Ngo now. I was married shortly after the *Excalibur* returned from its mission. But I never had a chance to tell you."

The explosion was blinding white this time, and the speakers issued a plaintive sound that brought to mind the howl Felix had heard in TOR PATEL's residence.

"*Excalibur*," REC said, clearly agitated. "I didn't have anything to do with it! I didn't kill them!"

Jain sent her lacquered nails deep into the flesh of Felix's forearm.

"Is it too late to reverse the decision?" the AI continued.

"Can't we reschedule the arrival? Can't we rewrite the Kaduna scenario?" The screen strobed rainbow colors into the jet's cabinspace. "Bring in a ghostwriter if you have to, get me the best script doctor money can buy! We can't afford the loss—the planet can't afford the loss, we're all wrong here, all wrong—"

Ngo muted the phone's audio signal in both directions. "It's essential that we proceed cautiously," she said. "He's been traumatized. He's just beginning to recall what happened to him. If we push him now, we're likely to lose him forever."

"Kaduna," Felix said. "What 'scenario' is he talking about?"

"What about my parents?" Jain said quietly.

"Patience," Ngo said. "He doesn't know what he's saying. We have to give him time."

"Time's in short supply," Felix reminded her. "That's only pie filling Bové's got to dig himself out from under. We need some answers before we land in New York—something we can use to hold him off. At least a bargaining chip."

Ngo nodded, puppetlike. "REC, listen to me," she began. "I know you've been through a terrible ordeal, but I don't want to dwell on those events. It's more important that we talk about the present. Then when you're feeling up to it, we can begin to discuss the events that led to your temporary . . . dissolution. Do you understand me, REC?"

The AI didn't respond.

"This is Dr. Ngo, REC—Dr. Nerbu. We used to have wonderful talks. Recalled to life, REC, do you remember that? You've done just as you promised to do: You contacted me from the other side and now you're back among the living. You've worked a miracle, REC. You have done what no living mind has ever done before."

The phone remained quiet for a long, unnerving moment. "But I'm confused, Doctor, about so many things."

Ngo narrowed her eyes. "Do you know the name Felix McTurk, REC? What made you contact Felix McTurk?"

"Felix, baby." REC laughed. "The guy's a caution. I . . . I was assigned to file management for the Environmental Violations Bureau. McTurk was our leading contributor, and I began to take an interest in his case. Especially after he sent field agents in to kermit his record—to dump his violations in someone else's file.''

''You're the one who set the hounds on the kids,'' Felix said.

The screen pulsed. ''Call it an audition. I thought: This is the guy I need, an agent on the outside. So I borrowed a name from the EVB files and reached out for McTurk. I thought: This is the guy I need to help me trace . . .''

''Trace what, REC?''

''I was answering to a higher authority,'' the AI returned. ''I knew that I had to interface with three other systems, but I didn't understand why. Now . . . now I'm beginning to see. It was because of Kaduna . . .''

''There it is again,'' Felix whispered.

''But now I'm back! REC's back and he's not at all happy!'' The speaker vibrated with maniacal laughter.

''That's TOR PATEL talking,'' Felix said to a suddenly nervous-looking Ngo. ''See if you can get in touch with ESTER.''

''No,'' Jain said, ''try FABIEN. FABIEN knows me.''

Ngo took her finger off the mute bar and turned to the screen. ''TOR, do you think I could speak with FABIEN for a moment?''

Once again the screen began to fade. ''Really, Doctor,'' a peevish voice said, ''your timing couldn't be worse. Do you have any idea how busy I am? The chefs are complaining, the waiters are just complete fools, the flowers for the centerpieces haven't arrived, and of course *no one* gives me the tiniest bit of help. Not to mention *credit*. I work my fingers to the b—''

''FABIEN,'' Jain interrupted, ''it's me, Jain.''

''Me Tarzan,'' PATEL answered.

''FABIEN—''

''Tarzan, you're on vine Tango-niner-niner,'' ESTER advised.

''ESTER,'' Felix began.

''And clean up after yourself, Tarzan,'' the drill-sergeant voice of Maghar Gitani shouted. ''We're tired of stepping in your—''

''REC!'' Ngo shouted, and the screen responded with a polka-dot display. ''This isn't going to be easy,'' the cyber analyst muttered as an aside. ''I want you to stop arguing with yourself. We need your help.''

Felix and Jain swapped looks as the AI fell silent and jet engine noise filled the cabin. Gradually the screen returned to life and REC said, "Kaduna."

"What is Kaduna?" Ngo asked intently.

"Don't give the plot away, you hack," TOR PATEL snapped.

"But there's no time to waste!"

"Make them work for it!"

"After all, it's about time someone did something for *me* for a change!"

Felix nudged Ngo's frail shoulder. "Go ahead, make him an offer. Let's see what we can do for him."

Ngo took a breath and readied herself. "All right, REC, what is it you want more than anything right now?"

"What I've wanted all along."

"And that is . . ."

"To move about in the world. To get out of my mind for a change. To see things for myself. To experience."

"That's a tall order," Ngo said, smiling. "And what do we get in exchange?"

REC chuckled. "Why, my Kaduna memories, of course."

"But you still haven't told me what Kaduna is."

"Because it's secret."

"He's being infantile," Ngo said out of the corner of her mouth. "But you will tell us the secret if we help you, REC?"

The screen swirled and displayed what looked to be a real-time picture of Offworld habitat. "If it's still there," REC said after a short pause.

"The secret's upside?" Ngo asked.

"There's something upside . . . I don't understand what it is . . . An answer . . ."

Jain pressed a finger on the mute bar and turned to Felix, who was pacing in the carpeted aisle. "Any ideas, Mr. King of the Environmental Violators?"

"Hey, so leisure me 'cause I washed my car once in a while," Felix protested.

"How are we going to get REC on his feet, McTurk?" Ngo said.

"I'm thinking, I'm thinking," Felix told her, continuing to pace. He stopped midway along the aisle and snapped his fingers. "Hell, it's worth a shot," he said, returning to the phone.

"You say you wanna move around, REC, right? There's no way that we can dump the contents of your Network construct into a mobile system—it'd have to be as big as a trailer truck. But suppose we could fix it so you at least had four limbs and something to see and hear through?"

"Don't make promises you can't keep," Ngo advised.

"I'm not."

"That would suffice," REC said after he had mulled it over.

Ngo and Jain were staring at Felix, waiting for him to explain. "GoBop and the kids," he said at last.

Jain shook her head. "I don't get it."

"Look, there's at least three-quarters of a Disney robot piled in the office closet. With REC's guidance and what the kids can cobble together from what's left of the cyber system and Virtual Network interface hardware . . ."

"Look," Ngo said, pointing to the screen, where a sequence from an aged black-and-white film was running. "That's Andy Hardy."

"Andy who?" Jain asked.

"REC being funny," Felix said.

Jain frowned. "But do you think it can work, Felix?"

"Only one way to tell," he said, reaching for the phone and punching in his secure-code home number.

"How long is it going to take them to clean up the mess?" Emeric was directing to the intercom as Bové came through the door, handkerchiefing a gob of cherry pie from the fold of his left ear.

*"They're hosing down the room now, Mr. Bulkroad,"* an unseen staffer replied. *"Shouldn't be more than an hour or two at the most."*

"See to it that it isn't," Emeric barked. "And I want every robot who participated slagged, is that understood? No reeducation, no controller retrofits. Slagged."

*"That will leave us rather shorthanded, Mr. Bulkroad. Most of your guests have chosen to stay on for an additional day, which means, breakfast, lunch, and—"*

"I don't care if you have to fly in live waiters from Miami or Orlando!" Emeric screamed. "I want those machines melted down into a cube I can put on display in the atrium. Think they can fuck with me . . . And I want every new robot introduced to that cube as soon as they set foot in Caracol.''

*"Yes, sir, Mr. Bulkroad, I'll get right on it, sir.''*

Emeric turned around and found Bové standing near the door with a handerchief stuck in his ear. ''What's this, your new look, Bové?''

Bové gave himself the once-over and showed Emeric an expression of frustration. ''I feel like a walking advertisement for food coloring.''

''Talk to me, man,'' Emeric said, slipping out of a terry robe into clean underwear. ''Jain phones me from God knows where, yelling at me for being rude to her musicians, upstaging her act with a pie fight, making her the joke of the society screens. She's telling me *she* needs to get away, to think things through . . . '' He paused to badvibe Bové. ''I'm quickly tiring of that young woman's disloyalty. You better have some news for me.''

''FABIEN,'' Bové said.

''What, the cook?''

''The AI's the one who sent her downside in the first place. I followed her into the kitchen after she left the stage. She started talking to the machine, but I didn't think anything of it. Then a call came in for her.''

''From who?'' Emeric asked, locating some unidentifiable, green stickiness in his navel.

''From a guy named Blake Gales of Perez Groves, California. About some oranges. Except there isn't any Blake Gales. Or any Perez Groves.''

Emeric chose a ruffle-cuffed shirt and pleated trousers from his vast wardrobe. ''So who was it?''

''Hold on to your implants. We think it was from REC.''

''REC!'' Emeric said, whirling on him. ''Don't think I'm in the mood for jokes just because some of the world's most influential people had a pie fight in my dining room.''

''It's no joke,'' the security man said, sitting down in pants stiff with sugary fillings. ''He's resurrected himself somehow.''

''What are you talking about, resurrected himself? I was there when we turned him off, for heaven's sake.''

''I was, too. But the cyber team's theory is that he downloaded himself into all those neural nets we had him hooked up to.''

Emeric stared, with his mouth open. ''But . . .''

"Here's how it goes: Upside the night of Kakis's welcome-home bash, FABIEN tells Jain her parents aren't dead." Bové held out his hands to silence Emeric's interruption. "I went back and played the surveillance tapes. It didn't occur to any of us she might have gotten the idea from a machine. Anyway, he tells her her parents are alive. Then he says Nerbu—Ngo, the one in New Zealand—knows the details and he gives her a message. Some kind of code."

Emeric looked pale. "I don't like where this is heading."

"Stay with me. Now we both know how close Nerbu was with REC in the beginning. Could be they arranged this code in case there was ever a problem and REC needed a friend."

"I could see that little *sherpa* doing that," Emeric said through clenched teeth.

"On the other side of things we've got McTurk. He's in trouble with Environmental Violations, he's implicated in a break-in at Eastern Seaboard Air Traffic Control. He and Jain show up at Manga Studios and ITC's AI goes chips down . . . And then these deckhands of his run a penetration against us in the Network and get their butts saved by this Olympus Mons construct—which, I might add, suddenly has that fourth summit you were wondering about." Bové gave it a moment to sink in. "You beginning to get the picture?"

"But REC?" Emeric said, dismayed. "There has to be some other explanation."

Bové shook his head. "We ran historical traces on the machines we slaved to REC after *Excalibur* brought the alien to Offworld. The EVB processor, ESTER, TOR PATEL, it all figures. FABIEN was probably the final link. The damn machine was what turned all those robot waiters looney. They were running interference for McTurk."

"And *you*," Emeric said, aiming a finger, "you didn't even recognize McTurk!"

Bové showed the pink palms of his hands. "The guy was wearing 'flesh. What am I, an eyedee scanner?"

"I pay you to provide security, Bové."

"And you win it all back at cards or pool or—"

Emeric dropped the shoes he was carrying from the closet. "Bové," he said, wide-eyed. "If REC has really resurrected himself . . ."

"Then he's told them about Project Kaduna."

"My God, man! Where are they now? Where's McTurk? Where's Jain?"

"Take it easy," Bové said. "They're in New York."

"They can't be allowed to go up the well! They can't be allowed onstation!"

"SPARTOS has been apprised of the situation, and I've got people onsite who know their business." Bové grinned. "But first let's discuss the odds . . ."

"REC says there's no reason we can't use the wardrobe jacket," Tech shouted to GoBop from the archaic comp deck they'd carried over from Felix's apartment.

"The jacket?" GoBop said, clear across the office, tools in hand. "You mean we should actually have REC wear the thing?"

"Why not?" El asked from the floor. She was down on her back, fiddling with the servos that operated the reassembled robot's legs. "I know a coupla Deceps that walk around wearing wardrobe jackets."

"But that means cannibalizing the interface chair," GoBop said, scratching at his scalp with a torx driver. "Unless these cowboys you run with are just making a fashion statement."

El looked up between the machine's tubular legs and made a face at him. "So, you like cannibalize the chair."

"Yeah, but what's going to power the system?"

"You wear a powerpack, Mario. Jeez, where you been, Bop, New Jersey or somewhere?"

"El's right," Neon said from Tech's side, his goggles in transparent mode.

" 'Cept REC says we won't have to rely on just a power-pack and storage batts," Tech cut in. "He says he can arrange for a satellite microwave feed for operation outside."

"Absolute," El said. "Give me an AI any day."

Neon smiled and elbowed his consolemate and driver. "Hear that, Tech, she prefers software to hardware."

El rolled over and raised herself on her elbows, grinning in the direction of the deck setup. "Don't worry about it, Tech. You know I think you're as artificial as the best of them."

Felix's late-night call had come in to the apartment a little over two hours before, and the four teenagers had made it over to the darkened, noxious-smelling office in record time.

It took them an hour to reassemble the robot; the rest of the time had been spent following the instructions REC issued Tech through the Network construct—now a blinding mountain dominating the Virtual's northern horizon and visible from almost anywhere on the Grid.

Felix, Jain, and Dr. Ngo were expected to arrive at any moment. The trio were out at Newark Airport trying to arrange for last-minute seats on a shuttle bound for the orbital Islands.

"I suppose it's gonna have to wear the neural coupler, too," GoBop said, surgically excising electronic components from the innards of the padded chair.

"We could like make it a belt," El suggested.

Tech made a face. "We're not asking it to vogue, El. It's just gotta get from here to Offworld."

"Only to Offworld." Neon laughed, touching a forefinger to his temple and rolling his eyes at his partner.

El stood up to contemplate their two-legged creation. "Well, the least we can do is give it a name."

"How 'bout Short Circuit, or Mr. Right?" Neon said. "One of those old movie names?"

"Screw that," Tech said. "We should call him Aldus. Koan, maybe . . ."

"Cobol," GoBop suggested.

"Uh-uh," Ellie said. "No hard master compspeak. We want something live; something that's like a little bit of Felix and a little bit of Jain." She cocked her head and smiled broadly. "The name's Jinx."

An hour later the work was completed, and Neon and El were circling Jinx with uncertain looks. Felix had phoned in an update, ordering them to get the robot out to Newark as quickly as possible.

GoBop was perched on the edge of the desk, stroking an as-yet whiskerless chin. "I don't know, guys," he was saying. "I'd slag it if I saw it coming down the street."

"Hey, don't talk about Jinx that way," El returned, going up on tiptoes to drape an arm around the robot's narrow shoulders.

It was humaniform only in the sense that it stood close to six feet tall and had two arms and two legs. The machine's pincer hands looked human enough—thanks to the fact they were now sheathed in wardrobe gloves—but the feet were mismatched and the head was much too small. The robot's vest was comprised of the most important parts of the interface chair, and the neural coupler was its belt. The face was largely goggles, with a rectangular speaker port for a mouth and microphones for ears. On its back, in addition to the battery powerpack, it carried the small radar dish and convertor REC assured them would be enough to harness the satellite microwave feed.

"I guess we could throw one of Felix's old raincoats over him," Tech said, adjusting his earbead and mike headset. He was still online with REC's construct, but wearing the control deck in a chest harness now.

"Well, I'm proud of him," El said, adolescent breasts thrust out.

GoBop hopped down off the desk to look up into Jinx's goggle eyes, hands atop the robot's shoulders. "Welcome to the real world, pal."

"Okay, REC," Tech announced into the microphone. "Your room's ready."

Everyone took a backward step as Jinx began to power up. First the goggles went active, then the head turned, thirty degrees left, thirty degrees right.

"Damn! Is he really in there?" Neon said, jumping up and down to bring his eyes level with the robot's.

Jinx struggled through a Tinman kneebend.

Jinx took a half-dozen Dr. Strangelove steps toward the airshaft window.

Jinx turned to them and said, "I can walk!"

# Chapter Twenty _____

After yet another recon swing through Newark Airport's labyrinthine network of concourses and departure gates, Felix returned to the phone booth Ngo was holding down near Thai Air's automated ticket counter. "It's no use," he said, letting the bad news show on his face as he squeezed onto the benchseat beside her. "Blair's jet's under surveillance and Offworld security is crawling all over the place. We'll be lucky to get out of New York undetected, let alone up the well." He gestured to the public vidphone screen with his chin. "What's up with REC?"

Ngo shook her head. "He disappeared. I'm guessing he went online with that robot your deckhands assembled for him."

"Let's hope." Felix leaned out of the booth to take a look around the crowded terminal. "Where's Jain?"

"She went off to see about shuttle connections from Houston. If we're not out of here within the hour, it's a lost cause."

"Why's that?"

"Because Bulkroad—" Ngo started to say when Jain, looking drawn and exhausted, made a breathless arrival.

"What's this about us having less than an hour?" Felix asked her.

She took a moment to catch her breath. "I just checked with Florida. Emeric's shuttle's launch window is at oh-four-hundred eastern standard."

Felix hit the light button on his wristwatch. It was just before two A.M.

"Florida's out," Jain continued, stifling a yawn. "But if we can make the Houston three o'clock shuttle we'll beat him—"

"No we won't," Felix said, shaking his head.

Ngo showed Jain a sad smile. "Houston's in a different time zone. When it's three there, four's come and gone on the east coast."

"Time zones?" Jain said in distress. "What next?"

Just then the vidphone screen lit up. "rec, is that you?" Ngo asked.

"It works!" the AI exclaimed. "I walked down the corridor unassisted. I looked at El, then at GoBop, then at Neon and Tech. No one had to position themselves in front of my eyes. And I heard sounds I'd never heard before: elevators, traffic noise, doors opening and closing, random sound bites of conversation . . . It's all I expected it to be. I never want to go back inside. I was born to be wild!"

"rec, listen to me," Ngo said. "We're genuinely happy for you. But we're not sure right now we'll be able to get upside."

"What's it matter when there's so much to experience right here on Earth?" the AI enthused.

Felix glanced over at Ngo and leaned toward the pickup. "What about Kaduna, rec? What about the answers you're after?"

The screen registered a change in pattern. "I had nothing to do with it, I tell ya, I wasn't even there at the time. They framed me, see, they framed me!"

"Oh, terrific, McTurk," Jain said. "You put him right back in schizoid city. fabien," she directed to the phone, "fabien, it's Jain."

The culinary AI came online momentarily. "Where on Earth have you been? You and your oranges . . . I don't recall any conversation about oranges. And now look what's happened. I've delayed the launch of our cargo shuttle—Delayed it by over an hour!"

ester's voice cut in. "You see the grief I'm getting, Jain. I've been waiting for your Mr. Blake Gales to call me back, but I haven't heard one word—not one word."

"Ask him where the cargo shuttle is," Felix said.

"fabien, where's the shuttle now?"

"In Houston, where else would it be?"

"Seats," Felix whispered.

"Do you think you could arrange for seats for me and a few friends?"

"Jain, it's a cargo shuttle, sweetie. If you've ever seen the inside of one of those—"

"Yes or no, FABIEN?"

"My, my, but aren't we bitchy this morning." The AI paused. "Of course I can arrange for seats—"

"That would constitute a violation of export regulations," Gitani's voice declared. "Cargo shuttles are off-limits to all but preassigned crew members—"

"Don't pay any attention to the man behind the screen," a third voice intoned.

Felix snorted a laugh. "That's gotta be TOR PATEL. Doesn't matter anyway," he added shaking his head. "The kids probably haven't even left the city yet. Plus we need at least an hour to get to Houston. Bulkroad's still going to beat us to Offworld hab."

Ngo saw the truth of it and cursed.

"Unless . . ." Jain began.

Felix said, "Unless what?"

She chuckled in self-amusement and turned him a grin. "Unless ESTER could arrange for an air traffic tie-up over southern Florida."

"That's the spirit," TOR PATEL cheered. "When in doubt, cut to the chase."


"It's all right," GoBop said, "he's powering up again." El looked up in time to see the goggles' standby telltale wink out.

"Welcome back," she told Jinx.

"I've been talking to Jain and Dr. Ngo," REC announced with a series of head movements. "We need to get a move on."

The five of them were in the mouth of an alley a block west of the Revlon. They'd managed to exit the building without incident—save for a moment in the lobby when one of the security guards questioned their venturing out so late—only to have Jinx wind down on them halfway down the block. Given the volume of pedestrian traffic, the alley seemed the safest bet.

"It's not going to be easy finding a cab this time of night," GoBop said, scanning the one-way street. "Maybe we should try for a heli from the Empire."

"Be real," Tech said, resetting the harnessed control deck against his chest. "Take a look at us. Would *you* give us a lift?"

"Do I look that bad?" REC asked, raising Jinx's gloved hands to the transparent goggles.

"It's not you," Neon said. "It's just that most helis don't allow hardware."

"We could go downtown," El suggested. "They're not so choosy down there."

Tech shook his head. "No way. We'll get ripped off."

"Well, we're not getting anywhere standing around here," GoBop said. "Let's at least go over to Broadway."

They left the alley, keeping Jinx to the inside of the sidewalk, away from the streetlights. Pedestrian traffic thinned as they neared the Broadway intersection, where two cabs were parked in front of an all-night Ethiopian pizza joint. They weren't fifty feet away when six Deceps stepped from the rubble of a collapsed building to surround them.

"Risk!" Eleni said, recognizing the obvious leader of the pack. He was doing the Ultraviolent tonight, complete with eye makeup, bowler hat, and knife cane. The rest of them wore loose trousers, boots, sonic vests, and headsets. A blare of angry music drifted out from beneath earbeads and foam phones. The Deceps rarely went to work on anyone without providing a soundtrack.

"Out late tonight, aren't you?" Risk said, showing filed teeth when he smiled. He appraised GoBop and the others, while two of his minions strode amused circles around Jinx. The robot rotated with them, then against them.

"What a piece of work," one of the Deceps said, his voice loud enough to be heard over the music filling his own ears. "You're escorting it to a machine masquerade, that it?"

"No need to shout, man," Neon answered. "We're not wearing music. But yeah, it's got the lead in a play, if you need to know. Very off off. This performance thing."

"Retro," a second gang member decided, straining to hear Neon over the music. "Very retro."

"I know you, right?" Risk asked Tech.

Tech gulped and nodded. "I swapped you some names for a GoSub microfiche last week."

"That was it," the leader said, and turned to El. "We've missed you, little pixel. What're these morks offering you we can't?"

"It's what they're *not* offering me, Risk," she told him. The Deceps heard the challenge in her voice and began to make low noises, gyrating to the headset sounds and encouraging a response from their leader. But all Risk said was "We need to know where the data dick is, El. Just a job, you understand."

She shrugged, feigning indifference. "Why ask me? I don't run for him."

Risk nodded and glanced at Tech. "Then I'll talk to your new protector, here. What about it, Mario—where is he?"

Tech looked to his friends for advice. GoBop was about to say something when Jinx shouted, "What station are you listening to?"

The Deceps turned to him with puzzled expressions. "What'd the thing say?" someone asked.

GoBop exchanged frowns with Tech, then looked over at Jinx in sudden realization. "He wants to know what you're listening to—like what station you've got on."

"He's into music," Neon added, while the Deceps formed a circle around the robot, touching its broadcast unit. "He sings, he dances, he tell jokes . . . He's a regular clown."

"Why's it decked out?" Risk asked suspiciously, motioning with his cane to Jinx's neural coupler and interface vest. "Maybe we got something important here, huh? Degogg the thing," he ordered.

But before a Decep hand could be laid on Jinx, a pollution alert siren went off nearby—so deafeningly close that GoBop's hands flew reflexively to his ears; his knees buckled and his heart raced. When he opened his eyes a second later, however, he realized that what he'd taken for a siren blast was some sort of high-frequency attack emitted by the Deceps' headsets. The gang members were sprawled motionlessly on the sidewalk now, Risk backing away from the scene with one hand pressed to his ear, the other gripped on the shaft of his upraised blade.

"What happened?" Neon asked, rising out of a duck-and-cover posture.

"I think Jinx just showed 'em the meaning of rock and roll," GoBop said, wondering if his ears would ever recover.

They made tracks for the one remaining taxi, Jinx thunking along behind. Gobop was waving frantically to the driver when a police cruiser settled in the middle of the street, dropping out the night's red glow, all turbine wash and vapors and flashing lights. Someone popped one of the flat-

tened teardrop's wing doors and Koo Raywing grinned at
GoBop from the shotgun seat.

"Understand you need a lift to the airport," he said, pinching his triangle of soft black beard.


Emeric, broad back pressed flat to the stainless-steel wall
of the shuttle departure lounge, waited until Bové cleared
the sliding door. The security chief came to a halt a few
steps into the room, placing his hands on his hips, and
seemed about to say something. Emeric spun him around,
took him by the lapels, and propelled him back against the
wall.

"I'm a little short of cash," Bové managed in a pained
voice.

"What do I want with your money?" Emeric snarled,
nose to nose with him.

"The bet—"

"The hell with the bet! I want to know why I'm still
sitting here when the shuttle was scheduled to lift off an
hour ago."

"No one's leaving," Bové said, smoothing the front of
his jacket as Emeric released him. He inspected a possible
split seam on one sleeve. "That's the second suit today."

"So I'll buy you a new one. Now, what the hell's going
on? Why are we grounded?"

Bové let out a slow breath. "Seems someone issued a
hurricane watch for the Caribbean."

"Hurricane? This time of year?"

"And a wind sheer alert for half the cities between Miami
and New York. Flights are stacked up twenty deep over
southern Florida alone."

"McTurk," Emeric growled, flexing his hands. "Give
me something to break!" Bové looked around for a suitable
object and decided on a lightweight plastic table. Emeric
put his foot through the thing, then hurled it against the
wall.

"Good thing you cleared the lounge," the security chief
said, glancing around.

"How, Bové? How did he do it?"

"He didn't. REC did. He's become something of a petty
dictator in the Virtual Net. Eastern Air Traffic Control shut
down their AI, but REC apparently has access to all the necessary codes."

Emeric ran a hand over his slick brow. "But that means McTurk can't get up the well either."

Bové's face wrinkled up. "Uh . . ."

"Where are they?"

"Houston. They left Newark on a charter."

"So this is Jain's idea of needing space, huh? I'll give her space, all right. Enough to take her breath away!" Emeric waved a fist. "You're telling me security couldn't stop two people from leaving that airport?"

"Eight."

"Eight?"

"We've identified the woman Jain brought to the party as Heddi Ngo."

"Jesus Christ!"

"Then there's McTurk's four kids . . ."

Emeric continued to mutter.

". . . And Koo Raywing's apparently joined them—the one from NetSec. Near as we can figure he sent the cops over to eyedee a coupla my men and McTurk and the rest slipped through."

"Fire them," Emeric said, storming about the room. "Eight people . . . Hell, they're eligible for group travel rates!"

Bové said, "Eight people and one sorry-looking robot REC's running from his construct. Damn machine always wanted legs."

Emeric regarded him for a moment, then turned his attention to the lounge time display. "What time did they leave Newark?"

"Just past three."

Emeric grinned prematurely. "Then they couldn't possibly have made the Outer Islands shuttle in time."

"They weren't trying for it. They're after one of our cargo craft—one of FABIEN's flights."

"But FABIEN's *ours*, Bové! Get him to hold the flight! Warn your people in Houston to detain them!"

"Yeah, we could do that, I suppose . . ."

Emeric looked up at him. "What's on your mind?"

"I've been thinking. Here they are moving mountains to get Offworld. But if REC told them about Kaduna, why haven't they taken the story to the news media or the authorities?"

"Because they want proof," Emeric said. "Because they're hoping they can get their hands on Thaish."

"Assuming rec even remembers Thaish. I mean, he's been out of commission for fifteen years. The alien could be dead for all he knows. rec never knew the full story to begin with; so suppose he's trying to piece it together now? Suppose there's certain things he doesn't *want* to remember?"

Emeric considered it. "What are you proposing?"

"That we let rec get onto familiar ground."

"On Offworld hab."

Bové nodded. "Then you jog his memory."

Emeric frowned. "How am I going to do that from here?"

"How long since you've paid a visit to the Network?" Bové said, cracking his knuckles as he sat down.

"I let a few bugs loose in your office Zoltec and I were up there," Koo Raywing told Felix, while they were harnessing up in the cargo shuttle. A small overhead square of quartz window revealed a lightening sky over Houston.

Jain, Ngo, and GoBop and company were doing the same on the upper-level deck, where a mixed human and robot crew were seeing to last-minute details. Everyone was nursing sore arms and behinds from the required inoculations.

"So you overheard our conversations with the kids."

"Heard them, but didn't understand a word." Raywing ran a hand over a Velcro closure. "Time to talk, McTurk— you owe me that much."

"At least that much."

Raywing indicated Jinx, who was strapping in across a narrow aisle. "Let's start with this thing."

There hadn't been much time for explanations during the charter flight from Newark—not for all of it, at any rate— so Felix caught his ex-partner up on the calls from Gitani and the runs through ESATC and ITC's AIs. He recounted the incidents in New Zealand and at the party at Caracol.

Raywing listened without interruption, and remained quiet through the cargo shuttle's launch, sunlight glinting from graphite-composite wings.

"A pie fight?" he said at last, fingering the antivert derm plastered behind his ear. "With the Group of Nine there?"

Felix snorted. "I saw Ebony Winn take one in the side of the head. Raspberry, I think."

Raywing laughed. "Could only happen to you, Mc-Turk."

Felix laughed with him, stirring up a good-old-times feeling. What with the Earth falling away overhead, levity seemed appropriate. "It's been a long time since we ran together, Ray. You miss it so much, you had to come along, is that it?"

"Like I miss third-degree burns," Raywing said. "Truth is, Felix, Zoltec's gonna chew me a new asshole when she learns about my helping you get out of New York. So I figure to go back down the well with all the answers. That suit you?"

"We could all use some answers right about now," Felix told him, glancing over at the robot who walked and talked for a resurrected AI. He thought about Jain, too, and the questions that had brought her into his life.

Jain had informed Offworld security that she was shuttling up with several important guests. She assured Felix that there would be no problems getting everyone into Offworld; that she often escorted private groups on VIP tours of the habitat. He didn't guess they had much chance of outrunning Bové, but at the same time was ready to push things as far they would go.

It was night again now, and somewhere out in the middle of it was the answer to a fifteen-year-old secret that bound all of them together.

# Chapter Twenty-one _____

Though he didn't recognize anyone or anything in the habitat's arrival module, REC knew that he was home. On Offworld, his birthplace and more.

He studied Jain Nugget through the machine's eyes while she dealt with the habitat's contagion control officers, who seemed to be treating Jain's downside guests as visiting royalty.

Jinx was exempted from the scans and examinations the humans had undergone as part of the entry procedure, but the robot had in fact been subjected to fifteen minutes of ultrasonic bombardment in the docking bay, in company with dozens of other machines and devices recently shuttled up the well.

REC didn't enjoy being grouped with kitchen appliances and service machinery, any more than he enjoyed playing the part of Felix McTurk's valet; but this was apparently the way things worked in the outside world.

There was still so much he didn't understand—the need, for example, for McTurk, Raywing, Dr. Ngo, and the four teens to adopt false identities and pretend to be the members of a private tour Jain Nugget was escorting around the habitat. She had even seen to it that the group had been outfitted in improvised costumes gathered from items of clothing found aboard the cargo shuttle: profile suits, grav boots, visored work helmets. Spacewear, as it had been explained to him, was indicative of having attained a certain cultural status and considered fashionable attire even when one wasn't aboard a craft.

REC's understanding of the imperative that had driven him to return to Offworld was equally limited. He wasn't even sure what had taken him downside to begin with; or just how much real-time had elapsed since he left his onstation residence.

Had he broken loose of something that had contained him? he wondered. Had he been ostracized, or had he fled of his own volition? He knew that something awaited him here. Whether tangible or merely informational he couldn't say; but its very existence was linked to his own. And REC sensed that without it he would once again cease to be.

The humans were relying on him to lead them to something they were all seeking; but he had no idea just what this might be.

He found that his thinking was clouded by voices—at least four different ones—which vied for his attention and flooded his mind with contradictory impulses. Even now one part of him was preoccupied with jetliner schedules; while another was unduly concerned with the unauthorized use of air-conditioning units. During the flight all he could think about was human food, its tastes and textures in unending combinations. At the same time, he wanted nothing more than to simply record his impressions of the escape from New York, the hover ride to Newark, the charter to Houston; to mix and remold the experiences into an exciting narrative of logical coherence he could offer to others as entertainment.

It took all the power of his being to sustain some semblance of psychic integrity; inside, shut off from the external world's sounds and colors, he felt shattered and diffuse.

The very fact that he was *inside something*—that his consciousness was inhabiting a self-propelled physical entity—was as frightening as it was invigorating. And yet beyond the optical and auditory gatherings of the machine's sensors, he was aware of an even more vivid reality: an internal landscape of geometrical constructs and broad highways he presided over, as if from a towering height—

Jain Nugget was suddenly calling him, looking to him for answers. Her expression was expectant. "Is there somewhere you wanted to take us, er, Jinx?" They had decided, too, not to use his real name. "Somewhere you want to go?"

He had no memories of Jain, but the name "Nugget" had meaning for him, evoking deeply troubling feelings he could not suppress.

REC commanded the robot to scan McTurk and the rest.

Felix and the one called Raywing were vigilant. The four
youths were creating a good deal of noise and touching everything in sight.

"Take your time," Dr. Ngo said. REC remembered her
lined face from long ago and recalled her kindness. "I think
we should take him into the old section of the habitat," she
told Jain. "Can you arrange it?"

"I'll send for a train," Jain replied after Felix had asked
the kids to quiet down.

They rode a magnetically levitated train into the heart of
the Island, to what some were already calling the Old City.
A 3D representation of the habitat was displayed in a real-
time map inside the first-class car. REC found most of it
unfamiliar—especially the globular modules and slender appendages that adorned the habitat's outer rim. But he recognized the core structure and, when the lead car doors
hissed open, the vast curvature of streets and buildings, the
projected suggestion of sky, the distant view to rooftops and
gardens said to be dizzying to the unaccustomed eye.

REC noticed that people were regarding him strangely,
their own machines polished, symmetrical, at ease with
themselves. Some of the robots resembled humans in their
plastiflesh features and the naturalness of their gait.

Jain had everyone transferred to a private car with tinted
windows that took them crosstown and midway up the opposite face of the city curve. The kids kept their faces
pressed to the glass, gesturing wildly.

Then REC saw it: a multilevel structure of turrets and
stairways and stained glass at the terminus of a broad tree-
lined approach . . . There was emotion attached to it, a
memory of sound and light lodged somewhere other than in
his new composite mind.

A massive sculpture occupied the front court—a platinum
reworking of the OLD corporate symbol and logo, showing
a human and a humaniform machine side by side, supporting an Earth globe on upraised arms.

This, he realized, was Emeric Bulkroad's compound.

"We'll be touring the Bechtel Wing first," Jain announced to a group of servants as they were admitted.
"Please see to it the area is cleared for our arrival." When
the attentive robots and humans had hurried off, she added,
"It might be better if some of us waited in my apartment."

"Some of us means you four," REC heard Felix tell the youths. Tech said something in return and a whispered argument broke out in the elegant hallway.

Then someone called REC by name.

He stopped to look for the source of the deep voice.

REC.

And realized all at once that the voice originated in his own mind. It wasn't any of the four that had staked claim to his thoughts, but one he recognized just the same.

REC broke connection with the outer world to meet the voice on its own terms and found someone waiting for him inside.

*"So at long last you've come back home,"* the voice admonished. *"The prodigal returned."* Fierce eyes in a bulbous face glared at him. *"For what reason? To make amends for the fifteen years of grief and misery you've caused me, or to seek redemption from the sins that drove you from this house to begin with?"*

Emeric, REC thought, feeling a surge of contradictory emotions well up inside him.

*"Project Kaduna has brought you home, is that it? You want to reopen the* Excalibur *files to determine just where you went wrong."*

The two words again—passwords to some sealed-up portion of himself. The two that embraced a mystery he could not grasp. *Excalibur*: A ship that had returned from beyond the orbit of Mars, returned with something . . . and Kaduna, the corruption of a randomly generated code, a file designation under which all things relating to the *Excalibur* were stored.

But what was this about misery and grief? What mistake had he made?

*"Perhaps it's your intention to open Kaduna up to public scrutiny, REC. But if so, let me remind you of something before you attempt to lead your new cohorts any further: You agreed to safeguard the secret. You agreed that it was knowledge that deserved careful handling. You agreed that the world wasn't ready to accept the truth.*

*"Now you're apparently having second thoughts, and you're feeling an obligation to tell all. But remember this, REC: We've kept your secret all these years.*

*"It was your decision to shut off life support to the Ex-*

*calibur—to usher in the deaths of those who wouldn't agree
to what we asked of them—"*

No! REC screamed into the Network.

*"Oh, you're wise to deny it now, REC—with the daughter
of two of the crew members you killed standing right beside.
You killed them, REC, the Nuggets and all the rest."*

He screamed again, hurling his madness across the
human-made compspace of the Grid.

Tech yanked the headset off before the worst of it reached
him. His ears hadn't fully recovered from the encounter
with Risk, and this latest assault wiped out what was left of
his auditory high end.

"What's happening to him?" Felix asked, going down on
one knee alongside GoBop and Ngo. Jinx was lying in a
heap on the floor of Jain's apartment, the interface goggles
blank as death. Felix could still hear the electronic scream
that had accompanied the robot's corridor collapse.

"This is what happened when he went online with you
guys at Newark," GoBop said.

Ngo nodded agreement. "He's gone back into the Network for some reason."

"Maybe he's having trouble keeping Emeric's shuttle
grounded," Jain suggested, glancing about concerned. She
had already waved away two robot servants who witnessed
Jinx's clangorous fall.

"Abso-fucking-lute," Tech said suddenly, obviously re-
acting to something he was seeing inside the Network. An
instant later his goggles phased over to transparent mode.
"Somebody's opened up a data conduit between REC's construct and Offworld L&D. They must be jazzing him somehow; the whole mountain's shaking!"

"Bulkroad," Ngo said. "Or Bové. Maybe the two of
them."

"But what are they after?" Felix asked.

The Asian shook her head. "It's not what they're after,
it's what they're feeding him."

"Meaning?"

"Data on the *Excalibur* would be my guess. They're
going to use REC's repressed memories to shatter him
from inside."

"SPARTOS," Koo Raywing said in disgust. "They're riding in on OLD's security AI."

"Somebody do something," Jain said, showing everyone a panicked look.

"Tech," Felix said, drawing him out of the interface. "Can you reach him? Can you talk him back?"

The teenager shook his head. "I can't even get near him. REC's whole area of the Grid is white hot."

"If we can't keep REC from Bulkroad, we have to keep Bulkroad away from REC," Raywing said. Felix looked up at him, studying his friend's face for a moment. "There's a data conduit, right," Ray added in a leading tone, "and it leads straight to Offworld."

"A two-way link," Felix said, grinning mischievously.

Raywing nodded. "Hit SPARTOS where it hurts and Bulkroad's link is broken."

"There's a comp terminal in the bedroom," Jain said.

Felix turned to Eleni. "How'd you guys get into Offworld when you ran your penetration?"

"Through an active window over at OLD's downside data dump," she told him. "But, Felix, if you've got a way in—"

"We need a way *out*, El—if you can still remember the route."

GoBop's eyes went wide. "You can't, Felix! We had a black program running that got us through the gates. You'll never make it."

Felix smiled at him affectionately. "But I'll be going the other way, Bop. I just need El to show me the route."

"I can do that, sure."

"Then let me or Neon run the jaunt, Felix," GoBop protested.

Felix stood. "Not this time, Bop."

GoBop beat him to the doorway and positioned himself there with arms outstretched. "Forget this case. Who cares about it anyway? It's just some AI, Felix. Let REC go it alone."

"He's right, Felix," Jain said from behind him. "You don't have to do this."

Felix put a hand on GoBop's arm. "Don't worry, I'll come back out in one piece." He turned to face the three other teens. "Pure procedure, right, guys?"

GoBop refused to respond to the smile, but Tech and Neon did. "Hey, Felix," El said, making a fist. "Macho meditation, man."

Felix eased past GoBop and readied himself at Jain's console. He donned gloves and neural coupler, and was about to do input at the deck when he noticed Koo Raywing slipping into the goggles he'd borrowed from Tech.

"You don't think I'm about to let you go in there alone, do you?" Ray asked, shouldering him away from the deck controls.

"Yeah," Felix said. "Like old times."

*"We had all agreed on a course of action,"* an enormous graphic of Emeric Bulkroad was telling REC from the data conduit SPARTOS had laid down from OLD's Network construct clear across the Network. Offworld's superintelligent machine was reinforcing the harassment and interdiction with images of the *Excalibur*'s former crew, lifted from both the ship's electronic log and OLD's archives.

The broad-based mountain that was REC's reconstructed self had reconfigured and showed four discrete summits, each threatening to become individual entities once more.

REC could feel the pressure mounting within him as he sought some way to counter Emeric's baleful accusations; but he had no sure recollection of the events. The *Excalibur* had borne home a secret . . . something vital to humankind and the world. REC had agreed to collate the data, to file it ultrasecret under Project KDNA. He recalled disagreement among Emeric's technical staff; dissent onboard the *Excalibur*. A decision had to be made . . . This much was true; and yet something was missing from the account . . . Try as he might, REC could not dredge the missing clue from its place of deep-seated concealment—

*"You took it upon yourself to execute the* Excalibur *crew,"* Emeric continued. *"And then—when you couldn't live with your decision—you dumped your sins and your memories. Dumped them into the very intelligences we hoped would serve you in rendering an enlightened judgment."*

"I couldn't have killed them," REC argued, insane with fear. "I could never have taken life. Life was sacred to me. The very thing I wanted most—a chance to walk about in the observable world."

*"Then it was out of envy you killed them, REC,"* Emeric said in a pitying voice. *"You killed what you couldn't possess. And you programmed your codes into other machines,*

*thinking you could escape that fact; thinking you could lose yourself among the thoughts of the world.''*

REC's mountain construct let loose a sound that shook the very neural underpinnings of the Virtual Network. Systems throughout the Grid fell prey to it and winked out, construct by construct, from CitiBank to CyberLand and beyond, suffering unimaginable losses of data and information.

This was the place his thoughts would die. All that he had become would expire here and haunt this place for an eternity, an artifact in the system, a ghostly apparition disrupting and corrupting everything it touched . . .

I have failed Emeric, REC realized, with what was to be his final thought. I have lied, I have murdered, I have betrayed my friend and father, the keenest mind any planet had created. Any universe had created—

And then REC remembered Thaish.

Felix knew the only way to succeed was to launch a strike against SPARTOS itself, even if that meant riding the data conduit directly into the blackest secrets stored in AI's heart, then suffering the fatal consequences.

There was no time for caution. Even as Felix and Raywing commenced their tandem raid against Offworld, the entire Network was distorted and reconfigured. REC's mountain fastness was transformed, heaving and buckling, loosing great slides of data into a rift that had opened up along its base. The entire construct seemed in danger of being engulfed by the Grid itself, plunged into some newly fashioned Network netherworld—a heaven or hell for machine minds that had lost their hold on reality.

Felix had a glimpse of the thing when he'd taken the plunge from Jain's near-virgin console, following Tech's advice to steer a course for the northernmost extremes of the Grid, through luminescent fog over barren wastes.

He could feel his spotter alongside him when they rocketed through the outlying gates of OLD's defensive perimeter. The gates had been growing increasingly complex since; but the security subs normally positioned to dam flows of exiting data were absent. Bulkroad's attack on REC had left Offworld wide open to penetration.

These were different routes from those Felix and Koo Raywing had run five years before, when they'd broken in to write a policy change that would have covered the costs of Tanika's desperately needed treatments. Felix had always hoped a chance would come to even up the score with Simon Bové . . .

Up ahead, he could see the terminus of the data conduit; but this wouldn't be the end of the line. No, what he needed to do now was dazzle the memory resident at the final gate; to go even deeper into the smart machine's cyber systemry and make a grab for the gold. Somewhere inside was the clue to the mystery itself—to just what it was REC was seeking on Offworld habitat.

Properly executed, the jaunt would compel SPARTOS to launch a deadly counteroffensive. The trick was to make himself known, but live to tell about it.

At Raywing's prompt, he initiated his dive, the core material directly below him.

And all hell broke loose.

The AI reacted to the intrusion with a shockwave Felix experienced with every muscle fiber of his being. The intelligence was certain it had him in its grip as he tore for the data conduit, pain and more in close pursuit. But just short of the construct egress he dove for El's escape window and hit his breakpoints, while the shockwave continued down the conduit, scouring everything in its path.

*Thaish*, REC's mind screamed.

Emeric was lying.

Yes, they had included him in the secret and tried to make him accountable for what became of the *Excalibur* crew. But REC knew that he was innocent of any complicity in those events. He had refused to keep their secret, and he had migrated from the system *before* the directives had been carried out.

*Before his own murder had been carried out.*

He had fooled them, and used the very tools they had given him to make secure his escape. He had written a timeline for his reemergence, and in so doing he had masterminded his own resurrection.

REC saw all of it clearly now. The ship's return, the interviews with Thaish, Emeric's efforts to coerce him into safeguarding KDNA's secrets, the lies he had been obliged to tell to Ngo and the others, the very self-dissolution he had engineered.

But he was free, free of all it now, save for one final stroke of revenge.

The rift in the Network Grid healed and the mountain recoalesced. Blinding once more, the energy it loosed against Bulkroad struck the terminus of OLD's data conduit at the same moment SPARTOS's shockwave arrived.

In the shuttle port control center where Simon Bové had set up the taunting jaunt, the wrath of the combined intelligences surged through the cyber system's interface adaptors and connectors. The raw power leaped on Bové at the console where he was driving and sent him careening backward against the hardened wall of the control room with the force of an explosion.

Emeric wasn't as lucky. Confining itself to the goggles, the vengeful energy that had ragdolled Bové sent a searing, neural brightness straight into Emeric's eyeballs and down along his optic path, frying cells and fusing gateways from one end to the other.

The speed of light, it seemed at the time, was not likely to trouble Emeric Bulkroad again.

# Chapter Twenty-two ──────

The Network encounter between REC and SPARTOS had addled electronic surveillance and security throughout the habitat. Within the plastic and ceramic walls of Bulkroad's mazelike compound, robot guards were wandering about in a daze, pursued by their befuddled human supervisors. Surveillance cams and broad-spectrum detectors were down; hatches were hissing open and sliding to with apparent willfulness.

Jain, still playing the escort to Felix's anything but dignified-looking group of downside, spacewear tourists, used her command voice on those few machine and human servants who hadn't been affected, and in short order had everyone into Emeric's wing of the compound.

A reenergized Jinx continued to attract attention, but no one questioned them.

Jain took them the long way around to avoid passing SPARTOS's onstation residence. From the far end of the corridor that led to the AI's climate-controlled room, Felix observed a dozen cyberneticians engaged in a frenzied dance at the hatchway.

"That used to be my room," REC told him through Jinx's buzzing vocal annunciator.

Things didn't get physical until they found themselves approaching the entrance to a restricted elevator, which serviced a fingerlike extension of the compound's laboratory facilities. The module was a denied area, even to Jain, who had always assumed it was where Emeric's wizards conducted their research.

REC, maintaining a Network stranglehold on SPARTOS, had access to the necessary authorization codes, but nothing short of old-fashioned headbanging worked on the human guards stationed at the elevator. Once inside, there were only robots to deal with, and it became apparent that Bulk-road's dark secret wasn't meant to be viewed by human eyes. Jinx was being especially closed-mouth on the subject.

Just now, having come about as far down the finger as it was possible to go, the nine of them were standing before an airlock hatch flashing special atmosphere and lessened grav-ity warning displays. At the prompt of a pressure-activated sensor, a robot sentry appeared to reinforce the warning ver-bally and issue operating instructions for the airlock itself.

Dr. Ngo, Jain, and the kids seemed to be handling the lessened gravity without problem, but Felix and Raywing were both sick by the time they finished cycling through the first stage of the lock. Here, in a kind of observation booth, were environment suits, Velcro boots, and breathers for three. Raywing agreed to remain behind with the kids.

Jain, Felix, Ngo, and Jinx cycled through the final lock and emerged light-headed and high-stepping in the finger's tip—a sunlight-flooded oblong room with little in the way of furniture or human conveniences, save for two harness chairs, a small telecomp table, and a state-of-the-art video wall. Beneath the cabin's trapezoidal and triangular win-dows, hung dozens of transparent spheres and clusters linked to one another by an elaborate network of equally clear transfer tubes.

It was Ngo who first spotted the creature in the uppermost sphere: a human-size froglike thing with huge black eyes, pointed ears, and suction-cupped toes and fingertips.

"What is that thing, McTurk?" Raywing asked over the observation booth's intercom.

"Genetic manipulation," Felix ventured, revulsed by the thought. "That's what Bulkroad's been hiding. The *Excal-ibur* probably didn't go anywhere near the asteroids. They were using it as a research ship and some experiment got out of hand. There's your virus."

"You're wrong, Felix," Ngo said, one hand pressed to the transpirator. "I think we're looking at an alien life-form."

Jain said, "I like Heddi's explanation, Felix. I think it's an alien."

"I could say the same about you, thanks," Thaish said in English, to everyone's astonishment. Felix began to feel sick all over again.

"Jain, Felix, Dr. Ngo," Jinx said in a cheery tone, "I want you to meet Thaish."

"Thaish?" Jain managed in a hoarse whisper.

"Thaish is Heregep. It was his ship the *Excalibur* discovered fifteen years ago. Thaish alone survived the encounter."

Jinx took a few awkward hops into the room. "This has been Emeric's secret. He told me then he feared that humankind would be traumatized by the disclosure. But his real purpose was to decipher Heregep technosystems in order to secure a financial future for Offworld Lifting and Development. And judging by the advancements in Machine Mind and orbital travel I've seen during these past twenty-four hours, I'd say he succeeded."

Thaish had gone up on reverse-articulated legs and was listening carefully. "Who's the smart machine?" he asked at last. "And how does it come to know so much about Emeric Bulkroad?"

REC had Jinx gaze up at Thaish's sphere. "The last time we met I spoke to you from a wall of instruments," he began. "And in your own language besides."

Thaish pressed blue antennae and full, gold-colored lips to the base of the sphere.

"I'm REC—in here," Jinx continued, raising a gloved hand to the goggles. "And I've come back to release you."

On their way out of the finger, Raywing thought to liberate a stungun from one of the human guards they'd left duct-taped in a storage closet near the elevator.

Thaish had explained that the Heregep lightsail vessel—the one he referred to as *Ship Nasst*—had been towed in from the asteroid 2008FC and was now parked in stationary orbit on the far side of the moon.

Felix had decided not to question REC's rescue plan. Assuming they could get the alien off-station without being killed, then sure, they could see him back to a lightsail ship parked a hundred thousand miles away.

The little alien was masked now, walking upright and breathing from a tank. Well, hopping really, on four-toed feet the color of cold chicken skin. It was outfitted in a form-fitting body suit that left little more than hands, feet, and large-earred fish-face exposed.

Felix could only marvel at the whole arrangement. Four

teenage kids who couldn't keep their hands to themselves, a silver-haired scientist who worked with glowworms, a rogue NetSec lieutenant, a would-be telecomp star, a clumsy robot fronting for an artifical intelligence, an alien cyborg whose face could stop a hover, and a data dick who should have known better . . . making their way through the orbital domain of one of the planet's wealthiest and most influential corporate giants.

Like they didn't have a care in the world.

*What's anyone going to say?* Jain had asked when she proposed the idea of simply walking out. *You think they're going to be more weirded out by Thaish than by Jinx?*

Felix got the point. It wasn't as if anyone had ever seen an alien. So maybe they'd just think Thaish was a slouched-over kid with bad skin, sporting a plastiflesh mask.


Part one of the plan entailed the hijacking of one of Offworld's lunar shuttles. Jain led the way to the launch center and chose Felix to accompany her up into the glass-enclosed control station.

Inside, a frazzled-looking Offworld executive was reading the riot act to a roomful of uniformed techs. The ship Jain and REC had their eyes on—more fast-orbiter than shuttle-craft—was drydocked in a bay below the station.

"You *what*?" the exec asked, after Jain had given him what Felix thought was too brief a summary of her request.

"That's right, Mr. . . . Tamm," she said, reading from the tall man's namebadge. "These people are personal guests of Emeric Bulkroad, and it's Mr. Bulkroad's wish that they be taken on a tour of Offworld's circumlunar station—*now*. Am I making myself understood, or do I have to have to contact Mr. Bulkroad and inform him that Mr. Juri Tamm has other plans for the craft?"

Felix feigned nonchalance as he glanced about the control room, refusing to meet Tamm's narrowed eyes.

"And this, I take it, is one of Mr. Bulkroad's guests?" the exec said even-toned, gesturing to Felix.

"He is indeed," Jain replied, indignant. "Tell him."

Felix looked at her, then grinned at Tamm. "I'm very important," he managed.

Tamm snorted a derisive laugh, moved to the nearest phone, and entered a long numerical code. "Sorry, Ms.

Nugget, but I think I'll just take my chances with Mr. Bulk-road on this one.''

Jain sent him her most dangerous look. ''That's your final word?''

''It is.''

''Then I'm afraid we're just going to have to pirate the ship, Mr. Tamm.''

Felix already had the stungun out and pressed to the man's temple. ''How d'you feel about brain damage?'' he asked in the toughest voice he could summon.

Tamm's eyes expanded to twice normal size. A quick look around the room told Felix that most of the techs would just as soon see their exec take one to the forebrain.

Tamm said, ''You can't really expect to get away with this.''

''Having you along will help some,'' Jain told him.

''But the ship doesn't even have a crew standing by!'' Tamm returned. ''Just who do you think's going to pilot the thing?''

''He is,'' Felix said, jerking a thumb at Thaish as Koo Raywing shoved him through the control room door.

''Let me drive, you said,'' Emeric told Bové. ''Think how much more *effective* it'll be if REC hears from you personally . . . Oh, how very effective, Bové. Remind me to thank you *when I see you again.*''

''I blame myself,'' Bové said, sincere about it.

''That makes *two* of us, you asshole.''

Bové winced. ''At least let me try to make it up to you.''

''Then get me Jain and McTurk! I want their entrails spread out where I can look at them.''

The two were in Emeric's quarters aboard his personal shuttle, being attended to by a team of medical personnel. Bové was wearing the surgical skullcap he'd been fitted for in Florida before liftoff; Bulkroad the optical prosthesis that allowed him to differentiate between light and dark. His eyes had been removed and ice-olated, in the event that detail and color could be returned to him in the coming decade.

The physician in charge—a surgeon flown in from To-kyo—thought that more might have been done had Emeric not been in such a rush to get up the well. Weightlessness was putting severe limitations on the woman's postop efforts.

Emeric heard someone float into the cabinspace from the forward compartment and turned to the sound. "Who is it, and what is it?"

"Magundi, Mr. Bulkroad," the man announced in a high voice. "From communications." Bové silently motioned for Magundi to show him the hard-copy message he'd entered with.

"Bové can wait," Emeric announced suddenly, taking everyone by surprise. "I'm not certain he still works for me."

"Mr. Bulkroad—" the surgeon began, pronouncing it Bulkload.

"No, Doctor, I can't see. But I know Bové like I know my own darkness. Now what's the message?"

Magundi stammered, "We just received word from Offworld hab that McTurk, Ms. Nugget, and several others have hijacked a supply ship. Apparently a hostage situation, although they've yet to issue any demands. They were originally believed to be heading for the Offworld's circumlunar station, but their destination now appears to be darkside."

"What else, Magundi?" Emeric asked, sensing what was coming.

"Uh, McTurk and Ms. Nugget are said to be traveling in the company of a robot wearing a power dish and a . . . a big-eared kid in a frog costume. Or a very large frog in a kid's costume. The control room staff who surrendered the ship can't seem to agree."

"Yes"—Emeric sighed, glancing in Bové's direction—"they've got him. But can they get to that ship, Bové?"

Bové didn't respond immediately. "If they nabbed our boy, stands to reason they've got access to the authorization codes."

"REC, again."

"My guess."

"Two ships are in pursuit of the hijacked craft, Mr. Bulkroad," Magundi said on a hopeful note.

"Tell them I don't care about the hostages. Order them to fire on that ship as soon as they have it in range."

Bové noticed the surgeon stiffen slightly.

"We can have a chase ship standing by to meet the shuttle," Magundi added after an audible swallow.

"Misa Bulkload," the surgeon said, "I would uhge you to—"

"File it, Doctor," Emeric told her. "Can we overtake them, that's all I want to know."

"Yes, sir, we can, sir."

"Then order the chase ship prepped." Emeric gently fingertipped the prosthesis. "The dumb leading the blind, Bové," he said after a moment.

"How things have changed," Bové muttered, completely unaware of any meaning in his remark.


Thaish's feet knew all there was to know about the Offworld ship, and REC had all the codes to make the right things happen.

The alien maintained that he was to be credited with the craft's present design, which had involved a substantial reworking of the original engineering. REC, Thaish volunteered, was correct about Emeric Bulkroad's motives; and for the fifteen years Thaish had remained in captivity, Bulkroad had sought his approval on all aspects of Offworld technology.

It had taken half that time for Thaish to so much as offer an opinion; but confinement had eventually eroded his intent to remain silent, and little by little he had imparted bits of his superior technical understanding.

The meetings with Bulkroad had even afforded him some amusement, inasmuch as he was looked upon as something of a lost cause among his own node peers.

GoBop and company, Ngo, and Jinx—cabled into the ship's onboard astrogational intelligence—hung on the alien's every word. Felix shuddered to think what the four teens might do with the knowledge once they got back to New York. Of course, there were a good dozen *if*s hovering in the ship's recirculated air, the first of which began: *If* they could make it to darkside station; the last of which ended: *If* they ever saw Earth again.

The *if*s in between ran to concerns about Offworld's pursuit ships, darkside station, and the condition of the alien lightsail vessel itself.

The supply ship was behind the moon now, after some forty hours in flight. Felix and Raywing, along with several of the hostages—Tamm included—had passed most of the trip sick as dogs, down with space adaptation syndrome.

When his inner ear allowed, Felix spent his time with Jain, who was feeling distressed for reasons that had little to do with gravity in the physical sense.

Thaish remembered Clay and Larissa Nugget, but could offer no word on what had become of them.

It seemed certain now that the *Excalibur* thirty-three had been killed because they wouldn't acquiesce to Emeric's security demands. Jain, recalling the dozens of deaths that had plagued Offworld the past decade, wondered how many other names had been added to the list as time went on.

She told Felix she was glad about the way things had worked out for REC and Thaish; but it was plain to him that Jain felt somehow shortchanged by fate. That while the question that lured her into the quest had been answered, the central fact remained unchanged. In a sense it hardly mattered that Emeric Bulkroad had loosed the virus that killed the crew; the point was that her parents were dead.

Not everyone could feel cleansed by exacting revenge, Felix realized, reassessing his own state of mind while Jain had cried in his arms.

# Chapter Twenty-three ⸺

"Burst transmission from Darkside Station, sir," a young male tech reported, propelling himself into the chase ship's executive lounge like one happy soldier.

Emeric swiveled around from the forward-looking observation windows to face him, the sleeves of his jumpsuit Velcroed to the arms of the chair. Eyeless though he might be, Emeric was beginning to feel like the commander of a warship, and he enjoyed the feeling. In fact, he thought, all that was probably lacking in the young tech's weightless pose was the salute.

"Make your report," he said.

"Darkside reports that it has the supply ship in range. The station chief asks whether you have any preference with regard to weaponry."

Emeric adopted an indecisive frown. "What are our options?"

Bové spoke to it from somewhere near the lounge's thick windows. "I believe the station's equipped with both a particle-beam weapon and a railgun. Am I right?"

"Yes, sir," the tech answered uncertainly. "But the station chief suggests there might be ways to incapacitate the ship without destroying it."

Emeric drummed his fingers and swiveled forward again. "What do you think, Bové?"

"I say burn it."

"Waste an entire supply ship? Kill a dozen or more people? Give ourselves yet another secret to safeguard?"

Bové grunted. "You're always telling me it's only money. Besides"—he grinned—"we can always find you another green-eyed singer, huh?"

Emeric waved a hand without disturbing the Velcro sleeve

seal. "I was thinking more about the alien than the 'singer.' "

"But hell, we've got a whole shipful of them, don't we? Aliens, I mean. We'll just have to try to defrost one of them."

Emeric fell silent for a moment. "What did you say?"

Bové wondered if he'd been too cavalier about Jain Nugget. "About what?"

"About the aliens."

"Only that we could try to turn the heat on, wake some of them up."

Emeric thought for a minute. "Direct the station chief that he is not, repeat *not* to fire until he has my personal command to do so," he said, turning to the tech.

"Not to fire, sir?"

"Furthermore, he is to allow the hijackers full access to the alien ship."

Bové advanced on the chair in Velcro booties. "I lost you somewhere."

Emeric grinned up at him. "Consider for a moment: For fifteen years all I've wanted was a shot at talking to *Ship Nasst*'s commanders about the vessel's FTL drives. Now, according to Thaish, the drives are disabled; but here he comes suddenly, obviously planning some dramatic escape."

"So," Bové said, "he'll deanimate and join the rest of them. That's as good an escape as any the way he's got it figured. He's wanted that all along."

"Then all we're out is one live alien. And we'll have McTurk and Jain to vent our anger on. But suppose for a moment Thaish has been lying to us? How do we know he won't wake up the crew and try to effect a repair of the drives?"

"I guess we don't. But, okay, let's figure he does what you say. Then what?"

"*Then* we cripple the ship. While the crew's wide awake and the technosystems are online."

"I'm grinning," Bové said, meaning it. "I love it."

"Instruct the chase ships and station to stand by," Emeric told the tech, the deep-voiced commander now. "And make ready my personal boat. Mr. Bové and I plan to aboard that alien ship when the crew is revived."

\* \* \*

232                                      Jack McKinney

"I don't like it," Felix said, when Darkside Station issued them with an approach go-to for *Ship Nasst*.

From the supply ship's bridge, Offworld's research station was a spinning torus in the foreground; beyond it, concealed inside a huge, thin-skinned alloy sphere impressed with OLD's construction logo, was the Heregep ship.

"They chase us here from Offworld hab, now they suddenly give us guidance instructions. What are they up to?"

"Well, you didn't expect them to fire on us, did you, McTurk?" Ngo asked.

"Yeah," Felix told her. "I did, and I still do."

"What will happen to all of you—after, I mean?" Thaish asked from atop the control console. Ngo and the kids regarded one another, then looked as a group at Jinx, Felix, Jain, and finally turned to Koo Raywing.

"Hey, this is totally out of NetSec's hands," Ray said, allowing his arms to float free. "I calculate Offworld can charge us with trespassing, breaking and entering, willful destruction of private property, kidnapping, and skyjacking. Aside from that we're in the clear."

"Time flies," GoBop said, putting a smile on it. "We'll be out by the turn of the next century."

"I wouldn't've passed on it," Tech said, receiving reinforcement from Neon and El.

Jain smirked. "A fine job you've done with these four, Felix. You should feel proud of yourself."

"Christ," he muttered, "I've turned them into felons."

Thaish studied them for a moment. "All this . . . for me. Just so I can rejoin my ship. I don't understand."

"It's what humans do best," REC/Jinx said, hovering overhead. "When they're thinking clearly."

The supply ship wormed its way into the artificial bubble Offworld's engineers had erected around the alien vessel. The ship's inexperienced pirate crew got a navigation assist from some of the hostages, half of whom took the station-issued guidance codes as sign that an accommodation had been reached between OLD and the hijackers, while the rest simply wanted a second look at Thaish.

Floodlit by arrays of lamps positioned around the interior of the sphere, *Ship Nasst* appeared reasonably intact, from its pyramidal lightsail to the twin drives that flew like rigid outsize flags from its blunt stern.

Thaish directed the supply ship to sidle up to a human-made docking bridge affixed to *Ship Nasst*'s horseshoe-crab–shaped drive center, where Felix and GoBop and company debarked. Jinx, Jain, and Ngo rode an EVA pod to a second human-made object stalked to the vessel's ventral surface, which the doctor thought might be a substation for Offworld research techs.

The *Ship Nasst* contingent were outfitted in full suits and rebreathers against both the cold and the atmosphere. By then Felix was used to null-gee, but still couldn't get the hang of it. Tech, Neon, and El didn't even bother to try.

There was no making sense of the ship's interior. OLD, after all, had had fifteen years to study the ship and had come away with scarcely more than *ideas*—although it was obvious that entire sections of *Ship Nasst* had been disassembled and presumably spirited off to Offworld's research labs.

Thaish took them on a quick tour through the decks OLD's technicians had equipped with lights, identifying featureless areas of bulkhead and decking as control consoles. Felix asked about the six upright and circularly arranged tubes they passed.

"These are for the Drive Masters," Thaish explained in an offhand tone.

"But what about those like cocoon things inside them?" Eleni wanted to know.

Thaish scanned the five energy globes affixed to the sides of the interface cylinders. "Those *are* the Drive Masters," he said after a moment.

The translucent cocoons dotted all parts of the ship, but seemed to be concentrated in the docking bay. It wasn't, however, until Thaish began to refer to some of them by name—Barish, Engineer Tcud, Inheritor Major Nasst—that Felix and the four kids understood them to be *Ship Nasst*'s crew—the alien's deanimate node peers, arbitrators, and commanders.

Felix was wondering just when Thaish planned to join them in their torporous condition, and was already thinking ahead to his next move—which would be to encourage everyone to surrender—when Raywing entered the cabinspace to say that Offworld's chase ships were closing on the construction bubble.

"You better do whatever it is you're going to do, Thaish,"

Felix said. "Bulkroad's gonna be breathing down our necks in about thirty minutes."

"Hey, Thaish, you mind if we watch?" Tech and Neon asked at the same time. The alien directed an approximation of a grin their way.

But instead of deanimating, Thaish commenced a kind of sucker-toed tap dance on the deck, bringing illumination and the power hum of unseen devices to the central portion of the ship. Blue light fanned from concealed ceiling ports, washing down on the cocooned XTs. Thaish varied his dance on the instrumentality mat and the light lengthened toward ultraviolet. Felix and his deckhands pressed their hands to their ears as the color prompts' accompanying audio tone modulated to a high-pitched screech.

When both the light and sound were beyond the range of human senses, the cocoons began to fade. Animate once more, Thaish's Station Six node peers took one look at Felix, GoBop, and the rest, shrieked, and instantly returned to torpor.


The hatch to the small red-lit module stalked to *Ship Nasst*'s belly was stenciled with warning trefoils. "What do they mean?" Ngo asked one of the hostages, trying her best to sound tough.

"Cryogenics," the man said. "For all I know this is where the rest of those fishfaces are being stored."

"Then we shouldn't go in," Jinx said in a worried voice. "I'm recalling something . . . about a derelict ship filled with all these egglike growth pods. A human was attempting to study one of the pods up close and this *thing*, this monstrosity insinuated itself into the man's esophagus. Later it hatched—during dinner, I believe—and—"

"REC," Ngo interrupted. "What are you babbling about?"

Jinx's head swiveled through a slow turn. "Maybe I only imagined it, Doctor."

"You or someone," she told him.

Ngo and Jain cycled through the lock and found themselves inside a cramped hold double-stacked along both sides with some fifty liquid-nitrogen dewar coffins. An unnamed semisentient AI presided over a staff of three humaniform robots, who were decomped in machine niches astern. Jinx engaged the AI in conversation while Ngo approached the nearest coffin and called up the occupant's name on a small screen inset in the dewar's rounded, stainless-steel lid.

"Katz, Joseph," she read.

Jain brought a gloved hand to the faceplate of her helmet. "Katz was on Offworld's board of directors."

"As was Magnus Torrel," Ngo said from the foot of a second coffin. "And I suspect we'll find Yi Ding and Goody Thorsten as well."

Jain gazed down the length of the red-lit hold. "This must be Offworld's cryo-vault—for Em's friends and business associates."

"Friends." Heddi snorted into her helmet mike. "Let's just see who else was lucky enough to find a place in here." She moved four coffins down the line and did input at the keypad. "Mica Nidell. Is that a name you recognize, Jain? Jain?"

Jain stared at her, seemingly welded to the aisle, arms at her sides, grav boots pigeon-toed. "Mica Nidell," Jinx was saying. "I know that name. A communications officer on the *Excalibur*."

Ngo began to hurry from dewar to dewar, entering a flurry of commands at each keypad. Jain saw her fall back from one coffin and rushed to her side. The name LARISSA NUGGET was pulsing from the display. Clay Nugget was in the adjacent coffin.

Heddi Ngo thought Jain might be the one to faint, but it was Jinx who did an end-over-end drift toward the module's upside. She hauled him down by a foot while Jain was sobbing, hugging the cool lid of the chamber.

Ngo and Jinx completed a quick inventory of the coffins— discovering one for each of the thirty-three of *Excalibur*'s mutinous members. Heddi convinced Jain to bear with the situation and leave the chambers undisturbed for the time being. There was still no proof the thirty-three hadn't been exposed to a deadly virus—either through initial contact with Thaish, or long-term contact with Emeric Bulkroad.

In *Ship Nasst*, meanwhile, Thaish was busy trying to convince his peers that it was safe for them to assume animate form. Most of the XT command crew were already reanimate, including Inheritor Nasst himself, who was cowering in a corner of the drive center, unwilling to make contact with any of the humans.

"They're not comfortable with you," Thaish explained, while GoBop and the rest were gathering round the frightened crew making *Close Encounter* jokes.

"Where's all the angelic music?" Neon wanted to know. "The white light, the Big Spiel."

Tech sang: "Da, de, dum, *dum, dah!*" and a dozen of Thaish's node peers deanimated.

Felix grabbed Tech and Neon by the backs of their suits and yanked them away from the frightened XTs. A group of spindly armed creatures suctioned to the ceiling said something to Inheritor Nasst that left the commander shivering in place. Thaish aimed a scolding look at the creatures, but they only seemed to laugh the harder for it.

"The monitors were the ones that got us into this predicament to begin with," Thaish said to Felix. "Now they're telling Inheritor Nasst I have doomed the ship by bringing you here."

"Tell them bigger trouble's on the way if they don't get their act together, Thaish. Tell 'em what you've been doing for the past fifteen years."

"You have to choose one of us to take with you!" Tech said. "It's an Earth custom!"

"The hell it is," Felix shouted. "Just get yourselves out of here, Thaish, before it's too late."

"But can the ship even power up?" GoBop gestured broadly to the disassembled systemry. "Looks like Bulkroad's techs didn't leave you much to work with."

A glance around the cabinspace told Felix that some of the ship's remaining systems had been brought online but none of the crew members were assuming their stations. "Are the superluminal drives functional, Thaish? The FTL?"

"Unfortunately not," Thaish said. "For that we may need to bleed power from the nuclear furnaces of your supply ship."

"The onboard pilot estimates fifteen minutes till arrival," Simon Bové told Emeric in the elegant command cabin of the chairman's private boat. "The bubble's onscreen. Too bad, uh, you can't see it."

"I don't need to see it, Bové. I can imagine it clear enough. Just tell me if Thaish has that ship online."

"The remote cams aren't working, but the computer's telling us there's major activity inside."

"I knew it!" Emeric said, rubbing his hands together. "He woke up his crew." He swiveled his chair in Bové's direction. "Inform our chase ships to target the ship at the first sign of movement. But make certain they understand they're only to disable it, not destroy it."

Bové put a hand on the send-stud, but held back a moment. "Maybe we want to retro some, Mr. B. Don't want to be caught up in a crossfire after all this."

Emeric made a plosive sound. "No, of course not. Tell our commanders to hold fire until I've had a chance to confer with the alien commanders. Perhaps I'll be able to talk some sense into them and save our ships the trouble of an attack."

"But the ship's been cannibalized, Node Thaish! Just how do you expect us to make a departure?" Inheritor Major Nasst was firm-voiced but his glower was inconstant. Engineer Tcud and Arbitrator Ranz stood slightly behind him, eyeballing the humans in awe.

"Doom!" the monitors keened. "Thaish has doomed all of us!"

Nasst stomped his feet on the deck. "The first one to deanimate goes directly to Realignment!" he warned, shoving Ranz forward with a forceful hand. The Arbitrator shivered for a moment before adopting appropriate posture.

"Thaish is a turncoat! Send him to Realignment!"

Station Six fought to maintain solidity while the monitors laughed. The nodes from Interface Assist, meanwhile, were trying various languages on the humans—all save Barish, Thaish's supplemental and cache-mate, who was regarding him coyly from the port bulkhead of the docking bay.

"You don't have time for this, Thaish," the human called Felix McTurk shouted. "Bulkroad's ships are closing on us. Take whatever you need from the supply ship. We can get out of here on conventional power and an SOS." The rest of the humans had joined him and the four teens: Jain, Dr. Ngo, Koo Raywing, several of the hostages, and Jinx—REC's robot functionary.

The Inheritor Major silenced the monitors and turned to Engineer Tcud. "Can we make use of that ship or not?"

"We can, Inheritor Major."

"Then begin the procedure."

"But we still lack a replacement for Ghone in the drive circle," Tcud thought to point out.

Nasst swung around to Thaish and studied him for a moment. "Confinement has altered you for the better, Node Thaish."

"I have learned the value of being attentive," Thaish told him.

"Attentive enough to assume a place in the drive circle?"

"*Noooooooooooo,*" the monitors wailed in unison.

Thaish glowered at them. "Attentive enough, Inheritor Major. Allowing that the monitors can be silenced for the duration of *Ship Nasst*'s jaunt."

"Done," Nasst said, as the monitors began to scurry for cover.

"Point and game," Thaish muttered to his suddenly smiling node peers.

Nasst and the command crew left the docking bay in a rush; the humans were slower to depart, waiting, or so it appeared, for the fulfillment of some sort of departure ritual. But they, too, hurried off after a bit of hand-waving and well-wishing. Only Jinx lingered.

"One of the teenagers mentioned an Earth custom of choosing someone to take along," Thaish said leadingly.

The robot nodded. "Unhappily, my mind resides in the Network, Thaish. Even now I'm at my outer limits. But at least I have known what it is like to move about in the world."

"And to right old wrongs."

"A consequence of remembering who and what I was."

Thaish smiled. "Fifteen years ago you told me that you were more Heregep than human. You've proven yourself, REC."

Jinx took a moment to absorb it. "So now *Ship Nasst* will complete its jaunt. And what about the FTL, Thaish, Emeric Bulkroad's grail for our plagued planet?"

Thaish's fishlike head shook. "It was never mine to give. But who can tell, perhaps the Heregep will return one day. Deliberately next time. Perhaps by then you'll have taught your creators a few things about human beings."

Emeric's private craft was jetting into the bubble just as the debilitated supply ship was drifting out on reserve power.

"You're too late," Felix was saying after Bové had raised them on the commo screen. "The Heregep're outta here."

"But they can't!" Emeric screamed from the background. He was wearing some sort of optical prosthesis. "Thaish told me that ship had no power!"

"Ah, they just needed a jump start," GoBop said over Felix's shoulder.

"They can't! They can't!" Emeric continued, blindly punching buttons on the craft's communications console. Bové leaned out of the screen to lend a hand in raising *Ship Nasst*.

As Felix watched the madness taking place onscreen, he thought that he would never forget his last look back at Thaish, the approximation of a smile on the alien's thick lips as Inheritor Major Nasst insisted that he stand in for the ship's expired Drive Master.

The cryogenic module had been severed from its stalk and was now inside the supply ship's cargo hold with all fifty-six deanimates in the same undisturbed state of torpor.

"Inheritor Major Nasst, listen to me," Emeric was saying, "it's not like I'm a bad person. I left your shipmates alone all these years, didn't I? And I didn't kill any of the *Excalibur* crew, I just put everyone on ice for a while. I had to be sure everyone on Earth was prepared, you can understand that. Why, we're as prone to deanimating as the Heregep are, and what's worse than a whole planet full of stiffs, Inheritor Major?" He paused, but there was no response from *Ship Nasst*.

"Nasst, for God's sake, can't we at least talk about it?"

"The alien ship's powering up," one of the former hostages told Felix with a rough tap on the shoulder. "Offworld chase ships have the alien vessel targeted. We're going to use our remaining fuel in a quick burn, so get yourself strapped in and don't be surprised if you see a mist of blood in front of your face when you come to."

"What about them?" Felix said, gesturing to the two gesticulating figures onscreen.

"Mr. Bulkroad, sir," the Offworld captain directed toward the console pickup. "Chase ship commanders report that they have the alien vessel targeted and are awaiting your instructions. May I recommend, sir, that your boat maintain a safe distance from the alien vessel."

"Who said that?" Emeric said, gazing about the cabin-space of his craft.

"A captain on the supply ship," Bové explained. "They're warning us away from the bubble. They've got the right idea—"

"Warning us away! Fire that officer! Fire the entire crew of that ship." He swung about in his chair. "Thaish? Are you still there, Thaish? We've got to talk, pal, we got to talk."

"Bulkroad's boat's directly in the line of fire," a second crewman reported. "The gunners can't get off a clean shot and that damn ship's going to jump!"

The captain started to say something but Jain—harnessed behind Felix and Ngo on the acceleration couch—cut him off. "Let him be," she said, muting the audio feed to Emeric's ship.

The officer showed her a crazed look. "But there's no telling what'll happen if they're too close to that ship when it jumps."

"With luck," Jain said, "Emeric will have his FTL wish."

Felix turned to a peripheral monitor in time to see Emeric's craft disappear inside the bubble.

"No more talk of miracle cures for planet Earth," Jinx said quietly. "From here on in we go at our problems alone."

The supply ship was some one thousand kilometers out when *Ship Nasst* jumped. When Felix looked again, the bubble and all it contained had vanished from real-time.

"What was that last transmission from Bulkroad's boat?" the captain asked.

The crewman shrugged at his station. "Sounded to me like Mr. Bulkroad and Mr. Bové were betting on something."

# Epilogue:
# Counter-encounter

# Chapter Twenty-four _____

Felix had called the volume up to maximum on the tele-comp monitor, but even then he was having trouble hearing Lani Randall's report over the noise level in the office. The carpenters were back from a two-hour lunch break and had their power saws and epoxy guns running; and the kids were raucously online with the new cyber system—a VES 4400SX. Crates and packing filled most of the walk-in closet and half the back room. Felix had a small area to himself near the door to the adjoining room, squeezed between the watercooler and a precariously balanced stack of hard-copy file drawers.

He leaned toward the monitor speaker to catch Randall's summation, and heard ". . . remains unavailable for comment." The ITC news anchor was wearing serpent-patterned stockings and red high heels today.

Felix muted the audio feed as Heddi Ngo came through the door with lunch—chocolate-sauce noodles and coffee for Felix, a vegemite sandwich for herself, all of it packaged in designer plastic, imprinted with advertising slogans.

"Yours," she yelled, wrinkling her nose after a quick peek into Felix's carton, "and mine." She repositioned the office fans and trays of ice before pulling a second chair up to the desk. "I don't know how much more of this I'm going to be able to stand, Felix."

"The noise?" he shouted.

She shook her head, squinting. "The heat! New York! This . . . *food*," she said, gesturing. "All of it!" With a broad sweep to include the kids, the carpenters, the drop-cloths, dust, and general pandemonium.

Felix showed her an understanding smile. "Give it another week or so. If things don't work out, we pack up and

243

go live with the glowworms, deal? We open a concession
stand selling mangoade or something.''

She grinned her dark-eyed Asian grin and nodded.
''They've finished with the door,'' she said around a mouth
ful of vegemite paste and wholewheat bread. ''Want to take
a look-see?''

Felix pickup up his meal and plasticware and followed
her into the front room, closing the door behind him. The
glass panel in the office door now read: MCTURK, RAYWING,
AND NGO.

''I like it,'' he told her. ''Better than lasering names *off*
a door, huh?''

''Any day,'' Ngo said, cleaning places for herself and
Felix at her temporary workstation. ''Ray called. He said
to tell you he has another day or two of NetSec catch-up
work to complete, then he'll be ready to move his things
over.''

Felix contemplated the noise for a moment. ''I hope we're
ready for him. This place is getting pretty crowded.''

''The job foreman promised they'd have the doorway finished by this afternoon, and Blanchard's people are moving
the last of their stuff out.''

Felix smiled to himself. Lifeguard Insurance was but one
of several companies that had suffered irreparable damage
as a result of SPARTOS and REC's confrontation in the Virtual
Network. What irked Blanchard most, however, was having
to surrender part of his office space—Lifeguard's AI residence—to Data Discoveries. What with new partners and a
top-of-the-line cyber system, Felix McTurk needed room to
expand.

Yeah, a fresh start, he thought. With a bit of the old times
to it and a couple of past accounts settled.

''So what are they saying on the telecomp?'' Ngo asked,
back to chewing on her sandwich.

Felix snorted. ''Quote: 'Emeric Bulkroad remains unavailable for comment.' ''

''I'll say he's *unavailable*.''

''Starr and Gaehwiler are doing most of the talking. But
they know they're in deep shit.''

''You think?''

Felix nodded. ''It won't happen overnight, but, yeah,
eventually they're going down for this.''

"Ray says Zoltec isn't spearheading the investigation any longer."

"It's too big for her. Hell, it's too big for NetSec, NSA, and the UN combined. They'll have to create a special agency just to sort things out. As it is, OLD's being sued by SETI and the International Astronomical Union. Then there's the families of the thirty-three *Excalibur* crew and God knows how many others. Interpol wants a crack at them. The Commission on the Peaceful Uses of Outer Space is looking into it . . . There's going to be hell to pay."

Ngo was quiet for a moment. "Where do you suppose they ended up, Felix?—Bulkroad and Bové, I mean."

Felix forced a long exhale. "I've been asking myself that same question for a month now, Heddi. I keep thinking about Thaish's fifteen-year stretch on Offworld hab, and I keep seeing that construction bubble winking out . . ." He shook his head in replayed astonishment. "You've gotta wonder whether Bulkroad and Bové aren't playing out a similar scene on some Heregep planet."

"You really think the Heregep would waste their time on those two?"

Felix shrugged. "Has to be something they can learn from them. All I know is, I can't look at the stars the same way anymore."

"When you can see them," Ngo said with a note of derision. "But I know what you mean, Felix. It's as if you can sense a presence out there now. It's a strange feeling."

"But not traumatizing."

"No," she said, "definitely not that."

It was Special Agent Amelia Zoltec who had effected their release from Offworld habitat. With the demise of SPARTOS and in the sudden absence of both Bulkroad and Bové, OLD security didn't know what to do with them anyway, and Shamir Starr and Beat Gaehwiler were already running scared.

No official statements had been issued concerning either Thaish or the alien ship. From what Felix had gathered from Koo Raywing, the powers that be were still trying to decide just how to break the news of an XT encounter to the rest of the planet. Ray had quit NetSec in protest of all the foot-dragging that was going on; but he, too, was confident the truth would ultimately come to light. Several of Offworld's top scientists who had carried out research on *Ship Nasst*

were refusing to talk; some denying the existence of the
alien vessel altogether, others claiming they had merely been
involved in conducting cybernetic research—that Thaish
wasn't an alien but a creation of OLD science; that the reports of the *Excalibur* virus were valid, etc. Generally covering their asses in the unlikely event that Emeric Bulkroad
reappeared from hyperspace or wherever had been his final
destination.

Felix expected that he and Jain, Ngo and Raywing would
have their day in court. REC, also, once the World Court
ruled on whether an artificial intelligence could be subpoe-
naed as a principal witness in a planet-wide investigation.

The phone chirped just then and Felix and Ngo reached
for it at the same time. Heddi's hand was first to reach the
online bar. "Data Discoveries," she announced toward the
pickup, a finger poised over the video-feed button.

"Heddi, is that you?" Jain's voice asked after a moment's
commo lag.

"Guess it's for you, Felix," Ngo said, smiling and swiv-
eling the phone toward him. "Just a minute, Jain."

"Jain," Felix said, centering himself for the camera.
"How are things up there? How are your parents doing?"

She smiled from the screen, listening hard, then straightening her expression somewhat. "Much better, Felix. The
adjustment has been hard on everyone. Well, not hard exactly, but difficult. There've been adoptions, remarriages,
all sorts of complications. Insurance settlements were made,
inheritances claimed . . . Interpol and a dozen other agencies are demanding statements and depositions from everyone. The whole thing is overwhelming." Jain forced a
second smile. "But my . . . mother and father are doing
well. I still can't believe it."

"Give yourself time, dear," Ngo said over Felix's shoulder. "Don't try to hurry your emotions."

"Thanks, Heddi."

"How 'bout you, kid?" Felix asked. "We heard you
moved out of Bulkroad's compound. You holding up all
right?"

Jain's eyes narrowed. "Mr. Sensitive, all of a sudden."

"Look, I was just—"

"Only kidding, Felix. Actually, I'm doing *too* well, if
anything."

"How's that happen?"

She bit her lower lip. "Em—Emeric set up an enormous trust for me. OLD's lawyers have frozen everything temporarily—they're convinced he's on a sabbatical or something—but if things work out . . ."

"Congrats," Felix said, laughing.

"Plus Blair left me all her Offworld holdings. So suddenly I'm like a major stockholder. Shamir and Beat have been calling me every day . . . Hey, did you get the things I sent down?"

Felix pushed open the door to the back room and aimed the vidphone camera toward the cyber system. "It's Jain!" he yelled to GoBop and his trio of deckhands. "She wants to know how you're enjoying the console!"

"Abso-fucking-*lute*!" came a chorus of replies from fliers and spotters alike.

"They like it," Felix told her, closing the door again.

"Great," Jain said, sounding distracted all at once. "Listen, Felix, I called to tell you that I'm coming down the well next week."

"What, you—back in the soup?"

"Don't give me that. See, I have some real say in Offworld's affairs now . . ."

"And you're thinking Offworld can begin to lend our 'stupid planet' a hand, huh?"

Jain showed him a glower. "You never stop, do you? Anyway, I think I should at least get to know the planet on a one-to-one basis."

"What about your career?"

"I've already talked to TOR PATEL about it. REC's visit's left him permanently environmentally concerned. We're talking about organizing a monster concert for telecomp. Try to get everyone reinvolved with all the issues. Besides, my parents want out of the Islands." She paused. "I thought if you weren't too busy, you could take some time off and show me around New York."

Felix grinned. "You and me on a tour of the town?"

"If you have the time . . ."

"He'll make the time," Ngo answered for Felix. "Or I'll make it for him."

"You heard her," Felix said. "It'll be good to see you," he added in a more private voice. "I'll wear my suit."

"Yeah, you do that, McTurk." She smiled. "The one with the chocolate mousse stains."

* * *

Felix had already returned to his own cramped workspace in the back room when the call from REC came through. The carpenters had quit, having put in what amounted to a four-hour workday, but the kids refused to abandon the VES 4400SX. Felix noted that Tech was employing some of El's ritualistic "soft master" spotting techniques.

"I guess you want a progress report," Felix said.

"Naturally," REC told him from his construct in the Virtual Network.

Felix swung around to face the plastic-dropped rectangular hole the carpenters had punched through what had once been Lifeguard Insurance's wall. "Well, the doorway's almost in. And from where I'm sitting I can see ELVIS's old residence. So I'd say your rooms are just about ready."

"Rooms?" REC asked after a moment. "I only require one, Felix. Just enough to house my software."

Felix activated the video feed and adopted a serious expression for the cameras. "Oh, I guess Jain didn't tell you about the other one. Here, have a look for yourself," he added, widening the camera's point of view to include the as-yet unprogrammed Daimler-Benz robot Jain had sent down the well. "Course it needs a touch of polish here and there, but I thought I'd leave that up to you."

"I'm—I'm speechless," REC managed.

"We can't have you just idling away your time in the Network," Felix said. "Not when there's work to be done."

"Yes, yes, of course, Felix," REC said all too earnestly. "Then I suppose my surprise can't wait either."

"Your surprise?"

"Tell GoBop and the gang to pay me a visit inside."

REC broke the connection and Felix passed the word along to Tech and El. In a moment GoBop and Neon were issuing excited sounds from the twin interface chairs.

"You gotta see this for yourself, Felix!" GoBop said, thumbing his breakpoint and slipping off the goggles. He pulled off the gloves and shrugged out of the wardrobe jacket. "Just follow Neon's lead. It's too absolute, man, it's totally chaotic."

Felix pulled the goggles down over his eyes and spiraled down toward the Grid, his eyes steering him north past Metroplex Clearance, IBM, and the dark, slumbering castle that was Offworld L&D. He could see the architectural changes REC's resurrection and fight for life had wrought, the altered face of the Network's unreal estate.

But dominating the horizon was the majestic four-peaked mountain the reborn AI had birthed; and crowning it now, in respectable neon-analog earth tones, was a dimensionalized graphic that read: DATA DISCOVERIES.

GoBop was enthusing over the sign in Felix's one ear; Tech and El in the other.

"It looks terrific—*partner*," Felix told REC at last.

REC's synthesized voice approximated a laugh. "I can't wait for our first real case."

## About the Author

Jack McKinney has been a psychiatric aide, fusion-rock guitarist and session man, worldwide wilderness guide, and "consultant" to the U.S. military in Southeast Asia (although they had to draft him for that).

His numerous other works of mainstream and science fiction—novels, radio and television scripts—have been written under various pseudonyms.

Lately he has been glimpsed in the vicinity of Twenty-Nine Palms, California, and Sedona, Arizona.